The Stories of
Ronald Blythe

LUCAS BOOKS

The Stories of
Ronald Blythe

First Published by Chatto and Windus: The Hogarth Press
1985.
Published in Paperback by Methuen 1986.
Published by Harcourt Brace Jovanovich, USA 1985
under the title "The Visitors".

This Edition Published by
LUCAS BOOKS 2002
Thorndon, Suffolk
www.lucasbooks.co.uk

British Library Cataloguing in Publication Data
A catalogue record for this book is available from the British Library

ISBN 1903797-19-5

Printed in Great Britain by
Brackenbury Associates
Ipswich, Suffolk

The Stories of
Ronald Blythe

For my sister
Constance

Introduction

These stories belong mainly to the first years of my writing life, when I seemed to be reading and writing and thinking about short stories much of the time. They all incorporate what I saw and heard around me from childhood on, even the ghost stories, for as a boy I lived within walking distance of Borley Rectory, later to be owned by my old friends James and Catherine Turner, and of M.R. James's house at Aldeburgh. My interest was not in ghosts but in the personality of those who saw them. The village stories are drawn from my grandparents' Suffolk, a wonderful, hard, rural world where gossip became tale - even poetry. Some of the stories are about the effect of isolation on the usually strong- minded people who never quite manage to fit themselves into the local conventions.

R.B.

Bride Michael

It was raining when Marian divided the curtains. She stared out resentfully. Yesterday's feeble soaking drift had turned into a torrent which hit grey Cambridgeshire at a thudding right-angle. Creating their counterpoint to the wet roaring, were the meticulous noises her father made in the kitchen, the squirt of the tap into the kettle, the clink of china, the radio mumbling the News under its breath, all the cheerful murmuration of his self-sufficiency. However hard she tried, 'things were always in control' - his control, of course.

'Coming!' she called, bundling herself up in a dressing-gown and clacking down the back stairs. They were all squeezed up round the kitchen part of the house for obvious reasons. Respectable Wilton tracks leading from it led straight to the Arctic. Her father was pouring tea and she bent to kiss a rough silver face.

'There really wasn't any need,' he said. It was a protest he made about almost everything she did to help him, and he made it justly. There really wasn't any need and, what was more, there never had been. Whether his hands were frying bacon or sewing up wounds they displayed total efficiency. Crustless slices of bread lay beside the toaster as orderly as instruments on a tray

'Busy day, Da?'

'Oh, the usual, you know. Hospital this afternoon. Incidentally, I can collect those pheasants from the butcher's on the way home.'

'But, darling, I was going to. . . You know I said I would.'

'What is the point? And making a journey on a day like this when I go right past the shop! Oh, and I've asked Mrs Wraith to clear all the stuff out of the porch room so that I can get the underlay down during the week-end.'

'There are a lot of Howard's things in there,' said Marian.

Her father's manner changed to one of fussy concern in a second.

'Love, I'm so sorry. I forgot. Leave the room as it is. It doesn't matter a bit.'

'Da,' Marian's voice was flat with patience, 'I don't mind. I never have minded. You must know it because I've told you hundreds of times. *I don't care.* Now do you understand? Not about suits and shoes and golf clubs - things like that. I wouldn't have brought them from Barnes except I moved so quickly after the funeral there was no time to get rid of them. You can't simply walk out and clothe the beggar at the gate these days, you know.'

Her father looked as though he was going to say something daring and then said it.

'I've hung on to all your mother's hats.'

'Hung on to them - *hats*?'

'Well, I mean they are still here, in boxes and things.'

'I should think a museum might welcome them,' said Marian, entirely without cruelty. Her mother had been dead for thirty-two years.

Dr Potter made a face which meant 'possibly' and leafed through the post. None for her, a fat pile for him. He sorted them into drug circulars, bills and personal. There was only one of the latter. It was in a red, white and blue airmail envelope and he tucked it, unopened, behind the kitchen clock.

'Don't you want to know what Robin says?'

'Not much.'

'Perhaps you find me equally. . . irrelevant, or whatever you like to call it?'

'One's children can hardly be irrelevant, my dear, but they nearly always tend to be dutiful, and that is pretty bloody awful. Your brother, my son - there could be some kind of answer there if we could find it -doesn't like me, love me or hate me. Yet he goes on writing to me. His letters are simply statements which go out on the first of the month. They never press me. I send a little something when I feel like it - and I am coming to feel like it less and less.'

'But you still love him. . . us, Da?'

'Oh, certainly. But that is not the same thing at all. My loving you and your loving me are unrelated matters. If you had had a child you'd soon realize this.'

'I'm going to get dressed,' said Marian, recognizing the approach of one of their good-tempered rows. She returned to her bedroom thinking 'no baby', though not at all in the way childless women are supposed to think; simply no baby. No Howard - now that was a profoundly different matter - a reality still not grasped. Flesh like his should have been resistant to everything but time, yet a blood cancer had toppled the whole flawless edifice in less than a year. People spoke of the mystery of the soul but for her the mystery had been all in the flesh. Their marriage had begun and ended as a carnal contract. Let her be honest, it was the mortal state which had been God's gift where they were concerned. 'I know why I miss Howard,' she told the scarcely wrinkled sheets. 'I don't deceive myself.' She squeezed at his cigarette lighter and coughed the first smoke of the day into the mirror. With critical fingers, she drew the skin tight over her cheek-bones. Her girl-face momentarily gleamed out. 'Pretty girl,' she said to the reflection. Beautiful, early forties-ish woman, would have been the basic current description. She noticed that her face was getting bigger - her nose was certainly. It was strange how age either gave one useless additions or whittled away at one until there wasn't a curve left anywhere. She brushed her hair. It had stayed thick and soft and rich, and had always given her endless pleasure. It was so cool and actual, although, contrary to all that was said about men's feeling for women's hair, Howard had not enjoyed it. Perhaps it was because it was the only part of herself which she could enjoy without him. During the early days of their marriage she had spread it over his bare shoulders as they made love, until, one early morning, she had caught a look of revulsion. Funny Howard! No answer and, sensibly, no more questions.

She dressed. Her Donegal tweed, which looked like a couple of knotty rugs but which had the effect of refining her, felt damp. With the dressing-table lamp switched off, her room became no more than an adjunct to the merciless dreariness outside. She returned to the kitchen and found that Mrs Wraith had arrived and was festooning the Rayburn with her drenched coat and scarf. This flight of comfort when it was most needed was a feature of the house. In the summer, when one could almost live in the garden, the rooms became perfection: there was hardly a corner which was not inviting. In the winter there was barely a habitable spot. Vintage damps took over. One room was still called the surgery, although her father did all his work in Cambridge now, driving in daily in the latest and biggest black car available in the popular price range. Changing the car had become an act of almost religious importance for him. The time for turning-in the present Consul was approaching and already certain tensions had begun to inform his driving. Could it be that Time's winged chariot could only be out-paced by the latest model? Certainly Marian noticed that the arrival of Motor Show hand-outs during the autumn had a tonic effect on her father. She couldn't drive and couldn't tell one car from another. She went to Cambridge on the bus. Seated on the upper deck, she could see what her father, in all his arrivals and departures, could never see - the tower.

It stood in the garden, all that was left of an extravagant Victorian church which had abutted the house when it was the rectory. The church had symbolically burned down in July 1914 and the new one was a mile away in the village, where it should be. The tower rose neatly from a lawn and would have been an eye-catcher, but a thicket of trees had been allowed to grow in such a way that, tall as it was, it was hidden. It was only on the top road, and in a high bus, that one could glimpse it. The lawn on which it stood was called the 'other garden'. Dr Potter was pleased to leave it at this. He was a natural closer-up of rooms, vistas, events and dossiers generally. He could have lived in one room but having been installed in what she termed a proper residence by his bride nearly fifty years ago, he found it less trouble to endure it than to leave it.

Marian would have made great changes had she ever felt that she had come home for good, but this she never felt, although it was over four years since Howard's death and the awful move. She needed a sense of the temporary to keep her sane. She tried not to notice that her father, for all his unspoken affection, was not averse to the idea that she would not be with him for good. He had only enough real consideration for his patients and a few bridge-playing cronies. His thoughtfulness where his daughter was concerned was a deliberate, extra thing, something he had to remember, like picking up the joint. He hedged and sheltered her as a duty. His dutiful fatherliness weighed her down: after Howard's casual adoration, being with her father was like going through life with a protector's arm breaking her back.

He accepted the fact that, being female, there would be a need to make alterations. And Marian, equally accepting his masculine contentment with things as they were, did her best to change what had to be changed without too much disturbance. But in no time at all she learned that the ease with which she got her own way revealed Dr Potter's total indifference to redecoration. He and Mrs Wraith spoke of it as her 'new interest' and were as indulgent of her wallpapers and colour schemes as they would have been of a sick child's muddle. Yet doing the house up had, momentarily, blotted out for Marian the memory of the most incredibly terrible sight she had ever seen, Howard's coffin entering the earth. Committal. Howard dead. Howard's weight causing the under-taker's men to dig their heels into pale mud. Death had not shown her his complete hand until then. If her father had seen her reaction to this fact he would have applied the correct medical term for it. Less than two months later he was staring around at her decorations, admiring everything yet seeing nothing. He didn't miss the pictures she had taken down because he had never noticed them when they were up. But the destructive climax of his tact came in simply never saying 'Howard', in case the word might upset her. She felt that she had to say it more and more to prevent it from becoming obliterated. Howard this, and Howard that, she chatted as easily as she could. Her father heard her forgivingly, just as he might hear a patient's obscenities under anaesthetic. The dead were not only no more to him, they tended to have never been.

He and Mrs Wraith were now enacting the happy farce whereby the housekeeper was made to feel indispensable. It happened every morning. The car was brought up to the front door and then Dr Potter affected male helplessness while Mrs Wraith hurtled backwards and forwards with his coat, glasses, case, books, umbrella, etc., and little cries of, 'You'd forget your head if it wasn't screwed on!'

'Now the letters from the hall table, Mrs Wraith, and I'll trouble you no longer.' 'Trouble! I like that - trouble!'

'Ah, you spoil me, my dear!'

'It's just as well somebody does!'

Conspiratorial laughter. Returning at that moment, Marian joined in. She was doing to Mrs Wraith what her father did to her, undercutting by her indifference another human being's reality. The housekeeper simply lacked importance where she was concerned - meant nothing. Having failed with bad temper, irritatingly good temper, innuendo, rude confrontations and plain malice, Mrs Wraith was reduced to carrying her indignation to her husband.

'You'd think she'd pull her weight - but not her! On the go from morn to night he is. Even makes his own bed. Or thinks he does, pulls it over more like. While she's painting doors and making the garden too big to manage. I mean, her own father! It's not right.'

'It's because he's used to it,' Mr Wraith had said.

'What?'

'He's used to it. That's why people go on as they do - because they're used to it.'

'So *that's* what you think.'

'It's not what I think, it's what I know.'

'Somebody was behind the door when they gave the manners out, wasn't they?'

'He's domesticated, if you must know.' Mrs Wraith wheeled around at that.

'What a thing to say about the doctor,' she exclaimed, shocked.

The whole question of her future had blown up with the October storm while Marian was dining with her father the night before. The suffocating silence surrounding Howard's death and her curious no-man's-land position had exploded into words. Neither angry nor what are called understanding words, but flat, ordinary words too thin to hide behind. The doctor laid his cards on the table. She had no cards. This was the fact which emerged.

'You're young,' he stated.

'Forty - forty-one in December?'

'That's young.'

'It might be to you, Da,' she said, smiling to prove that she was willing to discuss things academically.

'Well then, see it this way. Take a good long look at yourself in the mirror before you go to bed and then ask yourself, is it all over? Just try to say, "It is finished", to what you see in the glass.'

'You sound as if you are challenging me to find out for myself whether I'm a manic-depressive.'

Marian felt less easy now. She was proud of the poised manner with which she had coped with her disaster. If people - her father - were to tie one of their beastly psychiatric tags on ordinary dignity, how the hell was one to behave in the face of death?

'Who said anything about manic depression? I'm saying that a perfectly strong, healthy woman, such as you happen to be at this moment, isn't going to find it easy - or perhaps, possible - to switch life off like a. . . like a. .'

The hand he was vaguely waving at the artificial logs in the grate became momentarily powerful in the first lightning.

'I'm not one of your patients going through the change, Da. You don't have to talk to me like this.'

'How then?'

How? wondered Marian miserably. Her father was right. How else? 'Well, put it like this,' he continued, pleased to be allowed to go on developing his argument in good, strong clichés. 'The old machine is in fine running order and it is going to create energy, and energy must find an outlet.'

'*Father,* please!' There was a pause, during which thunder crackled distantly. Then Marian, with a grisly sense of sounding like Mrs Wraith, began to justify the four years. She listed all her good deeds and ended up with, 'But this is "nothing", of course!'

'I never said it was nothing. You had important reasons for doing what you did; therefore it was something.'

'But I did it for you.'

'You did it for your own peace of mind. And it is done. What now?'

'You want me to go away...' said Marian slowly.

'When did I ever say such a thing?'

'You're saying it now.'

'I'm not saying it. I'm trying to find out whether you are capable of saying it - and apparently you are not.'

The argument continued between mouthfuls of lamb. We must be an insensitive breed to go on as we do and never lose our appetites, thought Marian. The sensation of being in the wrong place grew quite mercilessly now. It was extraordinary that so small and fleshless a man as father should have the strength to propel such a vast crisis across the table. She observed his frailty with detachment. The rosy contusions in corner of eyes which stared only at his plate, the waxy temples, the glistening on his jaw-line; it would have been daughter-like and right to be moved to tenderness by such things - except, and she had to admit it, she was not. She thought of him as the dapper little medical officer behind the Menin ridge while her mother did her bit by making a home for him. The home which Marian had been unmaking. Her mother. A shingled ghost. A bird-voiced woman exclaiming indistinctly through her early childhood. Her mother, who was large, middle-class uncomplicated and who (apparently, according to her father) enjoyed enlightenment and plenty of Maple's furniture, housemaids and shibboleths. The only thing her mother had questioned were questions.

'When did you stop feeling, well, widowed, Da?'

'Oh, good God, Marian! You're ready enough to sit on *me* when *I* talk. Feeling widowed, as you call it, is an obituary-column attitude. I missed your mother - of course I missed her - but not in the way you think. I don't know that I ever felt widowed, as you call it.'

'I think you felt free.'

'Probably I did.'

'You could even have felt - glad.'

'I never said that.'

'I don't feel free. Howard's death has locked all the doors.'

Her father showed a hint of true pity, then became the good listener. Marian's next remark changed all this. He was genuinely surprised.

'Howard and mother were the same age.'

'I didn't know that - were they?' He recovered quickly. 'But we are not the same age, are we, my dear? And that's the way we've got to look at things, isn't it?'

'I know what you mean - what you are getting at. I am interrupting your freedom so you want me to go.'

Dr Potter assumed a look of idiot patience.

'My dear girl, let us get things straight and then keep them straight. You cannot interrupt my freedom, as you describe it, and I don't want you to go. What you are talking about is power and my refusal to entangle my power with yours in this house in some kind of life-giving struggle. If you need something positive and vital, then obviously you must leave here in order to find it. If not, stop mourning - for yourself, not, er, Howard.'

'You're heartless, Da.'

'Sentiment-less, perhaps. To me it's a killing disease.'

'I'm going into the garden for a bit. My head aches. It's the electric in the air.' Just as she knew he would, her father immediately began to clear the table and put the chairs straight.

'Didn't you want to see that horse-jumping programme from the White City?' she called back.

There was silence, followed by what sounded like a handful of cutlery being banged down. A light went on in the kitchen where the television set rested on the dresser.

Marian wandered out into a night which was fragmentary with summer. The approaching storm oscillated in the west, but eastwards, over the village, the moon blazed in a serene sky. Storm shadows and moon shadows were lined up like armies. Creatures bustled about in the seer herbaceous thickets and the trees quivered with nervous birds. Occasional preliminary bursts of damp squally wind tore in and out of the stillness, bringing down more leaves and promising violence before long. The house showed its mid-nineteenth-century confidence in every line of its jet windows, its velvet eaves, broad doors and custard-coloured chimney-pots. A distant flaming on the lip of blackness exposed the whereabouts of Cambridge. Between the garden and the city miles of fen exuded its own phosphorescence.

Marian manoeuvred herself through the kissing-gate leading to the 'other garden'. The grass here had been given its last cut before the winter and was formal and elegant. The tower looked extravagantly picturesque. Its door was wired-up. This was because children from the village, including Mrs Wraith's Gary, found it irresistible and might just as irresistibly tumble off it. I suppose I tumbled off it in a way, thought Marian. Several times. She thought of lying high above the burning garden with Robin during the summer holidays, their hissing secret talk, then no talk, then the singing silence as he touched her. Explorations. Guilt.

This recollection made her fretful - for Howard. This surprised her and caused her to come to a halt. She saw her shadow stretching across the grass, alongside the tower. The tower was the tower and she was a large well-corseted woman with well-groomed hair. Hers was a far more familiar silhouette in an English garden than anything else, she supposed. Had it been possible, she would have climbed the tower at this moment and made a claim for some kind of sanctuary from the desolation pursuing her. Her father was right, she decided resentfully. What he had been saying was, 'I don't want your emotional frustration served up to me as mourning every time I come into the house. I'm old. I want to sip whisky, watch television and back a horse or two. It's not very intelligent of me, it's not very gentlemanly either. But, being old, I no longer care. Leave me if you cannot share my indifference.'

She returned to the house and crept into the fluorescent kitchen, silently, as she imagined, but he heard her. Eye, ear, taste and touch retained for him an animal keenness.

'Javanese Boy got a clear round,' he said, not looking up.

Horse and rider were trotting out of view. There was a glimpse of rearing, side-turned heads, man above beasts, and of eyes dilated and shining; of mouths parted and trembling, and heaving breath. Storm sparkled on the screen and a military band throbbed amidst applause.

'If one wants to win, one has to compete - is that it, Da?'

'Mm? Oh, my dear girl, don't worry. Do anything you like. I'm the last person who should give advice. Here, have a snifter.'

'No, darling. But I think I will tuck-up now. 'Night.'

Her father didn't reply. In bed and shuddering with cold, she switched on her transistor. More storm and a sweet, thin male voice - 'O give me the comfort of Thy help again: and stablish me with Thy free spirit.' Compline. She switched off. That was one thing she could be certain of, she would never be one of those Christ-consoled women. She lacked the religious instinct as completely as some people lacked a colour-sense or a head for heights. A few minutes later the storm broke. She listened to it conscientiously, as one would listen to music, and passed through its involvement into drowning sleep.

It was amazing that rain and wind were still bludgeoning the world with the same intensity when Dr Potter's car squelched out of sight at half-past nine the following morning. There must be floods, though nothing on the News. The extremeness of the weather was vaguely enjoyable. Marian felt that it excused her from her more predictable reactions. On a day like this she had a right to be different. Not everyone grabbed at such an excuse, or course. Both Mrs Wraith and her father stuck to their sameness. The former cleaned the front bedrooms as usual, which was why Marian answered the door to a drenched figure clasping a canvas satchel. The deluge was now so fantastic that it simply washed out the usual niceties and the young man dashed for cover instinctively. An unbelievable amount of water poured off him and vanished into the carpet. A mass of hair, beaten flat and darkened like rotting corn, directed steady streams of moisture down a stone-white face. Marian found a shilling amongst the odds and ends on the kitchen mantelpiece and paid for the soggy magazine. What else could she do? She also said he could wait for a bit until it cleared up. Again, there was scarcely any choice. An hour later he was still there, seated on the hall chair and staring apologetically at the mess he had brought indoors, rather as an injured person stares at the dirt of his own blood. His raincoat hung from the doorknob and he himself hung forward with clenched hands and twisted legs, as though trying to close-circuit what little living warmth there was left to him. A cape-like stain of water had spread across his jacket.

He smiled as she approached. It was, as Marian knew it would be, the meek and maddening smile of the predestined. Her normal kindness as well as her acquired liberalism dissolved before it. A gipsy, yes. An escaped prisoner, probably; a ghastly old tramp, a child murderer (no, be reasonable) - but truly, she told herself, anyone could approach me and I would react with sanity and humanity. So what is it that makes me see red in this instance? For one unspeakable second what she imagined was the loathing of the exterminator tempted her and made her want to humiliate and insult the boy. His eyes met hers and then turned away, not with awkwardness or embarrassment, or any of the expected things, but with shock. Had he seen. . . ? How could he? Her filthy intolerance had been too temporary even for herself to have grasped the full meaning of it. He stood up and began to struggle into his coat. It was so wet he could hardly push his arms through the sleeves.

'Wait!' she cried.

Rushing upstairs, she began to heave her way through Howard's trunks and suitcases. His socks, still in the balls he must have rolled them into, bounced softly at her feet. Inside every shoe was the smudge of Howard's heel. But it wouldn't be in this kind of box. That hanging thing, of course! She dragged it out. God, it wasn't possible! The whole thing was becoming as gloom-laden as an old Bette Davis film - but there was a brown blob of something hanging from the button-hole and there were, more naturally, holes where a lieutenant's pips had been.

'This will keep some of the rain out until you get home,' she said. 'It's a mack belonging to my husband - which belonged to my husband...'

The young man put it on, pulled in the belt and turned up the collar. He was transformed. The metamorphosis from crank to hero was too much for Marian. It seemed terrible that someone such as he should have done so well out of something simply intended to keep out pneumonia. If he dared to say a word about his horrible religion she would demand it back! But all the young man said was thank you, a single thank you. When he had gone, boredom of the most hope-engulfing kind she had ever felt descended on her. She leaned against the banister, smelling the dead-house smell and also the washed, scented freshness of her own skin. 'What shall I do?' she asked herself. And then aloud, *'What am I going to do?'*

'Did you call?' shouted Mrs Wraith.

'No,' lied Marian.

Baxter woke with a start, saw that it was a quarter to eight, and jerked into action. Then he remembered it was Saturday. The room was small and hot and covered with bamboo-patterned wallpaper. The divan took up most of the space but there was also a hand-basin, a line with drip-dry shirts on hangers, a little table with hair-brushes, shampoos and combs at one end, and a writing-pad and Bible at the other, a fawn-coloured easy-chair with pointed wings, a calendar with information such as: 'The sun will reach its greatest activity in recorded history around 1970 C.E.' and 'Charles Taze Russell puts out the false fires of Hellenism, 1870 C.E.'; a chest-expander, a bust of Churchill with a place to strike matches, a small cupboard full of cups, plates and tinned food, and a picture of the Stoning of St. Stephen.

After reading from the Bible for a few minutes, having first found what to read with his eyes closed, Baxter slipped back into bed and lay looking at the bumpy ceiling. This was the best time, the moment when the angel held him, when the hopes he had seemed neither presumptuous nor impossible. Michael Baxter – he was saying his own name – Michael Baxter of the divine Bride Remnant, one of the 144,000 elected by Jehovah to become the Wife of Christ at the marriage whose consummation had already begun but -which would not be completed until after Armageddon. Bride Michael! Hope, presumption, which was which? Where did one end and the other begin?

'Jahweh! Tell me. I am your Michael. But Christ's Wife, am I

19

that? Yes? But perhaps only a Witness. Make me glory in the only-ness, Jahweh...'

'Breakfast, Mr Baxter!' called Mrs Jones through the keyhole. 'Sausages, and it's simply pouring.'

Baxter waited until her footsteps had died away, then opened the door just sufficiently to pull the tray in. He drew the curtains, just enough to lighten the room. Outside, everywhere, slate and tarmac had been scrubbed an obsidian, glass-bright black by the storm. Rain was hitting the pavement so hard that it buckled, hook-like, and shot upwards again. He watched it, fascinated. The gutters were rushing like little brooks. He thought suddenly of Swaledale and for the first time for months tasted home-sickness. He fought against this taste guiltily. The morning had begun as badly as it could. So far he had preoccupied it with dreams of his personal standing with God and nostalgia for a little Earth bliss, a farm on the hillside where the names Eliphaz, Zophar, Bildad - and even Job - might only recommend themselves to cows.

He cleaned his teeth. He didn't see his mother's letter until he was half-way through his breakfast. Mrs Jones had used it for a table-mat.

My dear Son,
You have not written to me but I don't worry because I know you are very busy and if you were queer I would have heard, wouldn't I. Dear, your Dad has finished the shed and it is just what we needed. I expect your Digs are very nice but not like home though we all have to leave the nest. Three pounds is a lot but perhaps not for all in these days. Spot misses you he still jumps when the gate goes. But it is only your Dad. Mrs Pallett asked how you are I said nicely thanks. Her Terry is going to be a Detective at York. We don't get much sun but mustn't complain. Dad says fine weather for ducks!! I bought you a shirt in Smedly's sale and will put it in the parcel. We read the books like you told us to. Did I tell you that I once came first in scripture at St. Johns? They are hard but not dry. I love you because you are a good boy. Dad says cheerio. Where is

Michael asks Mrs Pallett at Cambridge I say. You should have seen her face. I must close now. Dad says Cambridge is 182 miles.

Yours faithfully,
Your loving Mother xx

He tried to forget the letter as he shaved but it lay like a great block in the very forefront of his mind, squeezing out every other thought. His eyes burned back at him in the mirror, hateful with love. The Word was full of references about children honouring their parents. If loving parents was such a normal thing, would the prophets have needed to mention it so often? The last time he had gone home his mother had taken his face in her hands as if it was a piece of her own property. When it looked as though she might kiss his mouth he had fought back a scream.

Her letter had spoilt the day. It had been a good night. They had been very near. They had approached him in the hot room in the great silence between the late and early traffic. Their hands had touched him; his body sang in the knowledge of its privilege. He was a vessel for the Bridegroom and had been drawn from the context of all that was average and ordinary. He was Chosen. He had prayed, Jahweh, Jahweh, most precious, precious Name. And then - hardly daring to say it - *Jehovah!* Constellating sound.

Yet it could not have been very late because the city was still awake when the voices of the Kingdom were hushed at last and he had switched on the bedside lamp and gazed in fear and wonder at this temporal self, his long, naked, newly adult flesh to which he came at moments like this as an inquisitive stranger. He read. The book was called *Babylon the Great Has Fallen.* While he read, a lorry drew up at the café opposite and soon the fruit machine sounded, making its bomb-crunch mimicry, and sometimes spitting out its little fortune in mockery. More lorries drew off the A45 to find the café, which was a popular one, and women dashed through the rain with high, clopping steps. The lorry drivers did not call out: they had come to the café for food and each other. Sometimes they grew thunderous in the flimsy room, like bullocks in a truck. Baxter knew that the angel did not come to array him in the Bride-clothes but to wake him from meaningless mortal sleep and send him into Jack's Place to witness. The very thought of doing such a thing terrified him. Sometimes St. Stephen's fate seemed the easier one. Youth is the easiest time for death, after all. He touched the nakedness which the stones would have struck, his restless self. Beautiful. The temple. More clopping heels, then cries. Mrs Jones had come home. She would put on the kettle and a record just as soon as she could. She did. 'Reach out, I'll be there,' sang a man. Mrs Jones sang too. She had been to the Young Wives' Club, but she was fifty. She was good to him but she opened his window. Her husband had been killed in the Battle of the Bulge, so that was why she was a Young Wife. She said she only took in grads when he first came searching for a room. Then she changed her mind. Her music throbbed him to sleep. Bom-bom-bom in his heart, in his mind, at his finger-ends. The largeness of the day was absent in the sound. What Baxter heard last night and every night was the futility of the World's argument in miniature. But now and then he danced to the beat, silently in his socks, twisting pleasantly and thinking of nothing at all, and certainly never thinking of himself as some David before the Ark. Underneath, Mrs Jones never danced, although she sang all the words. She knew all the words back to 'Mona'. 'I'm nothing but a mother to that Mr Baxter,' she told her friend. 'Well?' asked her friend.

There were other sounds: they came from what Baxter thought of as the 'other Cambridge'. They were made in towers stretching up from perfect grass growing beyond the marshalling yards and the radio-parts works. The Congregation warned him of this splendid place. It was Babylon in one of its myriad guises. He must watch and pray. He watched, all one lunch-time, outside Great St. Mary's as the priests of Bel and their followers passed from King's Parade into the pointed interior with sluggish solemnity. A pretty girl standing opposite caught his smile and smiled too. All this fur and wigs, buckles, wands and lace stopping the buses, and for what purpose? Damnation. The religious empire passing by, not one member of which had heard the angel over the water say, 'You, the One who is and who was, the loyal One, are righteous.. .' The bloodspillers with their sensible faces. O Babylon! He should witness in this Cambridge, in the very courts of apostasy - but how? He was new to salvation and the Congregation was being patient. But he knew why they had directed him to Cambridge - because he looked like so many of the young men here and could pass among them without suspicion with his gift of light.

But not today. Today he could choose. He dressed hurriedly, not in the jersey and jeans he wore to work at the drawing-office but formally in suit and tie. He counted the magazines. He had sold twenty-eight last Saturday, eighteen the week before and there were fourteen left. Cramming them in his satchel, he ate some cornflakes, put on his coat and ran all the way through Randolph Road, Rosebery Road, Dilke Lane and the railway siding to the bus stop. He went to Durlingham because that was where the first bus was going and the rain forced a quick decision. He reached the village a little before ten. Surprisingly, there was no shelter, no shop or pub, no barn or shed, nothing but two grey rows of council houses lined up in front of each other on opposite sides of the road. He hardly knew what to do. The rain was flooding him like a river. He could feel it running down his shoulders under his shirt. He noticed a dense little lane turning off the main road and hurried down it. He could not remember getting so wet in so short a time and felt angry and helpless. Pheasants floundered out of the undergrowth with chottling screams as he ran. Just ahead lay a house. Before he had made up his mind what to do, he was standing in a big, shining hall smelling of furniture polish, and a tall woman carrying a copy of the magazine in her hand was backing away from him. She was saying something.

'You'd better wait for a bit. You can't go on through all that.'

He scarcely heard. He was crushed by the look she had given him, the momentary first look before a more reasonable and ordinary one had thrust it out of her eyes. No one in all his life had looked at him like that before. It was the look you had when you turned over a putrescent bird with the toe of your shoe, before the pity set in. He felt sick and surprised. Also vaguely relieved as another part of the Teachings fell into place; he had seen for the very first time Babylonish hostility. So this was it. Not the lies to clear him off the doorstep, nor the leers to lead him on. But a look which said, horrible . . . destroy, destroy! He sank on to the chair, long legs sprawling, the rain running away from him in worms on the black floor. Bride Michael. After a few minutes he took off his coat, hanging it on the back of the chair to dry, and then began to shiver uncontrollably. Far away, at what seemed like a planet's distance, he heard saucepans clanking and a wheezing of Music While You Work. Then – it could have been hours later – the woman reappeared, walking clown the purple staircase with strong, deliberate steps, and holding out something in her hand. He avoided looking at her but noticed that her voice had somehow changed.

'It certainly wasn't doing anyone any good hanging in the wardrobe year in, year out. It will keep a bit of the wet out.'

'Thank you - very much.'

Howard's old H.A.C. mackintosh sat squarely on Baxter's shoulders. He tugged in the belt and the skirts rode out, stiff and confident. With something like the same suddenness as he had entered the house, he now found himself hurrying away from it. Diamond-bright gravel cut into his sodden shoes. The sun sped from behind a mauve barrier and shone gaudily. When he looked back, he saw the woman standing like a statue in a niche under the porch. One hand seemed to be stretching towards him and had then become fixed and irresolute. He did not like to wave back in case waving had not been its intention. He looked back again when he reached the drive gates and this time the woman moved swiftly back into the interior. *Durlingham Old Rectory,* he read on the gate; *No hawkers, no circulars.*

While waiting for the bus he discovered the things left in the pockets of the mack. There was nothing much: half a cigarette, half a pencil, a paper-clip and some cherry stones. Also a piece of ruled paper,

Home

Howard,

I managed to get two tickets – dress circle – do say I'm clever. Going to have my hair done now but will pick you up from the office about six. Aren't we happy, happy people? - M.

Have I witnessed? wondered Baxter. He was back now in his Cambridge. Mini-skirted dolls with hair like shredded wheat were whirled along in the Saturday flurry. In Randolph Street, old men in alpaca coats wrote up chalk bargains and lined the path with second-hand television sets and wash-stands. Trains pipped distantly. Undergraduates carrying books, wine and cauliflowers exercised their self-confidence. The shop next to Baxter's lodgings was selling paperbacks, Durex, frozen peas and Brylcreem. He strode towards it. 'Yessir!' - Oh, you...' said the assistant, suddenly seeing Baxter's head above the handsome collar. He took the loaf they had put by for him. He spent the rest of the day reading and dreaming. Opposite, in the room across the road, the undergraduates and their girls sang madrigals. Beneath him, ironing her dress for the Olde Tyme do, Mrs Jones listened to Radio Caroline. The pleading cry ran from transistor to transistor, all along the road, *Love me, please, love me.*

'The singers went before, the players on instruments followed after,' read Baxter. He had burnt his mother's letter, he had sold one magazine, he had endured derision. His eyes pricked with sadness. He wrote out the Promise in large round letters on a clean sheet of paper, 'Praise Jah, you people, because Jehovah our God the Almighty has begun to rule as King. Let us rejoice because the Marriage of the Lamb has arrived. .'

A few minutes later, Mrs Jones knocked on his door.

'Everything all right?'

'Yes, thanks - everything.'

'I thought I heard a sound?' No answer.

'Funny boy,' said Mrs Jones to her cat.

* * *

The little talk about her future cleared the air, which was for

Marian a disaster. It had always suited her best not to see where she was going. There had been no plans with Howard. Purpose, yes: every month and hour of their marriage had its purpose. Nineteen years of purpose? she asked herself. There was no answer to this, nor to all the other beastly questions which had begun to spring out at her. But looking back, the everlasting now of her life with Howard grew very plain. Never once had they put out feelers into the future or held inquests on the past. This was what had made each living day so valuable - and what now made each dead day so worthless. Bitter fact that it was, she was beginning to have to accept that Howard had been emotionally improvident. Nothing remained to sustain her from out of all that extravagant loving. He had left her destitute.

This was the appalling truth to which her father had felt obliged to draw her attention. So what was she going to do? Dear God, what a question!

The week which followed fed her sense of nightmare uncertainty. She found herself not only demanding, 'Who are you?' and 'What are you?' of the reflection in her dressing-table mirror, but demanding an answer to these questions from the sane and well-dressed woman who accompanied her about the house and garden, working so efficiently and without a hint of stress, while another, inner, Marian cried out into great, cruel silences. She fought against her sudden and surprising unhappiness by listing the various things she could do. A job. But she had never had a job. This very ordinary fact made her feel extraordinarily abnormal. She would write books, children's books, but she did not like children. Was this really so? The backlash to this question was so awful that she had to give an impromptu drinks party to drive it from her mind.

For an hour or two the house lived. At least it twitched and jerked with noise. Her father had enjoyed himself tremendously. 'It worked! It worked! ' he told himself. 'A bit sulky and down in the dumps at first, of course. That was only natural. But look at her now, laughing and talking. It was like the old days. Give Edie her due; she always knew how to make a party go. If things were going to be like this in the future, perhaps it wouldn't be such a bad thing after all if Marian stayed at home and kept house for him. A lot of it had been his own fault, anyway. He was not only an old widower he had got himself unmarried and had become a fussy old do-it-yourself bore. If he made the house usable she would use it. Storage heaters, maybe. Spend a bit. Distantly, on the other side of - what? - he heard his wife's loud and confident jolly approval. But Marian's cheerfulness departed with her guests.

Thursday was a strangely wordless day. Her father matched her silences with his professional reticence. Their talk became like two little tracks crossing a quagmire - perfectly safe so long as one did not stray from the beaten path. Sometimes she caught him looking at her with an expression of cautious humanity. He would always love her, of course, but he was not going to have what remained of his life ruined by a depressed female. Both he and Marian recapped on what had happened since Howard's death. Only tacitly.

The weeks immediately following Howard's funeral had positively glowed with her stoicism, her apparent inability to crumble. Had her London friends seen much of her at this time - they had not because she had retreated to Cambridgeshire to make what she could of her misery -they might have found it easy to question her famous happy marriage.

The friends were not any more vindictive than ordinary people tend to be, but Howard and Marian's bliss had rather been thrown in their faces. 'Hardly a tear,' they said wonderingly at Kensal Green. And the way she waved them good-bye from the undertaker's Daimler! Smiling and waving - awful! Only Mrs Wraith, who had come up from the country to take charge, watched with dread as the car returned to the Tresham Court flat with Marian turned to stone on the back seat and unable to respond to a helping hand for what seemed like the best part of an hour. It was actually six minutes.

'Just like she's been struck by a stroke,' said Mrs Wraith to her husband, later. 'All as cold as butcher's meat. Thick shock.'

The London friends came to see her at the Old Rectory after a tactful interval. Most of them had never been to her childhood home before. The size of the house and its gardens, also the size of her position locally, seemed to them far too large an extension of her personality to have had tucked away unmentioned. Some of them could have felt uncomfortable, except Dr Potter made sure that they did not. He loved these week-ends and encouraged more of them. He took the friends off on excursions to the Gogs and the Backs, showed them how to play croquet and drank a bit too much. 'But he's a *duck*,' they told Marian.

Howard's City colleagues were another matter. They had never been more than names on the necessary workaday fringe. They had stood well back from the intimate mud at the graveside, pale with cold - after their cosy offices - rather than pale with grief. A muster of partners, directors, clerks and chophouse faces. They had all vanished by the time the dear ones had finished jostling one another to see what Marian had inscribed on the coffin. Nothing. *Nothing?* Are you sure? Here, let me look. How amazing! Poor old Howard - nothing. Not even a flower pulled from her own spray. People usually did that. Just a board shining with drizzle. Well.

Then, of course, there had been countless other things to prove that her life had gone on, letters and telephone calls, and trips to London, which became a strange place. She kept in touch and the dear ones kept in touch. Except the 'touching' no longer created the old pattern and became more and more like odd bits of jigsaw catching against each other. All the fun and meaning of her London life had obviously depended upon its casualness, on the juxtaposition of Barnes, Hammersmith and Castelnau, and in clinging to the banks of the river. She now walked alone in a landscape stripped of casualness, where every friendly intention had to be as purposeful as the dykes holding back the fenny swamp if it was to succeed. Worse, there was a harshness in the local light which deprived old situations of their warm and fuzzy edges. Disagreeable though it was, she was slowly forced to admit that most of those she claimed as friends were really her set. It was not the same thing.

On Friday she went to Cambridge to make the most of herself, as Mrs Wraith described her monthly visit to a beauty shop and hairdresser in an alley behind Petty Cury.

'You look lovely,' said Mrs Wraith, when she returned.

'I don't feel lovely.'

This was not true; she did. She had never been vain in the way that Howard had been vain, holding off time and hoarding his youth to the very end, but every now and then she experienced an animal satisfaction in the sheer vitality which was so natural a part of her that she, too, remained unmarked. At this moment, with the bland yellow October sun drying up a week's rain and the beeches scattering gold, she certainly felt lovely, as Mrs Wraith called it. All the way home on the bus she had balanced one plan on another. Right at the top, daringly, like placing the King-roof on a playing-card house, was something she had never planned before. Marriage. She might, could, get married again. It seemed a reasonable plan for nearly the whole afternoon. But late that night there was neither reasonableness nor loveliness left. Only the dark and the fact, as incontrovertible as the damp in the air, that she loved Howard. That Howard was love. Howard had died and so love must be . . . She allowed herself to equate the fact with such calm truth that it became sustaining. She listened to Mozart's *Lucio Silla* overture and Britten's *Gemini Variations.* Howard's hand was on her breast, then on her thigh. The sweet music continued long after her own hand was thrown, with disappointment and revulsion, into the waste spaces of the bed, where the cold sheets burnt into it.

She rose next morning to an uncannily silent house, then remembered that her father had said he was making an early start for Newmarket and that Mrs Wraith had the day off to visit her sister at Fen Ditton. She felt faintly sick and unequal to anything. With no one left but herself to control it, the house was now openly wolfish. Its big square cold rooms gaped, determined to make a meal of her. It would gobble her life up as it had devoured her mother's existence, and then it would go on existing in its own indestructible way. Thank heaven it's fine, thought Marian. I can get out into the garden.

It was dry only in the sense that no rain was falling; indeed the sun shone with surprising heat. But the garden had been soured by so much wet that tidying it was a greasy, saturating business. About eleven, she made some coffee and sat on a bench to drink it. She still felt faint, but no longer sick. The faintness was not unenjoyable. Ash leaves flopped into her lap. I've been upset, she thought tranquilly. Poor old Marian! Countless rooks shrieked their way out of and then back into some hedge elms for no discoverable reason. Mad, they seemed. She strolled to the tower and tugged away the wire-netting frame nailed over the door, without too much difficulty. Her girlhood rushed back to her as she climbed, unbelievably memorable gusts of it drawn from cool damp stone, bat musk, imprisoned air and ascending nervousness. It was the summer holidays before the war. She and Robin were mutually blinding each other as to the real intent of their climb, acting characters from King Arthur, being innocent for all they were worth. This innocence they simply dumped the moment they reached the leads. Discarded too, as well as they could, was the guilt which took its place. 'Suppose I have a baby?' she asked once. It was a fat, grown-up question and Robin resented it. 'Don't be daft,' he scoffed. 'How can you? I'm your brother.' Later, they smoked De Reske cigarettes, compounding their wickedness.

Marian heaved up the trap door and clambered out on to the roof. She walked gingerly from the side, peering across the battlements. A prickly smudge to the west could be King's College Chapel. She saw for the first time the extent of the new development along the Cambridge-Durlingham road, but the lane leading to the house still only had Mrs Wraith's cottage in it. The lane twisted, only broken reaches of it could be seen. A figure strode in and out of view, swinging along with confidence one minute, vanished the next. She waited for it to reappear. The mackintosh gleamed, clean and fresh; hair bounced with each step 'Like a plume on a liberty horse. Howard!' Now and again an arm went out to take a slash at a nettle, or something. Then, vanish again. This meant he must be near the gate.

'Howard, Howard, Howard...' sang Marian lightly under her breath all the way down the stairs, giddy with descent and blessedly mindless. The ground floor came up slap against her feet. She ran along the back path, through the shrubbery and almost into him just as he was closing the gate. Her hand was on his arm, her eyes saw nothing for what seemed an eternity. Then she recovered herself and began to explain. She saw him smile to show he understood. Yet there was no understanding. No mirth either. Just the patient grin of the predestined and a display of childishly pearly teeth.

'It's all my fault,' she said. 'I do feel awful. I meant you to keep the mack. You didn't understand because I simply didn't care whether you understood. I *hated* you. Can you imagine it! I've been a bit worried lately,' she added. She was aware that he was looking at her curiously. Probably thinks I'm crazy, she told herself.

'I - I wore it all the week, before I knew it was mine.'

'Well, now we've both proved that we are no better than we should be - so come and have a cup of coffee. I've been having mine in the garden. There's plenty left.'

She was quite recovered now and miraculously herself. Sauntering along by his side, she could see the little holes in the epaulet where the lieutenant's pips had been. Something was drawing his attention. He was staring at the sudden glimpse of the tower.

'The church?'

'Only a tower. The church was burnt down in 1914.'

His air of studied vacuity vanished in a second. His face became eager and involved. A deep inner excitement informed him. Until now he had accompanied her with an annoying wariness which one would have had to have been a clod not to have noticed. She had endured it with grace, knowing that for a second at least he had received the full force of her intolerance. Had taken it straight in the face as once, in a photograph, she had seen a Viennese Jew being defiled by four sedate middle-aged Nazis. She had done everything she could to make amends, though far more for her own sake than for his, but it was not until he saw the tower that she sensed caution desert him. He was changed, free, adventurous. His face wore the expression worn by all young men in the intangible pursuit of Grails, True Crosses, Fleeces or perhaps just their own identity. She knew he would not turn back now.

'It's nice, isn't it? We - my brother and I - used to play in it when we were children.'

This did not strike her as a false description of what they had done.

'Did many churches burn down in 1914?' he asked.

Marian had to glance at him to see if he was being serious.

'Well, only in Belgium, I suppose. What a funny question. Our church burnt down because somebody left an oil stove on in a draught. 'There was nothing mysterious or Act of God about it. They just claimed the insurance and built a new one. You can't see it from here'

They were now at the front door, which stood open. What next? wondered Marian. She supposed that she would have to give him some kind of hearing. Perhaps, if she didn't ask any questions and just looked interested, which wouldn't be easy, he would get it over quickly and depart. He was standing in the doorway and looking into the large glossy hall and up at the arc of purple stairs, where they fled away richly beneath gilded picture-frames.

'It's beautiful,' he said.

'Not really.'

Yet seeing it as she imagined he was seeing it, it nearly was. Beautiful. She noticed the North Country voice for the first time and thought of black industrial sprawls.

'I lived in the country once. On a mountain.'

'On a mountain?'

'Yes,' he replied gravely.

'How you must hate Cambridgeshire!'

'No. It is beautiful.'

'Nonsense.'

He smiled, showing childishly pearly teeth again, but no humour. She recognized this smile as the one which nearly all the committed young people wore these days. Poor dears, she thought, so many of them became committed long before they discovered that they had no talent for the loneliness involved in their commitment. Cambridge was full of them and one friend of hers who was connected with Welfare spent a great deal of time keeping their world-care-carrying heads away from the gas taps. Now that she understood this young man, she liked him. Howard and she had somehow missed commitment. They had had the war, and after the war they had the peace. It was as simple as that.

'Come and see the tower,' she said. 'There isn't much to see,' she added, 'but I've always been fond of it - probably because it is the only thing which makes my home special.'

He followed her up the spiral stairs. She heard Howard's mack cracking and crushing against the stone, and a light easy tread.

'There!' she cried, when they had clambered out into the midday brightness, presenting him with the enormous view. 'Now this is beautiful!'

He was enchanted. His hands half stretched out to the distance. And it was marvellous, she had to admit. The Cambridgeshire plain for as far as one could see - twenty miles? - was the barest, fractionalized degree immersed by the recent rains, so that every grass-blade, every shedding tree reared individually from glittering water. Cambridge itself was a chunk of quartz sapphire lodged on the finely honed horizon. There was no smudging; nothing which could be seen could not be seen entirely, unless brilliance itself blinded. The young man was rapt. Or this is what she imagined he was. She had never actually seen somebody in this state until now and felt rather at a disadvantage.

'Well?' she asked at last.

'I was imagining the Chosen Ones,' he said.

Oh hell, thought Marian, here it comes. Though how exciting when one came to think if it, to stand on a tower and imagine the Chosen Ones. She had been imagining lunch. Wondering how he would react if she suggested it. An alien strength was guiding her, rushing her at times, promoting schemes and completing decisions which her normal self could neither agree to nor resist. She tried to put it all down to boredom or vertigo or a ghastly week of what her father called 'facing up to facts', but what she felt now was really quite unmysterious. Desire.

'They speak with Jahweh's voice - they always have,' he told her matter-of-factly. He could have been describing the rooks swaying in their stick city at eye-level.

Marian watched him uneasily.

'What do they say?'

'Many things. Everything for the true listener.'

'Tell me one of these things.'

She was pleased to see shyness. Awkwardness. He wouldn't be glib like her Aunt Marjorie, her mother's sister, who was a Catholic convert and who pattered out answers like a machine-gun. He probably wasn't a proselytizer at all. He had no actual words to describe what had happened to himself because it was a wordless business. But this had not stopped his sect, or whatever it was, forcing him to use words. That was the worst of the Christians, they never ceased talking. A Brahmin ban-the-bomber who had come to some of the Barnes parties had never needed to say a single word. Everyone somehow *knew* when they were with her. Howard had known most of all and laughed the knowledge off. Marian saw them still, Howard four months from his death and Meta whatever-her-name-was in a pink and silver sari, dancing the Bossa-nova! 'What fun!' they all cried. Fun. Fun had been her and Howard's holy Word.

The young man, who had been searching for a text, began to quote. Their eyes met for the first time and Marian felt a shuddering jolt, as sense-threatening as a shooting toothache, disrupt her sanity.

'Curse not the land, no not in thine thought; and curse not the rich in thine bedchamber: for a bird of the air shall carry the voice, and that which hath wings shall carry the matter.'

'Please do go on.'

'I am not an actor,' he said quietly. The happy look had gone. He was defensive, critical.

'Oh, of course not!'

Their eyes were still staring and her hand was covering his as it lay on the parapet.

'We must go down,' she said unsteadily. 'I'll get us some lunch - you will have some lunch, won't you? Just eggs or something.'

'My name is Michael,' he said.

'Come and have something to eat - Michael.'

Don't be afraid, she longed to add. Don't think, don't analyse, don't flinch. He's probably queer anyway, she thought. He almost looks it. She hoped that he was, that the tower would topple, that her father, who liked everybody, would return early from Newmarket and send the young man off with cheerful advice on any question he cared to ask.

'Your husband is dead?'

'Yes, dead.'

Dead, dead, dead, reverberated down the stair-well. They were climbing down hand-in-hand, herself first. Sometimes it felt that she was leading, sometimes that she was being thrust from step to step. At the bottom he whirled on her in the confused and flurrying manner of a lover in a baroque painting whose movements are hampered by art traditions. His face banged against hers until, to steady its wildness, she held the back of his head in her hand. Her fingers crept into the soft thick hot hair as he kissed her, rocking her against the wall. He lifted her other hand and kissed it, palm upward. He bowed his face until his brow fitted into the slope of her shoulder, bearing down on it with such unexpected strength that it hurt. She bore it for as long as she could, then forced herself free.

'Come and see this beautiful house, as you call it,' she said.

She switched both bars of the electric fire on in her room and drew the curtains. A most extraordinary calm contained her. She expected to be stupid, even ugly in her demands and was prepared for some subsequent humiliation. Hatred even. Or pity. That would be perhaps the most unbearable, yet she was prepared to bear it. She expected confusion from him, certainly, and was nonplussed to see his clothes, one by one, being folded and piled on a chair. The thick curtains, marigold and Grecian urn chintz backed with old black-out material, hid the sun. The firelight made deep rose shadows on their bodies which, in the oval mirror, looked remote and classical. They lay side by side on the top of the old-fashioned honeycomb quilt in a room which had become luxurious, whose corners were richly indistinct and whose furniture glistened sumptuously. Suddenly, without warning or any progression from the simple breathing contact of their flesh which until now had been their fullest love-making, and breaking a gentleness she was beginning to enjoy, he was in her. In her and with her. More than she could endure. Her hands prised against his shoulders, but uselessly. His mouth remained on her face, leaving cooling wet patches and a faint sweet smell. The little brass travelling-clock which had been a wedding present ticked in her ear. It was afternoon outside but outside was a far country. They need never journey to it again. Whether he slept or had just become quiet and lost in thought afterwards, it was impossible to tell. His eyes were closed and there was almost no movement. She smoked, puffing each mouthful away from him. The cigarette travelled to and fro like a messenger. When it was finished, she turned on her side, half leaning over him, staring down, her breast lightly on his and spreading softly.

'Michael.'

'Michael!' he repeated, gently bitter and with eyes tightly closed.

She hugged him. 'You're getting cold.'

'I'm all right.'

She pulled an eiderdown across them and waited for what seemed like an hour for the exact breathing to change. Then she said, 'I can't just not talk.' Her head felt full of weeping.

'Did you like me?' he asked.

She heard herself make an ugly gulping sound and then her face was crooked uncomfortably in his arm and he was feeling it like a blind man. When his fingers slid on her tears there was a moment of shock and incredulity.

'I thought you liked me,' he said. 'I liked you.'

She turned away to cry unrestrictedly. The noise she made no longer seemed to matter. She wept with complete selfishness and indulgence for herself alone. She just curled into a foetal lump and shook and moaned with her crude sadness. The impetus of her grief promised to carry her from depth to depth, to where any reasonably kind human being could no longer follow her. She would become deranged with weeping and there would be nothing for it but to be left to get on with it. But as totally as her crying began, so it stopped. There was no breath-catching, no gradual rise to the sane surface. She passed from storm to measured composure in a second, sat up and wiped her face with Kleenex.

'I must get up,' she said. 'I'll make some tea.'

She felt his arm tighten on her waist. She didn't attempt to force it away but simply patted his hand, expecting to be released. The pressure remained. She bent and kissed his temple. Lightly.

'Come on, Michael. People will be arriving.'

She wanted him away and herself bathed and dressed. An inconceivable number of tasks demanded to be done, gardening tools to be put away, the tower door wired up, the elevenses tray brought in, the barrow emptied, the fire made up and her bedroom.... Surely he had the sense to realize. He wasn't going to be awkward?

'Michael!'

She spoke with her face turned away from him, for now she minded about her blotches. He sat up suddenly, pulled her round and began kissing her so fiercely that she became frightened and beat at him. He was eating at her, hurting her mouth. She had to stop resisting him to stop the pain. The soft sweetness which followed filled her with gratitude. She held his fingers to her lips; they tasted bitter. Love - sex -was less cloudy this time.

'Crying like that!' he scolded in her ear. 'It's not fair... fair.. fair...'

Later, he hung around while she tidied up. It was only ten to four when she drew the curtains and let the late sun in. Their room fled, hers returned. He sat in Mrs Wraith's chair in the kitchen while she made some tea. He chattered about Carr and Inces where he was a draughtsman and told her about Swaledale. His ordinariness now perplexed her. It seemed tragic that he should be so unaware of having lost the thing which made him extraordinary. Not his chastity, or whatever they called it these days; he had not valued chastity, she was certain; but there had been some hope, some grounds for privilege, and these had been surrendered. She felt nothing when he left because there was nothing in the thin, tall figure, carrying Howard's coat now and loping out of sight with firm defensive steps, to incur her further hate -or lust.

Her father brought his partner back to dinner and while they talked she could scarcely believe it had happened. Howard, too, lost a scrap of his reality.

'I knew there was something I wanted to tell you, Da,' she cried, opening a second bottle of Médoc, 'I stupidly opened the tower door and now I can't get it to close.'

Baxter walked slowly and took deep breaths as he tried to conquer what he would like to believe was a mild attack of upper-deck sickness caught on the swaying 835. There was one plain, dull and respectable reason for his faintness, but this escaped him. All that he had eaten since a beans-and-egg supper the night before was a plate of cornflakes and two pieces of Mrs Wraith's cake. To avoid a slight dizziness he held himself very erect, but the placing of one foot before another had suddenly become a great matter and the probability that he must slip down on to the sticky pavement if this wavering nausea increased brought him to a shocked halt on Magdalene Bridge. The steady flow of the river dragged serenely below him. Its powerful limpidity became mesmeric and stern. It commanded Baxter's nervous system to adopt its own calm continuity while strictly forbidding him to throw-up in its face. The feverishness left him. He strolled on, relishing an unfamiliar feeling of convalescence and the sense of his body being marble clean and cold under his clothes.

Summer-time had just ended and the new dark was novel and festive. Lights, record-players and voices poured into it, as though trying it out. The lanes groping their way down to the Backs smelled of toast, stationery, wet stone, smoke and garden-rot. Baxter kept his path when dim gateways suddenly let fly a swarm of young people, not because he felt proud or defensive, but because to dodge about and laugh and shout 'Sorry!' as they did would have involved him in their happiness. This - if genuinely existed - was not for him. The river beneath the new Garrett Hostel Bridge showed no perceptible movement. Baxter imagined he could feel the stresses in the bronze parapet. A drowned self looked up at him from among the motionless licked-toffee rushes. Gradually, this prostrate self turned into her body. Her map of flesh lay below him. He studied it with privileged deliberation, retracing the paths he had taken. The woman, the thrust and the slack of her, the great soft weight of her legs, her mouth rubbing its way into his. And her hair! He had never seen such hair; it could clothe them both. 'Do you really like it?' she had asked. He had liked it in fistfuls. Kissing it had blinded him. It had been immediately after this that the woman had risen above him, adored him in some way, said all the things he couldn't hear because of 'Michael, Michael, Michael' - her endless saying of his name.

'Michael,' murmured Baxter to himself in the water. The woman had gone; there remained the huge problem of his reflected self. Was that wavering image the shadow or the substance of Michael glorified? In Him, of course. He would like to pray, to put into words the day's facts, beginning with his mother's letter carbonizing in the hand-basin. Ending - where? Not here by the river where everything was beginning again. He strode abruptly from the bridge. Just at that moment all the Cambridge clocks chimed seven. He could, if he hurried, reach Kingdom Hall. He slowed down so noticeably that people passing glanced at him with faces which said, 'Forgotten something?' His mind was now like a see-saw, with the dark side soaring up to the light and being exposed by it, and all the brightness plunging to the earth and being blackened. A college window was slammed-to and then a door.

'Jehovah - Creator!' said Baxter. He would have liked to have added 'Mercy' but the Witnesses did not plead for mercy, finding it superfluous to their belief in the reciprocal arrangement between God and themselves. All the same, doubt terrorized Baxter as he entered King's Parade. Jehovah. . . Jehovah. . . have I rejected? Am I rejected? And then, sublime loophole, *Can I reject? Or be rejected?*

He passed the Chapel. Garnet windows hung serried between the branching stone, telling no story. Inside, pressing against the glass, was the special gloom of the reliquary, the bolted jewel-box, of great sights lying fallow. Outside, a beatific hull continued to break its original promise to sail away beyond architecture. Baxter looked upwards in order to see the haphazard stars between the finials of the skyline. But the marvellous building drew him to the tenderness of the earth. Its beauty hardened in his head just as the woman's breasts had hardened in his hand.

Some undergraduates approached, saw Baxter staring and also looked up. 'Ye men of Galilee. . . ?' one of them said after a pause. 'A flying saucer!' 'Buzz Aldrin!' 'Batman!' The answers rattled down on Baxter but yet hardly disturbed him. He was, like the devout of all times and all places, beginning to comprehend the nature of the deal he had to do with God. 'The waters of the Shiloah that are going gently' were turning out to be too gentle where he was concerned. Knowing his own nature - for which the Creator must accept responsibility - he had permitted swifter currents to flow through the tabernacle of the Most High. There had been no blood-guilt. He remained Chosen. 'Chosen.' He said it softly aloud and the undergraduates walked away.

There was a lavatory in the Market Place. He ran down a slippery little staircase into its acrid depths and washed his face and hands in the bowl, re-tied his tie and combed his hair with a piece of yellow comb he found lying there. Outside, the problem of where to go and what to do loomed greater than ever. He sat on a corporation seat and the low country breezes from the river lands, which still smelled strangely to him, whipped over the market cobbles, shifting celery fragments, straw packing and scraps of newsprint. A man came and sat beside him and lit a cigarette. Baxter rose and walked across the square to a restaurant with filmy net curtains and a menu in a brass frame by the door. It was called the Moomin and had been opened only recently. He had read about it in the paper. Inside, it was soft and shining at the same time, as though plush had been polished. A waiter about his own age took his coat and pushed a table into his stomach as he sat down, lit a candle and handed him a menu with scores of dishes written on it with a Biro. People eating alone watched him and there was a juke box playing Bach's *Coffee Cantata*. The food came too quickly: he felt that a dish costing 16*s*. 6*d*. should take its time. It turned out to be knobs of liver, kidney and mushroom under a milky-tea-coloured sauce. He ate a lot of bread with it. He felt better, steadied. The people eating near were now far less impressive and Baxter found himself joining in the watching game in which the whole restaurant was involved. Some of the eyes were like the clegs from the lake near his home, stubborn and clinging. Others sped over him like swallows. All, however, told him one thing, that they were together and he was apart. Those that said 'join us' did so not out of compassion but to see what would happen if he did. 'Who is the belle of the ball tonight?' muttered his waiter to a friend. Baxter paid the bill 28s. 9d. - it was the most he had ever paid for a meal in his life, yet it was only half past eight.

The meeting would be over now. Had they missed him? Their Judas? A sudden craving for the room itself filled him, the God centre with its misted ochre distemper, stack-chairs and its mystery. He began to long for it as an exile longs for the commonplaces of his own country. Upper room and catacomb, these were the places which Jahweh chose. Not the clergy temples of ever-recurring Babylon. Not the wine and the music beneath the spires, but the God-filled cave and the blood tryst.

Mecklenburgh Street, where Kingdom Hall was, still retained its gas-lamps. They sent a stagy glimmer down the cratered tarmac and gave a mews-like elegance to doors which opened only on to miniature warehouses and mattress repositories. It was a cul-de-sac, holding a special fascination for policemen and lovers. A policeman now watched Baxter approach, saw him try the door of *Kingdom Hall: Headquarters of the Watchtower Society,* then saw him spread imploringly against the dun paint, hands outstretched, head pale and fallen, crucified.

'You've had it, son,' said the policeman.

'I must go in,' said Baxter, not moving. 'I belong - I *belong.*'

'You're too late, mate. It's all over.'

'It can't be, it can't be!' said Baxter. He was shouting.

'Here, here,' said the policeman. He punched Baxter's shoulder gently. 'You a grad, son? You been drinking? You all right?'

'I.. . I'll go home,' said Baxter slowly.

'You do that,' said the policeman. 'Home is where you belong

41

right now.' He had noticed the epaulets and the pip pin-holes. 'You one of them, then?' He nodded at the Hall.

Baxter hesitated. Witness! Witness! screamed rook-like voices somewhere near his heart. A porous face with silky cheek-hair was close to his own. 'Good night,' he said.

'Good night, sir,' said the policeman.

The house was empty. Mrs Jones was at the pictures. It was pleasant being there without her, to walk about without stealth, to avoid inquiry and solicitude, bang doors, run the bath, whistle, hug her cat and make tea. But she had opened his windows. He closed them, drew the curtains and put on both bars of the electric fire. Later, he wrote to his mother. He then read, Acts XX and Revelation XVI. An angel had poured a bowl of blood out of heaven on to the earth, so that it could not affect Jehovah and His living waters. This blood had poisoned the River Nile. The fish had died and stank. Baxter lay on his back thinking about this. If an *angel* could be blood-guilty. . . All his certainty fled. He tried to pray but as he had never approached the Throne without the confidence of the Bride Remnant his words seemed cringing and despicable. He would not crawl - even to God. I am Bride Michael, he reminded heaven and himself. He fell asleep with the light on and the door open for the cat. He lay on top of the bedclothes in his pyjamas, breathing into the pillow with a noisy, jarring force. The woman's hands were touching his back, hesitant, stirring.

'No!' he said.

The word in the pillow was like a stone in a well.

'It's only me,' said Mrs Jones.

'No...'

'You all right, Mr Baxter? I'll put your eiderdown over you and switch the light off.'

Something touched Baxter's waist, his bare feet. He swung round, hands backwards against his eyes, yet seeing the woman all the same.

'Get out! Leave me! Don't touch me. Great whore! Harlot! Bitch- -bitch-bitch . .'

'You do see, don't you, Mr Baxter?' said Mrs Jones. It was about an hour later and they were standing together at the bottom of the stairs with his luggage neatly stacked. 'I mean, I'm all on my own, no hubby and all that. I mean it is difficult for me, Mr Baxter - even you can see that. You young fellers, well you get excited. Het up. It's only natural. Don't think I don't know that. But you do see, with me being all on my tod - Ah, here we are. Must have been waiting on the rank. Tell him the Y.M.C.A. It's only until you get settled - have worked things out. You know what I mean? And then on Monday you have a chat with the Welfare. It's nothing to be ashamed of, you know. Couldn't you feel me being a mother to you, Mr Baxter? Couldn't you? I was, you know. Only there you were, up there, undressed, no friends, reading the Bible. I worried I can tell you, Mr Baxter. Say good-bye, pussy, good-bye and good luck, eh? Say it nicely. No hard feelings, we don't want any of those, do we, Mr Baxter! It's being on my own - you do understand, don't you?'

'What shall we do for Christmas?' asked Dr Potter.

'What we always do, I suppose,' said Marian. 'Eat, drink, wash up; listen to the Queen.' And take good care that there are no horrid empty chairs standing around, she added to herself. 'Why?'

'Why? Oh, I just thought that it was a lot of damn work just for the two of us, so why don't we try the Blue Boar?'

'But we'd never get in. Christmas is next week.'

'We *could* get in,' said her father, as though pulling a rabbit from a hat. He waited for her to look pleased.

'Then you must have made inquiries some time ago. Why haven't you said a word until now?'

'I - I don't know,' answered her father.

He didn't. Some kind of atmosphere in the house, a sense of enclosure and a resultant sense of his being unenclosed and unimportant, had made it difficult for him to plan the most ordinary things these past few weeks.

'Not a hotel Christmas, Da,' said Marian, gentle now.

'Not if you don't want it. I just thought...'

'It was sweet of you, Da.'

She kissed him. He had another thought.

Then how about getting the Londoners down here? Push the boat out, if you like. How about that?'

'Now who's piling on the work?'

'Oh, we'd all pull our weight. Come on, let's give 'em a ring!'

'No, Father.'

There was a pause during which a coal spun from the grate, flaming exultantly.

'There's a reason?'

She nodded.

'Well, come on, out with it.'

'Da, how are your professional nerves?'

'They are all right in a professional situation. Stop being so bloody obscure.' His voice changed. 'You're ill, is that it?' Thoughts of Edie at Marian's age careered in his brain, revealing the bitter facts. 'You've been to see somebody else and, now you know, you've got to tell me. Is that it?'

'That's almost it. I'm going to have a baby.'

She saw him trying to believe, watched him summon every agency, his rationalism, his humanity and all that was left of his ordinary male surprise after half a century in the surgery, but an imbecilic incomprehension held its ground. He looked at this moment like one of the meanest of the mean-faced old. Habit brought recovery at last. Shock - to him - what the hell was he thinking about!

'Do you want it?'

It was Dr Potter speaking. Not God.

'I've always wanted what I got before,' said Marian, glancing backwards for the last time.

At Swan Gates

The first word I ever spoke, they said, was 'dark'. They were retiring, it seems, and were sunk into those repetitive banalities which close the day. 'How dark it is,' they murmured to each other as they strolled the long low rooms in the travelling lamplight. 'Yes, dark,' agreed my father and dark, dark, dark whispered Miss Willaby - although whether she meant myself, a tiny new thing lying there in the cane and rosewood cradle, or just the night, no one can be certain now. But the sad, quiet word must have faltered about me for, to their astonishment, I echoed, 'dark'. Could this have been the night the huge white bird crashed down the chimney and beat against the looking-glasses in terror? It is possible. They say they cannot remember and I am not surprised! My father and Miss Willaby were perfectionists in the art of abdicating the memory of their English experiences. But the bird hurling itself against the faded garlands on the wallpaper like a screaming shuttlecock and the solitary word were the only two things which lingered from that lost year at Swan Gates, my birthplace.

As soon as he could, that is, when the mourning was over and a granite cross of Ionian shape had been sentinelled at my mother's grave, my father took Miss Willaby and myself to India. There we lived until I was grown-up, in Tanda, which is in the Provinces, and in a white house fretted and pierced for light and air. There was a garden which ran down to the Gogra River. My father kept it Indian as he despised the brown travesties of Surrey and Gloucestershire with which our English neighbours surrounded themselves. It was all so bright, so gold. We lived and moved in a perpetual jewel. The lawns were like thin yellow carpets flung down under the mango trees. Nothing soothed or cooled. Everything one saw or touched set up a shallow disturbance in the mind. And the white dazzled endlessly, whether it was the gleam of walls or of blossom, or the classically folded linen falling from the narrow shoulders of the house-boys.

In summer we retreated deeper and deeper into the house in our endeavour to island ourselves in shadow. We penned in corners with shiny screens and dragged tubbed pomegranates into the dark after us, and Miss Willaby would trail through the aromatic gloom like a Goya lady, all black and heavy in skirts and shawls. We gained very little by all this. The fierce serrated gold stabbed through the lacy trellises. It was inescapable. It was gold in the water-garden, gold the rotting figs and the mangoes bursting under the sun, golden-black the boys' eyes and the night, when Miss Willaby would drag her soaking skirts through the drenched marigolds shouting, *'Butti jaloa! Butti jaloa!'* - light the lamps! - in her hard Edinburgh voice. From the punt-shed on the banks of the Gogra River I would look up and see the garden lamps jerking in the trees and a hatred of India would fountain up inside me like a bilious sickness and I would long for the cold, meagre stream which looped Swan Gates.

How weary they must have been with my endless questioning. Frightened too - although it was some time before I realized this. 'It was an old, old house - the house I was born in?' 'Yes,' they would answer. 'And you had to cross the fields to get to it?' 'It was pleasantly isolated,' my father would reply with satisfaction. 'Didn't you like living there?' A lizard-like dart of intelligence would scuttle from my father's eyes and take shelter beneath Miss Willaby's hooded lids. Then one or the other of them would laugh greyly and say, 'Of course we did!' Only once did I follow this up logically with, 'Then why can't we go back. . . ?' because I never wanted to feel my father's astonishing anger sweep over me like that again. However, this last question was settled once and for all when I was about fourteen. A letter came from England which gave my father so much happiness he propped it up against the fruit-dish at breakfast and read it gradually, like a poem.

'Murray's have got rid of it at last,' he said. 'Meadows and all. Lock, stock and barrel! No more tenants. No more mention of it. . .' He smiled long and deliberately at Miss Willaby.

'There were six bedrooms,' she volunteered in a strange, emancipated voice, such as the voice people use when they feel they can at last speak freely of the dead. 'The one your poor mother. .. the one you were born in was at the end facing the apple orchard.' She returned my father's smile. Her mouth and eyes jigged in the unresponsive flesh of her face. Shall I go on? she seemed to enquire. 'All the other rooms faced the water,' she said. 'You could see the swans when they came up. Now there's something I'll not forget! There must have been a guid fifty of them and all of them so white. They say they had been there since before the Stuart kings!'

'The Tudor,' my father corrected.

Miss Willaby hitched her dress and stared privately around her.

It was very shortly after this that I realized Miss Willaby was my father's mistress. She had been all the time, of course, but the conscious transition of her status in my own mind from a tall, plain Scottish housekeeper to a woman my father touched, wrecked not only my faint affection for him, but even the mere obligation of appearing dutiful when he was around. Curiously enough, there was nothing in this revelation which changed my attitude to Miss Willaby; if anything I liked her better. What lessened my father, improved her in my eyes. I was not unaware of the injustice of this, but the detestation I felt for my father was too robust a thing to be shaken by such niceties as equity. I retreated from him and took refuge in a dream. The dream was Swan Gates. I gathered together the few simple, trustworthy images they had let slip from time to time - an orchard, a straggling thatched house, a bright day and a dark river - they snapped together and made a wholeness. Once I talked of it to Miss Willaby.

'Going where -?' she asked, lowering her rough gingery brows.

'Home,' I said cruelly.

'And where might "home" be then?'

I faced her with embarrassment.

'England's home,' I said.

'That house?' she asked swiftly. 'No good going there. It isn't ours anyway.'

'I only want to see it. I was born there. I-' 'Hoo!' she exclaimed, the gravelly look coming into her eyes. 'Why tell me? I was there. Anyway, being born in a place doesn't make it sacred - or not usually it doesn't. Go and swim. You read too much.'

My father came in just then and Miss Willaby swivelled round in her stiff cocoon of muslins and shouted, 'Arnold thinks he's a saint.'

'Time will tell,' my father answered, heavily playful. 'He's hardly ready for temptations yet!' He squeezed my arm and I shrank.

'I am going to Cambridge, aren't I?'

'Cambridge? I suppose so - although you could learn as much at Jalalpur if you had a mind to.'

'Cambridge I think,' I said in an affected adult manner, 'it will make it easier for me to get to Swan Gates sometimes . .'

I waited. My father scarcely stirred. He had his back to me and I could see his hands as they gangled by his sides, white and red still, in spite of all the Indian sun. They were like a racial covenant resisting his ex-patriotism. Then he swept round in a paroxysm of temper and grabbing me by the shoulders, shook me until my hair fell down over my face and my eyes stung with tears. 'Keep away! Keep away!' he cried. *'You understand?'* The flesh on one side of his neck was discoloured and folded like tortoise-skin. There was a pink bubble on his full lower lip. Instead of being intimidated by his flaring anger I gained a desperate courage from his loss of control and I heard myself say, loudly and distinctly, so that my own terror was increased as well as his, 'Why. .'

An incantation could not have produced a greater effect. For a full minute we all stood with the silence pouring over us - our own silence, not that of the house, from which we heard the distant creak of fans as the punkah-boy cooled the dining-room and the childish, private gaiety of the kitchen servants - and then Miss Willaby saved us.

'There's one thing I wouldn't mind being in England for myself,' she said. 'Those blasted cicadas!'

This was the only time I ever heard her swear in any shape or form. My father's hands dropped away from me. 'Leave the room,' he said with fantastic dignity. I did so, but slowly enough to hear him mutter grudgingly to Miss Willaby, 'Thank you, Blanche.'

A very odd thing came out of all this. From that day neither of them made the least effort to conceal their relationship from me, although they still avoided any appearance of intimacy in a thousand experienced ways when the house-boys were around. Occasionally at evening I would meet them strolling in the garden alleys and Miss Willaby would have one hard little claw-like hand caught up in the bony crook of my father's arm. And once, returning from a midnight swim, I looked up at the house and saw a yellow oblong engraved meticulously against the furry darkness. An oiled silk curtain had been lowered instead of the usual Venetian drop-blind and in unbelievably perfect profile, I saw them approaching each other like a pair of magnified praying mantises. Their rigid bodies were so arid that seen in the single reflected dimension, love or affection between them became unthinkable and when they at last drew together, it was not so much an embrace, as an awkward piece of geometry. But for all that, I realized I was witnessing the preliminaries of their guarded bliss, and returned to my room abashed and bewildered.

Now more than ever I thought of India as a cage. I became obsessed by the thought of England and instead of enjoying my last year at the Jalalpur school, I retreated into a furious self-pity. Like most self-pity, it was highly irrational, for while I thought of the dank water-meadows and meadow sweet streams of Swan Gates, I still enjoyed lying naked under the swirling mosquito meshes in my bedroom and listening to the slazzle-slazzle of lizards confused by starlight and the brilliant shrieks of invisible birds. Just as the mountain paeonies, the peach-boles mellifluous with beetles and the sensuous strumming of oleander-gorged bees could never be equalled, I was bound to tell myself, by East Anglian apple blossom. Every Friday evening I returned from Jalalpur and as I sat at dinner I would observe Miss Willaby and my father with an almost clinical detachment, finding it incredible that there should exist in either one of them that passion, the way to which could only be discovered by a desperate act. I was encouraged to talk about the week at school. As we chattered, myself inwardly aloof and my father mysteriously aware of my being so, however adroitly I gossiped, Miss Willaby would rush to and fro from the kitchen to the veranda - or to the linen-cupboard where she stored all the bottled apricots which we never seemed to eat. Intensely, embarrassingly busy, she took to smiling woodenly as she passed and stretching her long, discoloured throat.

It gradually dawned upon me that their 'India' was a charade. It was literary. It was as if a Calcutta lawyer had set up house in Bath and had insisted on being served with roast beef every night and having *Pickwick Papers* read to him while he ate it. It was all part of their elaborate hiding, or, more particularly, my father's hiding. And this more an escaping from his own nature than from any fear of retribution. Time was already comfortingly on his side. If he still knew horror it was the kind which came from a realization of the evil within him which had allowed him, either by a careful neglect or some swifter action, to let my mother die. So he hid from that worst of all accusers, himself. His secretiveness had flattened him into a cardboard figure, too neutral even to be thought of as 'eccentric'. Only his grotesque love for Miss Willaby was left to remind him of the continuity of life and kindle his chilly gaze. With me he was polite, rather than kind, and if at any time he let go and the beastly shouting, shaking onus of his temper descended on me, then it was usually more my fault than his.

My future now worried him stiff. I was going to Cambridge. It was all settled. As the day for my sailing drew near, my father extended the delicate antenna of his friendship to the full and I would often find him at my side, puffing away at the feeble warmth of his lizard nature in a final effort to draw me to him. I began to realize that it was less the possibility of betrayal that worried him, than that I should, as his son, add to the burden of his self-loathing. Miss Willaby, too, emphasized during those last few months in India that her kindness to me during all of my nineteen years had been a consistent thing. An unlooked-for thing, too, as it happened, since I learned from her in her one indiscreet moment that my being born alive had been considered impossible. She had laughed if off with, 'And look at you now - a braw laddie! Six fut or all but nigh!'

I was at Cambridge a whole term before going to Swan Gates. It was late April. The house, like almost everything else in England, was smaller than I expected it to be. I think I had expected to see a manor or a hall, or at least something which could be called a country-house. Instead I found a large, low cottage in a narrow valley which could only be reached by scarcely discernible bridle-paths. There was a very elaborate garden all round the house, too elaborate really for the kind of house it was. As I got near I could hear the sound of a piano being played rather flamboyantly, as though the pianist suspected an audience, or at any rate hoped for one. Suddenly the music stopped and the door flashed open before I had time to knock. A round, bouncing little man, like one of those smooth Chinese dolls which recover their poise however much they are tumbled, beckoned me in.

'Ah!' he cried. 'I thought I heard the bell!'

I mumbled my reason for calling. 'I was born here,' I said, sensing at once both the absurdity and the grandiloquence of the statement.

'Exactly!' the man said.

'Why "exactly"?' I demanded. 'How could you know why I've come? I hardly knew myself until this morning.'

But he just repeated his 'exactly, exactly' adding, 'You've come to tea, of course?'

I said it was very good of him and so we entered Swan Gates. I murmured it under my breath, 'Swan Gates.. . Swan Gates. . . Swan Gates. . .' I stared around, carefully, so as not to be offensive, yet all the time hungry for a glimpse of what might still be mine, some scrap of the past, a feather-touch of that first year; a sign; a whisper. A revelation. The room was comfortably furnished, in fact almost luxuriously so. The walls were covered with books and pictures. Slender, lady-like cabinets glistened with china. The piano I had heard stood in a raised recess and made a shining isthmus of wood and ivory. A reproduction of Donatello's *David* stood on a side-table. Over the fireplace there was a big blue summery painting by Tuke of thin Edwardian fisher-boys pinkly exercising against a vivid sea.

'Sit here, will you? I expect you find it cold after Africa?'

'India,' I said.

'Yes, yes; India. And your name is-?'

I told him, but could see that it meant nothing. He had obviously heard that the previous owners had gone abroad and that was all.

'In that case I shall call you Arnold - if I may, of course!'

1 nodded. Wondering how to continue I said, 'It's ridiculous - this atavistic thing. I mean wanting to come back to one's birthplace.'

'Oh?' he said. 'Why "ridiculous"? Why shouldn't one want to go back? Beginnings and endings are what matter most, although sometimes I wonder if they are not one and the same...'

'You mean that the moment of our birth is also the moment of our death?'

'Exactly.'

'Isn't that pessimism?'

'It might well be, except who is to say what anything is!'

'If birth and death *are* the same,' I persisted, 'I - I . . .' A sudden terror shook me.

'Tea! tea!' cried the Chinese-tumbler man. 'We mustn't be morbid in April!' He tugged a bell rope.

A nervous-looking young man entered pulling a trolley of cups, bread and butter and cakes after him.

'You staying?' the little round man demanded, turning to him. For answer the young man swung on his heel, a pettish movement, and was gone.

'My secretary,' it was explained. 'My name, incidentally, is Sandell. You wouldn't have heard - I hope.' He began to pour tea most carefully, using a multitude of silver things.

I talked about the swans.

'Yes,' he said in a deeply apologetic voice, 'I can really say that I'm truly, genuinely sorry about the swans. But I had no choice. You'll not believe it when I tell you, but in January the water often got right inside the house. Not flooding, you understand, but a more mysterious entrance. It rose in damp wraiths and crept through the plaster - gallons and gallons of it crawling all over the walls. So I had to do something. Ah, I can see you are disappointed. A pity, a pity!

Come with me.'

We carried our tea-cups into the garden. It was all drearily neat and contrived. Beyond the knife-edged lawn the ground fell away into a ragged shallow. We walked to it and as we got near it became fastidious and elaborate like all the rest. It was full of shrubs and standard roses. Its sides had been terraced and away in the distance, just before the parched stream-bed turned out of sight, stood an enormous stone figure which looked as though it had seen better days as part of a Victorian railway station.

'That's Zeus - heard of him?'

I put out my hand to touch a great mossy post rising out of the finicky turf like a totem.

'Stanchion,' explained Mr Sandell. 'Where they tied the barges up.'

'I suppose you dammed the stream? You diverted it; turned it away?' I felt that I could never forgive him.

'That's about it,' he said lightly. 'A pity, as I say, since I'm told the swans have been coming by here ever since the time of the Plantagenet kings...'

I was too miserable to say, 'the Tudor'. We returned to the house. Once again I tried to see things as they were, my father and Miss Willaby strolling in the garden, talking in this very parlour. *And how was it done?* I asked myself. And how were they not discovered? A picture of missal -like clarity fixed itself in my mind. I could see them sitting opposite each other at Tanda with their narrow legs sprawling across the rush mats, and their faces all puckered with watching and waiting.

Mr Sandell was saying, 'Well now, let's show you. the famous room!' He was bouncing along on his short fat legs.

'I really shouldn't stay - it's awfully good of you. . .' Then realizing my mistake - after all, he was only letting me see my room; there had been no suggestion of a visit - I floundered into silence.

But he was a seismograph registering the faintest disturbance in the nature of others. 'Of course! Of course! Why not?' My protests were swept away. 'Indeed, I should have thought of it myself. Come all the way from Afr - India, to where the sun came peeping in at morn and not stay the night! Terrible!'

I followed him as he chattered, through the hall and up a twisting staircase. The bedrooms opened off a narrow passage. From one of these doors the young secretary burst rather suddenly and brushed past us without a word.

'Sulks, sulks, sulks,' commented Mr Sandell. 'Overlooking the apple orchard, you say? Well that is still there!'

I felt the curiosity creeping back. So this... . this little room... ? In the absence of tangible evidence I took refuge in some kind of classical proof- Rizzio, Robsart - and my gaze automatically turned to the floor. But the only red there, was the legitimate flush of the boisterous roses on the carpet. I listened intently for something more than Mr Sandell's bright patter; my own 'dark, dark, dark', perhaps. The apple boughs crossed their fingers against the window. There was nothing. Nothing. Not a smudge of all that darkness to dim the barbed St. Sebastian simpering in his copied Florentine frame. Nothing but the fal-lals and the pale sprigged bed.

Mr Sandell was speaking. 'I have never done it myself- the going back, as you might say. Mine is the inheritance which doesn't call for introspection. It is, now I come to think of it, quite surprising how little I remember! Practice makes perfect, they say.'

'You would recommend that I just went on?' I asked.

'You really haven't much choice, have you?'

'N-no. But if I chose to go back, there are others I could carry with me.'

He smiled. 'My dear boy, the *bore* of it! Personally I have never had enough energy to "carry with me", as you put it, those I care for - and heaven knows *they* should be light enough! Those you don't care for would be a dead weight. Believe me, there's nothing so heavy as hate!'

'I'm not sure that it is hate . . .' I said slowly, realising all at once the truth of this.

'Then it is love?'

I wavered. I saw the Ionian cross in the little churchyard with its formal lie, 'Beloved wife of - ' , and the daffodils in their unkempt profusion. 'No,' I said with certainty, 'no, it isn't love.'

'What a relief' said Mr Sandell. 'How well - if I may say so - how well I know your feelings. They have been my own so many times. Not hate, not love. Something in between - which amounts to nothing, you know! Nothing. The joy of finding *that* out! To be able to get *on* with life!'

I wanted to cry out against these short-cut sentiments. To shout at him, 'It's nothing of the sort. You're wrong. It is my entire existence that you are settling so glibly; my life and my mother's death.' But Mr Sandell was twinkling round the room, patting things straight.

'There, there,' he was saying comfortingly as if he were talking to a child, 'you should be all right. Dinner's in half an hour.'

I don't know what the time was when I awoke. My watch had stopped. The plunging darkness of deepest night made me feel disorientated, so that I found it difficult to recall the position of things in the bedroom. I closed my eyes and tried to sleep, but all the time I kept thinking about Tanda and the two stem-like people who had to stay there because of what had occurred under this low invisible ceiling. Much against my will, I began to see my father and Miss Willaby with a remote charity. It was Mr Sandell, of course, with his twittering tolerance. I fought against his cheap kindness. My eyes hurt and for a moment I thought that I was going blind. I sat up, bewildered and rather afraid. The room was desperately hot and I remembered that I had left the window closed, thinking that it was India. I rose, peeled off the clammy flannel pyjamas Mr Sandell had insisted I borrowed, and felt my way across to the window. I dragged the curtains apart and thrust the casement out on its curly latch.

I think what I noticed first was the way the water swept in an ashen wake about the plinth of Zeus, and the way the roses had their budding stems tugged along on the swift current while their roots remained anchored. The big lawn was a dead, lustreless silver and the hills and meadows beyond the stream, fleecy, grey and indistinct. But the stream itself shone and its edges were combed into brilliant scallops which lapped and splashed against the terrace stones, and cast up jets of greenish-silver spray against the emerald stanchions. Because I knew what I had to wait for there was no element of actual surprise in my heart when the great cortege of banished swans swept by. I saw their orange eyes and immaculate breasts and their wand-like throats waving. I leant out, my bare arms icy, and heard a purling wire-thin sound, which could have been music, except it was incomparable. After the sound the sloe-blue darkness returned and it was night and silence again.

I returned to Cambridge as early as I could the next morning. Before breakfast I walked for the last time in the garden. The sun poured down on the carefully laid turfs which lined the bed of the stream. I strolled between the dry, mathematically planted roses and kicked the dusty mold at the base of the azalea bushes. Later, as I walked away down the bridle-path, I turned, knowing I should never come to Swan Gates again. Supposing my father and Miss Willaby should see that fussed-up garden! How they would loathe it! But they were in India, their spindly affection reflected across more golden grass. There was another barren shoot of my life which would have to be pruned away! I would leave them to their peace, such as it was. Tanda and Swan Gates, heritages it would be more prudent not to claim. Look what happened to poor Hamlet! The young secretary was staring at me from the parlour window. I thought he laughed. If he did, then he had no reason to. It was I who was free.

Period Return

For the last ten miles they had the compartment to themselves. Nicholas pressed his forehead to the sun-warmed glass, his eyes dutiful and searching, though aching with travel. Nothing must be missed. Although he had been asleep when Malta had been sighted and had always occupied the wrong side of the seat when declaimed-at castles had faltered by, now it was imperative not to miss a cottage, a post, a gate. Opposite to Nicholas sat his father, as though asleep. His face was moist and white and the flat gold rims of his glasses glinted richly in a broad lane of sunshine which stabbed into the private shadows of the carriage, making Mr Plenderist's head like a detail in a dissected painting. In a third corner with her shoeless feet stretched out upon the opposite seat, sat Nicholas's sister Deva. Reading, never speaking, thought the boy. He noticed again with distaste the avid, paper-eating moue of her mouth. Strange, he wondered, how plain Deva looked when she read and how beautiful she was when she spoke. Yet she rarely talked.

'We have just passed Buriton,' he said, remembering the name from his father's reminiscences. 'Buriton,' he repeated sadly, 'where Thompson shot the fox.'

But his father continued to make soft blowing noises from his sleep-loose mouth and Deva turned her page like a whip.

'After Buriton comes Tanney,' he continued, not quite to himself, 'and after Tanney, Forbes and after Forbes...'

'Mendleton,' finished Deva, her face tilted in mock-kindliness. 'It will be here soon enough and now, if you don't mind, I'll read, for goodness knows what chance I will have to do so in the next few weeks!'

'But you've read for *ages*,' he retorted daringly.

'Please do be quiet, Nicholas,' she said, evenly enough although her fingers jagged into the fluffy edges of the book.

'She's old ... she's old ...' he sang voicelessly, and the train-song joined in with '*twenty*-nine, *twenty*-nine...'

He looked at the corners of the compartment, three filled, and one empty. Or rather the fourth contained a small part of Deva - her slender feet. Always this unhappy angularity of relationships. Never the completeness of the square.

Nicholas wondered for the millionth time what his mother was like. She would be sitting where Deva's feet were resting. Like a puppeteer he lifted Mrs Plenderist from the faded steps in the photograph and sat her beneath the view of Framlingham Castle on the carriage wall. She had on her tall-crowned hat, without which he could never imagine her. It had artificial roses crowding under the brim and the hem of her dress went up and down like pennants. She wore the chain which Deva sometimes displayed at dinner. Even her shoes stood plainly on the dusty floor but when he searched for her face the features came and went like the *cat* in *Alice*, sometimes a nose, sometimes the eyes, or the sweet mouth smiling. Never the completed image.

Wearily then he would acknowledge the autonomy of the moment when the shutter fell on an Indian April the spring before he was born and she had died.

They were nearing Mendleton now and still Deva read. Nicholas wondered if she was exercising an enormous will power not to look out of the window where evening lawned the land in strands of grey and gold. They were riding slowly by the river. Long necklets of trivial houses threaded out from the lavender-dull centre of the town. A bus travelled parallel with the line beyond a row of bungalows. Nicholas could see the people inside in foolish profile, like painted passengers in a toy bus. It occurred to him as almost wonderful that they should have been going backwards and forwards thus each day all the time he had been alive in India.

Mr Plenderist opened his eyes and blinked weakly as the latticed shadows fell across his view.

'You'll see the church in a moment,' he said.

Nicholas waited. Distantly, above every other building, arose the stepped heights, the dizzily poised lead steeple of the parish church.

Deva stood up, a graceful figure, and began to jerk luggage off the rack. Nicholas felt suddenly very tired and small and dirty.

Mr Plenderist held his spectacles away from his face and shouted, 'Porter!' in his thin peremptory voice. The door hung open, swinging against silence. From a smudgy panel of the ticket office, Mr Todd watched Mr Plenderist emerge from his compartment. Then he watched Miss Plenderist pull a bag to the edge of the door and heard her second her father's cry for the porter, who was gardening.

Finally, Mr Todd watched Nicholas, observing him with a special interest, his thin legs, his dark drooping hair, his yellow Indian skin and his neat, nervous features. 'Un'ealthy,' he decided. 'But then it was them 'ot foreign places. And 'is poor mother dead and 'is father older than he, Mr Todd, was, which must make him, let Mr Todd see, sixty or more...'

He was thus calculating when Mr Plenderist put his worn, half-seeing eyes to the pane and said:

'Nice to see you, Todd.'

' 'Ome for keeps, sir, I 'ope.'

'We hope so indeed, Todd.'

'We was very sorry to 'ear, sir. *Very* sorry. .'

Mr Plenderist looked puzzled and then remembered.

'Oh yes, oh yes. Thank you, Todd.'

The worst of people of that class was that they remembered everything. Not for them the sliding doors of forgetting. To go on. One must go on. Be selective. Taste and understanding and a unique selfishness had allowed Mr Plenderist to quieten and lessen the broad echoing halls of experience. Before the disturbing likenesses, the images once worshipped, he drew the comforting curtains. From his earliest days this had been his practice. Like the wounding edges in Wagner's house every hard corner of his mental furniture was swagged and swathed in reassuring illusions. Less invidiously it might be asserted that Mr Plenderist's existence was the finest cultured pearl imaginable, and that in his own estimation he was justifiably annoyed when such folks as Todd stared through the nacreous orb and saw only the fidgeting grit.

Soon they were in the car with Bull gravely driving, shut off from them in his little glass room as if he were part of the engine. One minute it had been streets, the next it was fields of spring corn running the way of the wind.

'There's the pillar-box,' exclaimed Nicholas.

'It makes a walk,' said Mr Plenderist, who was thinking of far Behar. 'And those are your grandfather's limes. Very pretentious. But an approach was once considered more essential than it is now. People live on the path these days. You won't like the house, I'm afraid. Your mother didn't.' He paused, angry with himself. Helen was in the English cemetery at Behar - thousands of miles away - and years and years ago. He comforted himself with the thought that even if the pillar-box was evocative or the limes rustled her name, the house would be as he wished it. 'She never liked it,' he said, suddenly pleased.

As he spoke Bull swung the car round to the stone porch, upon the steps of which Mrs Bull waited. Nicholas had a sudden vision of symmetrical windows and angular bastions of faded brick. All one side of the house was dark with ivy which was already beginning to creep like a stain across the front. There was a fearful blankness about it all. So many windows and all of them blind. Suddenly he espied, riding upon the back of the dark roof, the greyest, sun-held howdah, a copper cupola with a bell.

'Oh, *do* ring it for tea, Mrs Bull. We have all come home! Just for once, Mrs Bull,' he cried, surprised at his own sudden happiness.

'How do you do, Master Nicholas,' said Mrs Bull, looking across at Mr Plenderist. 'How do you do, sir. How do you do, *madam*.'

She seemed to be bursting with information of some kind for which, when she had imparted it, she felt assured of certain rewards, the never-doubted thanks for one who, though she had trespassed beyond the functions of her sphere, had by her gamble for the solicitude of those she served achieved results, which though impertinent, could by their eventual felicity be accorded nothing but praise.

'I met Mr Plainshaft in Mendleton,' she said in a rush. 'He wishes to be remembered to you...He...I...We talked of your being home and, er, Master Nicholas ...'

As if in a dream the boy heard the housekeeper's apology jerking over them like an uncertain fountain until the unhideable relief of Mr Plenderist and Deva soothed her agitation, reducing her flood to a narrow, articulate trickle. . . Deva's face beamed pleasure. Her father wagged his head in admonitory approval. Above them Nicholas saw the cupola wither away and then return again uncertainly, its frail pilasters jigging a silly fandango. He longed to be the grass. A bird. Something which would die within the hour. When they spoke to him he dared not answer for fear the rattle of their approval would bring down the shameful wretchedness balanced so precariously upon his lashes. But they needed no answer.

'Really splendid news, Nicholas,' reiterated Mr Plenderist. 'Term has been held up for a couple of weeks by sickness... An ill wind indeed... For it means that instead of kicking your heels about the house for months, you will be able to start with all the other chaps. Tomorrow in fact. Mrs Bull says that you can start right away!'

'Won't that be fun?' urged Deva.

Between them they drew him towards the house, Deva with her arm close about his thin shoulders, its warm efficiency compelling him home.

A Bit Simple

Rose woke with a start. One second she was lying high up on the striped grey bolster from which the sheet had escaped, the next she was scrambling off the bed calling, 'Jaunty....*Jaunty!*' Her cries of alarm, of why and wherefore too, were always muted, as though she had long given up any hope of an answer. Jaunty certainly did not hear as he heaved up the tail-board of the lorry on his shoulder. His whistling, a monotonous two-noted blowing in and out, never stopped. Rose then heard the whistle above the moor wind and immediately felt appeased and content. She sat on the edge of the bed and smoothed the bit-rug with her small grubby feet. Her face was moist and sweet with sleep and there was a silvery shine on her skin. She was twenty. Her hair had been cut off just on a level with the lobes of her ears and created a dark helmet, inches thick, and her little features were made even more diminutive by their cloudy frame. Her pink winceyette nightdress was frumped vaguely around her narrow body and one cone-shaped breast of a thick, deliberate magnolia whiteness thrust vulnerably from its folds.

So he was still here. She was relieved. A grateful kind of happiness seized her as she dressed. There had been times when Jaunty just went – no wave, no honk at the bottom of the lane, no word of when he would be back. And when he came back, often as long as a week later, there would be the crinkled excitement on his face because of what he hoped to find. Did find.

'There, there, Rose gel, so you missed me, did you! That shows old Jaunty ain't so bad, don't it? A man has got to have a bit of pinin' after him, Rose gel. That's all he's got have, a bit of pinin'. And his mumble, Rose gel - mustn't forget that!'

And he would watch as she lit the paraffin oven and began to peel potatoes and shake stewing-steak out of a tin, the fear slipping from her, the forgiveness taking over. Soon she would be skipping about, laying the table, making up the fire, asking questions.

'Where've you bin this time, Jaunty?'

'China.' (Or Tipperary or all-the-way-there-and-back again.)

'Oh, *Jaunty!*'

Daft as lights, he thought. But he would smile the surprising new smile given him by his National Health teeth, the kettle would boil and he would fumble in his pockets and drag out various pencil-scrawled bits of paper and spread them on the table, the records of his deals.

'You're a good gel, Rose,' he would say, adding wordlessly, and if you had a bloody tail, you'd wag it.

She now combed her soft bunchy hair and drew it back from her face with a big iron clip. The white skin was concealed by a faded cotton dress and a print wrapper. She pushed her bare feet into bunny slippers, only bunnies with their eyes dangling out on threads and their ears trodden to rags. Then she looked out of the window at the moor. It swept out and up to the most impossible distance and as usual its heights were plunged in sodden swathes of cloud. When she had first seen this drifting darkness it had delighted her, particularly when the clouds purpled into vast pieces of jig-saw puzzle, or when the sun fell like a hot penny down the crack behind Exe Head.

'Jaunty, look!'

'You keep away from that, gel. That's where the wrath is. It's soft up there, Rose. Black and soft. If you went up there, down you'd go into the softness.'

Sometimes she would hear the frenzied blare of a sheep, far off and already outside the world of bird-song, and she would imagine its furry head gently sinking into the mat of yellow sphagnum, its eyes crazed and golden. Men, too, Jaunty told her. There were patches of the moss in a hollow near the cottage and she had walked over it, high and safe, stepping from tussock to tussock of springy deer-sedge. When she prodded the moss with a stick it gave a slight beseeching little tug and she had dragged the stick back suddenly and had seen with fear the inches of oozing blackness where the peat had gripped. She thought of Ted Allen who had sat next to Jaunty in Standard Four and who had vanished under the moor while searching for skylark's eggs.

'Wicked he was,' said Jaunty, 'only he'd have done to fight in the war.' Rose wriggled across the huge double bed and fumbled for the watch on Jaunty's table. It was five to seven. So early! She lay back in Jaunty's place, catching his rank smell and still able to feel a little of his warmth creeping from the blankets. The ceiling bulged with whitewash and brownish-pink roses streamed down the wallpaper. Above the bed, pushing its way through a fretwork shield, was a set of cast antlers shed by a red deer and swooped on by Jaunty during one of his endless days of collecting, foraging and picking things up. They threw a proud shadow by sunlight or lamplight.

'It's a Royal, a twelve-pointer,' he told Rose.

He hung his cap on it. It had no significance for him. It was an object and he had picked it up. He was acquisitive rather than greedy. He could not be accused of piling up treasure on earth - Jaunty would pile up anything. He was a scavenger bird and his lair some two miles off the main South Molton road was an object lesson. Now and then, though only in the summer, a holiday-making couple would follow the un-made-up track which twined so hopefully between crumbling shale walls still tall enough to hide the view and expect to arrive at some pretty farm with hens scratching near an ancient linhay and puffballs and lichens growing in the old peat workings, only to be confronted with 'Fernside T.P. 1887'. They would draw near to one another as they read it. It was inscribed on a recessed tablet a foot or so above the front door. There were four large blank windows containing four variously extended lace-edged blinds with dangling acorns, a steep slate roof and a central chimney stack fissured and agape from having to support an enormous flag mast. The moor behind the cottage was infinite and glorious; scarp capped hill and mountain, scarp, in a crescendo of rising land and colour. It was a view which should have taken any reasonable human being past Fernside without another thought. Except that no one was ever swept by. They halted, stared, wavered. They felt what Robinson Crusoe felt when he saw the naked footprint in the sand, and turned back to ponder what to do now that their whole reckoning of existence had been challenged and changed. They had not expected to meet desuetude in such a place. Not on such a scale. A disused drill, perhaps, and the general mess and muddle of the farm. But not Jaunty's iron mountain or his universe of rubbish. Oil drums, pig wire, a mesh of scores of bedsteads which said everything, lathes, axles, cogs, springs, gas-stoves, yellowing enamelled baths rearing up like blanched sarcophagi, sheets of corrugated iron flaming with rust, spokes and pails and chassis and chains, marine fittings, kitchen ranges, boilers and hurdles were multifariously represented, and weight and weakness slowly welded them into one. The moor flowers climbed over them mockingly. Thrust themselves beautifully between the motionless wheels and the withering steel. Foxgloves and cow-wheat, woodruff and spiky bog asphodel, St. John's wort and stray sycamore suckers, valerian and convolvulus did their best to draw a veil over what had been so mighty and was now so mean, but only succeeded in exaggerating the ugliness. Jaunty's 'sorting-houses', the shacks in which he tossed lead and brass and bottles, were overflowing and gave off a sad pungent odour in which midges danced thickly when the weather was close.

Rose was pleased to see these occasional visitors and sorry when they turned back. She wanted to run out and say, Hello! and perhaps offer tea but at this moment her legs grew stiff and strange, and she couldn't have moved or said a word if she had been offered a fiver. Her paralysis suited Jaunty.

'Don't talk. Say nothing, gel.'

So she watched them from the interior blackness, though not out of obedience to Jaunty, who often as not was far away, but because she knew that she had no talent for ordinary behaviour. Had she not tried it, at school, in a bus or a shop, in the chapel porch at Grosbesk where all the handshaking was, and seen the wrong kind of interest come into people's faces?

'She'll do on the moor,' her father told Jaunty, and although he was dying, and knew it, he laughed like a boy. Jaunty laughed too. His teeth had not arrived then and his mirth was a void. He had laughed with her father all through life, through school, through the Aisne and the Somme, and all through forty years of rag-and-bone partnership. Her father had only ceased laughing when the surprising pain began to eat away at his belly, an agony which exactly coincided with Jaunty's purchasing the new tip-up lorry with *J. W* (John William) *Puttock: Scrap Metal Merchant* painted on the sides. Rose's father came to the door to see it, his left hand pressed into the soft flesh above his belt, fighting the darts.

'Just. . . "Puttock"?' he said slowly.

'Just. . . "Puttock",' answered Jaunty equally slowly.

That evening her father told Rose, 'You'll be off then to keep house for your "Uncle" Jaunty on the moor. Man and wife, of course. Everything right, Rose. Everything straight.' He didn't mention the look on Jaunty's face when he had said, 'Just Puttock', any more than he ever mentioned all the other times when he had seen this look, at school when the frogs were blown up with straws, in the trenches when they found the small weeping German lad, in the fields when they came across some timid fluttering thing and Jaunty's stumpy brown hands had 'put it out of its misery'.

It was the pragmatic absence of feeling which made Rose feel safe with Jaunty. A month later she heard him, still laughing, upstairs in her father's bedroom.

'Me and Rose . . . Me and Rose!' And then 'ha-ha-ha-ha!'

She crept up the stairs and settled herself in the gloom on the landing. Her father's laugh was different. She could scarcely recognize it. She thought it must be the pain. Jaunty was noisy and confident. She imagined him smacking his sharp little knee with the palm of his hand, as he did when he made a bargain. Her father was saying gentle things about her, putting ideas into Jaunty's head. The ideas tickled Jaunty pink.

'Me wed your Rose!' and then the stuttering amusement, the sort which made him wet round the eyes. Then a pause which was hardly an apology. 'Well now, I shouldn't laugh, should I, Fred?'

'No,' said her father. It was a strangely spoken word and it produced an equally strange silence.

When at last Jaunty answered his voice was thick. No laughter now. 'What do you mean by that, Fred?'

'I mean she can't exactly come to any harm, that's what I mean. Not unless things are mighty changed.'

The quietness which followed this was fantastic and was only broken by the quavering hoot of the Barnstaple train. Then Jaunty and her father laughed together for the last time and the sound came skirling through the thin door, a confident enough noise coming from a man who could gain nothing by making a lady's bid and a man who was to die in the morning. Rose listened to it and then went downstairs and put the kettle on. Fernside! Where she had paddled in the splat. Where she threaded daisies while Jaunty and her father had unloaded the tanks and cisterns, the bottles and broken thrashing tackle from a lorry which said 'Gregg and Puttock' on its side. Humming contentedly, she took four bursting cream-cakes from a bag and set them importantly on a plate.

Life with Jaunty was little different from life with her father, except that she woke in Jaunty's bed, and except the moor, of course. An incalculable and crushing exception, she found it. Of one thing she was certain, that it was another moor and not where she had played her solitary games in the sunshine while the men worked. If that moor had presented such an engulfing silence she would have remembered it. That moor was small, with paths leading to familiar terminals. This moor was immense, it flowed like a land sea. It had its awful vortexes, which was why she could never wander across its tracks and be forgetful. Its main swell rose up and lipped over Fernside in a crest of suspended granite which made her head split and this was something she most decidedly had never observed before, neither this nor the way the rushes behind the splat shivered incessantly.

Jaunty watched her nervousness with approval.

'Always keep inside the hedge,' he told her.

The hedge was a wall built round Fernside by Jaunty's father. It rose out of the bedrock and was quite foolishly thick and strong. Fernside was flimsiness itself compared with it. But it gave her no sense of security, only of tightness. Sometimes she climbed over it by the slate stile, turned her back on the concave hill and ran wildly down one of the haphazard tracks until her heart thumped and her legs grew weak. Once she found a gulf which led to a combe full of black-faced sheep, a hundred or more there must have been, and many with rooks taking rides on their backs while they dipped their heads imperturbably in pastures a yard high. Honeysuckles streamed down from thickets surrounding the combe and their scent got right inside her and made her sway with a delicious giddiness, while the grasses pressed high and broke coolly between her naked thighs. She had returned with a fat bunch of the honeysuckle, all heads and brief stalks, no leaves, the way she picked flowers, and was arranging them in a vase when Jaunty grabbed them. It was a gesture which goes with 'presence of mind' kind of bravery, like taking an adder from a child.

'Don't ever let me ketch you bringing that stuff indoors again,' he said.

That was all. No reason and none of his spite. The honeysuckle died fast high up on the dump and already she could see that it was nasty.

Weeks, maybe months, later she was helping him clear the lorry when Jaunty's finger pointed to another narrow smudgy shape thrust against the skyline. It was an upright stone which both pointed and beckoned. As the sun set it swelled monolithically and ruled a shadow to the edge of the Forest. Rose wondered why she had not seen it before.

'No need to fret about that,' Jaunty had said. 'You may not have seen 'un but 'un has seen you. There are graves up there, too, Rose. Graves as big as hills. Have you ever reckoned what kind of folk would need that kind of dirt to cover 'em? Don't ever walk towards the stone or 'un will walk towards you.'

She had tested him on this advice and had once set off in the direction of the barrows and at first had little opportunity to look upwards because of the sucking uncertainty of the ground, which shifted voluptuously every now and then, and which, although her foot frequently sank deeply, showed no imprint. Then came firm stretches of heather and a blankness which compelled her to lift her eyes, and it was as Jaunty said, the brooding stone was moving down the hill. She and it were locked on a parallel. Frightened as she had never been frightened before, she turned and fled, and slipped and plunged her way through the cotton-grass, each footstep too quick and violent for the bog to take hold. No one was in the cottage when she reached it and fell into a chair. But there was the brown teapot where she had left it, still warm, the oilcloth with the corners of the table poking through and the huge photograph of her father and Jaunty in the army, all made of millions of dots. I won't tell him, she thought. He mustn't always be right... She kicked off her muddy shoes, swirled the tea round in the pot and poured herself a cup. She drank like a child, drawing the cold tea up in big gulps. As she drank, a small persistent movement began to hold her attention, vaguely and meaninglessly at first, then terrifyingly. Something glistened and went dark, climbed and fell. She wept and the twisting thing grew jewelled, unfocused and bespangled by her distress. She thrust a hand at it and it held it like the marsh. Glutinous, and nauseous with victims, it revealed itself, the fly-paper which Jaunty had suspended from the lamp.

He bought a dog and chained it to a barrel behind the linhay. It was full-grown and had a good bark, Jaunty told her. It had. It barked with a steady, undeviating insanity, its head shooting back after each effort like a field-piece on its carriage. Its legs were splayed stiffly and its eyes were two fat black glass marbles bursting expressionlessly from its skull. It was Labrador and something else. It had beautiful large cushioned feet but everything else about it was repellent. The barking impressed Jaunty; he felt he had got his money's worth. He said it would be company for Rose when he was away. The dog never barked at night but seemed to spend its time then climbing in and out of its barrel, for Rose had often awoken to hear the gentle endless clinking of iron links and an exhausted breathing, both amplified by the dense mists which rolled into the valley when the daylight ended.

The breathing was once so close that she woke Jaunty. There was a sad glottal wuffling right up against the window and then a clambering kind of bounce. Jaunty listened with interest.

'Rats,' he said.

'Rats! Oh, Jaunty.'

Once more he was sincerely puzzled by her horror. There were things called rats and they scuffled at night. A fact. A truth. The sun rose and set. There were rats. How could there be astonishment? All the same, her jumpiness was beginning to worry him. It was also a criticism of Fernside, and he did not like that. His father had built it and it was a marvel to him. She should be thankful.

'It's all right here, Rose gel. You know that, don't you? You're going to be all right...'

She felt his hand, all bunched up and hard as wood, on her waist. The fingers remained tense and retracted. There was no embrace and little comfort, only heaviness. She let is press into her until she knew he was asleep again. Jaunty rolled over in his usual position, an old little boy, foetal and mindless. She remained wide awake and once more pushing with all her strength at the strange barrier inside her head. Sometimes it was like a thick windowless wall, sometimes just a muddling insubstantiality, like the mist on the moor. The latter was best for through it she occasionally glimpsed the ordinary lucent paths. To reach these she would try to begin at the beginning. Her mother in the churchyard at South Molton. No face. No voice. But definite in death, and that was the main thing. Her father like Jaunty, only closer, nearer. Uncle Jaunty skinning rabbits. Off with his fur coat! He made her laugh when she wanted to cry. And herself, who was she? 'Mrs Puttock.' She said it out loud in the darkness and her name rose clumsily to the ceiling through the sad tobacco-urine-face-powder smell. Anyone else? No one else. Girls at school: Rosie, you're daft! Boys at school: let's have a look, Rosie! Or, Rags and bones! All up the street. Who else? Nobody else, but Jesus. She turned her face on the pillow, ready for sleep after she had said the important words.

> 'Lord keep us safe this night,
> Secure from all our fears:
> May angels guard us while we sleep
> Until morning light appears.'

The dog - it had no name - clattered its chain. 'Damn dog!' she murmured, and slept.

Jaunty worked haphazardly. Not so much when he felt like it as when it occurred to him. Then he was away. Rose, hearing the departure sounds, jacks and levers being thrown into the lorry, old coats and jerseys being snatched from behind doors and bundled into the cab and the dog utterly silent, would hurry out and stand in the yard. She no longer cajoled, wept or even spoke, but stood there mutely frantic with her hands clasped and her entire body tremulous with a despair which Jaunty could not see. When would he be home? He didn't know. This was honest. She was left with all the luck. His mottled little face twitched with a tacit enumeration of it, the house, the good dog, money in the vase and the wireless. She could have had the telly but they were too far from the electric. Not his fault that. She was left, too, with his moor. He had forgotten that he had given her this. There had been nothing when she had arrived, only the scenery, flowers and crab-apples, bracken and birds above it. Her innocence offended Jaunty. He forced her to see the moor, to recognize its power and reality.

The mist, for instance, was real insubstantiality. Its arrival filled him with interest and gaiety. He liked the way it clapped down on the hard decided edges of things and either obliterated them or made them fanciful. Not only Longstones, but the dripping granite crest itself could advance in the mist. Sometimes the moor mists would last for nearly a week and Fernside would become a toy house thrown down in the corner of a quiet white tent. Outside, the whiteness was the darkest dark imaginable, and when the evening came with its own obscurity the white and black darkness would fight for precedence, and writhe just above the inky middens in sodden whorls. It was easy then to see the Brocken, one's own small timid self turned into a wraith in one's lifetime. Jaunty had seen it in Flanders, whole battlefields a double mass of men and spectres, and soldiers searching the new silences wildly because they could not tell where life ended and death began.

Rose pulled down the blinds when the mist came, and turned the wireless up loud. At night, lying on her side of the bed with Jaunty's watch, which he never carried, ticking busily in her ear, she tried not to hear the moor sounds, the howling that could be an owl, but might be, and eventually was, a wild cat from Room Hill. Jaunty sought these creatures as other men sought the Yeti and had spent whole nights on Room Hill looking for them. They were as big as dog foxes and striped, and they possessed strange thick tails and fangs which held up the skin at the sides of their mouths in wet folds. They ate pet cats and once a young shepherd had been found on Curr Cleeve with all his stomach eaten away.

'Licked out holler as a drum,' Jaunty told Rose. 'Very clean and tidy creatures they are.'

Sometimes she would wake and hear a swift exhilarating kind of thudding, a noise which was so insistent that she was driven to the window in a paroxysm of inquisitive fear. The double darkness of black on white was utterly opaque and eyes were useless against it. But behind it, as though behind thick ice, the ancient horses from the heights swept by with stony eyes and dark manes. They came from Broken Barrow – escaped, Jaunty reckoned. If you rested your head on Broken Barrow it would tremble with the trampling. Never a minute's peace, said Jaunty. He took Rose up to the height to demonstrate and while she was lying there stroked her body timidly. The fine summit grasses blew feathery against her skin.

'Hear that, gel? Listen, hear that?'

But Rose only heard a bird singing.

They returned, slipping and sliding down the terrifying gradient, hanging on to the rock where it had bitten through the thin soil. Soon, the brief moment of serenity gave place to sullenness and shadow. Jaunty hurried ahead. There was still a cocky ebullience in the way he walked, enough for his nickname to retain some relevance. The distrait girl and the stiff bouncy old man moved downwards across the descending hollows in silence. It was a scene of morose departures – small creatures rustling in the bracken, small birds winging languidly above the sedge plateaux – and absolute negation. They never walked on Broken Barrow again.

He left about eight that morning, and for a while she 'busied herself' as he had advised.

'No need to fret and mope.'

'No, Jaunty.'

'Saunders comes today, don't he? You can get me some more plasters and tell him we don't want no more o' that green bacon.'

'Yes, Jaunty.'

'I've left you all right, ain't I, gel?'

She tugged two or three screwed-up notes from her purse and nodded. He added another.

'I never see you short, do I, gel?'

'No, Jaunty.' When he had gone she lit the copper and did the washing. The reek and steam, the jolly bubbling and the froth as she scrubbed away pleased her. She worked in a cosy moist muddle with silky grey water sploshing over the edge of the galvanized bath and making puddles on the lino. She stripped the bed and pushed the mattress half out of the window to air. She carried the washing to the line in a blue plastic bowl and stared around for rain. But the moor was glass-clear and groups of mice-sized sheep and cows shone on the hedged-in pastures as bright as flowers. It was hot and the wet patch all down the front of her pinafore felt pleasantly chilly. Her fingers were like the pink crinkled insides of budding flowers and the exertion had brought out a waxen gold in the normally dead white skin exposed by the low neck-line of her flimsy cotton dress. Humming softly, she returned to the house and began to carry out the dirty water, bowl by bowl, to the drain near the lilac clump. She was almost content. A few minutes later the contentment fled, vanished, dissolved, had no existence even in her recollection, seemingly had never been. She backed into the shadows without astonishment although nothing about her had changed one iota. Mr Saunders always came on Wednesdays, didn't he? His swaying van teetered along the track, winding its way cautiously between the mounds of scrap and came to a standstill near the linhay.

He swung himself to the ground, a gesture which was a travesty of its earlier fetching boyish grace because of the runaway meatiness of buttock and thigh which pushed out the faded R.A.F. trousers grossly. His hair was a tall reddish-brown mat, stiff with cream. He walked to the back of the van with heavy deliberation, opened its smart rear door and let down a little pair of steps. Just inside was the wire basket which the customers had to fill as they walked down the narrow passage between the racks. Brushes, saucepans, toys, cellophane bags full of dusters, socks and other haberdashery, and plastic pails swung from the roof. Beneath the floor of the travelling shop was a copper tank full of paraffin oil.

'Morning, missus. You've chosen a good day for it.'

Mr Saunders nodded towards the washing. Their eyes did not meet. Rose scarcely heard him; she was struggling with that clouding within herself when the elusive order or spark or certainty - she had no name for it - was so desperately needed.

'I thought I'd get it finished.'

'You do that, missus.'

He held out the wire basket to her.

'I must get my list . .'

'You ought to know what you want by now, missus.'

'He don't want none of that green bacon.'

Mr Saunders laughed without malice. His pale brown moustache lifted to show square stained teeth. His neck, prickly with wide-spaced oiled hairs, flushed enjoyably and made a startling contrast to the advertiser's-white perfection of his shirt.

'No green bacon, eh?'

His eyes met hers for the first time. Rose saw the familiar red lines. Mr Saunders's eyes were like the eyes she had once found lying in the back of the head of a broken china doll.

'Come on,' he said.

She took the wire basket and entered the van. He climbed in behind her. They walked slowly along the narrow passage and in a chatty, het-up voice he said,

'Pilchards are on offer, Mrs Puttock. You got flour? Marge? That's a new line, you get a pastry-cutter with that. Yes, that's the one you always have, Mrs Puttock - only one we've got left as a matter of fact. Pineapple? Baked beans?'

The basket was filling up and the plump hands were holding her waist, holding her up against him. There was no strange new shock. A ritual had begun. She knew the moves and succumbed passively to them. She knew the scent, sickly sweet, as though Mr Saunders sucked sugar-cubes. It lay right at the front of his mouth and it engulfed her with its gentle rotting intensity. He felt her relax and the slightly mocking tone he had used outside the van returned.

'Steady on... steady on! Where's the fire, eh? You've got to take things easy, you know! We can't have you all upset like, can we? Old Jaunty wouldn't like that now, would he?'

His hands moved up and her breasts stiffened under his touch.

'Corned beef? Oxos?'

They were up against the far end of the van now and Mr Saunders was turning her round, taking the basket from her, pulling the cotton dress up when an independent strength within her bewildered self broke out, broke free. The next thing she knew was that she was sitting in her own kitchen and Mr Saunders was leaning against the table, and his glistening cheeks and lively red-cracked eyes were dull and muddy.

'Why didn't you say? You had only to say...'

Say what? she wondered.

His apologies and self-justification poured out of him. All those other times, had he ever hurt her? Had he? Not once. It took two to make a bargain. What bargain? wondered Rose. And why was Mr Saunders in her kitchen and where were her groceries?

'I didn't get my biscuits,' she said.

He carried the basket back to the house for her and emptied its contents onto the kitchen table. When he drove off he waved his old one-of-the-boys wave and she wondered if he would come again and if he didn't, who would?

She walked round the garden, picking her way past heaps of old machinery and snaky bits of pipe crawling through the grass. Her face was wet with tears and because she wept so seldom it gave her a bitter kind of satisfaction to feel them there, drying on her skin and brimming against her lashes. Crying was an achievement. Like death, it was definite. Something profoundly important was happening to her, as when the calyx at last divides and the petal unfolds. The dog rose to its feet as she approached. She eyed it cautiously and noticed that it looked different. The normally smooth fur round its throat was all hackled up and its mouth was opening and closing soundlessly. But it flew at her as it always did, and, as always, she reacted with pointless fear since its leash was too short and the animal could not reach her. Her bare wrist touched a nettle and tingling white mounds appeared at once on the soft skin. The sudden pain drew everything into harsh focus, the washing sagging from the line, the acre of muddle and Mr Saunders's sugary breath.

'Now look at what you've made me do! Now look! Damn dog. Damn bloody dog. I'll kill you - you'll see!'

Usually when either she or Jaunty abused it, the dog rolled over and over in ecstasy, but this time it continued to stand there in its bristling silence. Its unnaturalness horrified her.

'Bark then!' she cried. 'Bark, bark, bark! I'm not loving you, I'm hating you. Can't you see I'm hating you? You're mad. Mad dog, mad dog!'

She searched around frantically for the kind of small stone with which Jaunty usually concluded his rage - 'training', he called it - when she saw the young man pushing his bicycle up the path at the side of the house and wheeling it in and out between the kitchen ranges and chunks of machinery with obvious amusement. The stone fell listlessly from her hand. Had he heard her, she wondered? What did he want? Why was he in the garden? Nobody ever came into the garden, except the other dealers. She then realized that he must have heard her because he was looking at her with an elaborate mock reproach which implied 'we all go off the deep end occasionally!' He was tall, startlingly tall after Jaunty, and had long bare legs and arms which should, because of the size of them, have looked very naked but didn't because they were covered with a mixture of tan, dust and fine glinting down. He wore a check shirt and brown shorts, dirty white tennis socks and shoes with curly leather tongues. A camera swung from his neck and a St Christopher medal on a chain shone beneath his unbuttoned shirt. In contrast with his odd confusion of dust and freshness, the bicycle glittered like a jewel. It was so bright and elegantly fragile that it seemed to dance at the end of its owner's arm like a sparkling toy. It was a geometrical exercise carried out in flawless aluminium and multi-coloured enamel. The young man looked about him for a place to park it and then, to Rose's consternation, he ran it lightly over the weeds to the main scrap-heap and rested it against an amorphous pile of rubbish. He returned, looking rather ruthful.

'May I have some milk, please,' he said.

'Milk?'

'Milk,' he said. 'Travellers always stop at lonely cottages and ask for milk. It is one of the inflexible rules of picaresque fiction. Everything depends on it. But water will do.'

She looked at him shyly.

'I think there's some milk,' she said.

'That dog looks as though he needs something, too. What did Blake say - ?'

> 'A dog starved at his master's gate
> Predicts the ruin of the State...

'He isn't starved!' said Rose indignantly. But the young man didn't apologize.

'What is his name?'

'He - he hasn't got a name.'

'I see. No name. Just Dog, like Diogenes.'

He walked to the barrel, tumbled the animal on to its back and tickled it, but got a rigid reaction. The dog lay as if dead, its bursting eyes were whorled with white and it was helpless with fear. A look of concern and bewilderment came over the young man's face as he undid the heavy collar.

'Well, there's a way to treat a saviour!' he said. 'Some people don't deserve a nice long run on that beautiful moor!' He gave the dog a little slap and it righted itself from its crazed posture and fled. Rose saw it scramble over the hedge and race away into the distance. I should be worried, she thought. But I'm not, I'm glad.

'Did you ever see such a craven beast?' said the boy. 'No dog has ever behaved like that to me before. No wonder you swear at him. Only you shouldn't throw stones, you know. Never throw stones. Did you notice the way he got over the wall? You'd have thought he'd seen a ghost.'

'He's all right now,' said Rose, shading her eyes. The dog was zig-zagging through the gorse and looked transformed by a new joy. Such obvious, blatant happiness somehow rankled.

'He bites,' she said.

'Whom has he bitten?'

She thought for a minute and then turned her tear-marked face to the boy. 'No one,' she had to admit.

'I thought as much.'

'I'll get you the water,' she said slowly.

He followed her into the cottage, stooping his fair head as he entered the door. The wash-day muddle and the damp, musky indoors smell forced a critical and slightly humorous appraisal from him which he made no attempt to conceal. There were cold ashes in the grate and the draining-board was the working model for one of Jaunty's scrap-heaps, with its stack of empty food tins.

'I could make some tea,' she said.

They drank it sitting on the wall outside while the sun burnt down and scents from the moor, the first Rose had smelled since the old days, were distilled by the heat. The young man told her that he was doing a postgraduate course at London University. He said that last year he had hitched his way to Venice but this year he had set his mind on exploring Exmoor. Only the bike had been a mistake. All the best parts of the moor were accessible to walkers only. Those paths at Castle Hill, for instance - had she seen them? She should. And the

Winbarrows on Winsford Hill? His easy familiarity with the moor rather offended Rose and when he mentioned Room Hill she thrust her special proprietorial information at him. He listened to her describing the great cats, saw the fear overtaking the words and watched the set and intense pallor of her face. When she had finished he grinned, cleared his throat with mock pomposity, took her hand in his and said,

'Now look. Cats as big as sheep having shepherds for supper, must you believe that?'

'Jaunty saw them.'

'No, he didn't. He couldn't have done because there aren't any.'

'Are you sure?'

'Of course I'm sure. They'd have one in the Zoo, wouldn't they, if they did? *Felis terribilis*, diet, shepherds and gorse. It would have been one of their most interesting exhibits and I would certainly have noticed it. I'm always in the Zoo. It's the saddest funniest place in London.'

Rose half smiled. It was his way of speaking, eyes nearly shut yet vivid and seeing, mouth thoughtful, even when he laughed. The medal swung from the chain round his neck and when he saw her looking at it, he took it off and slipped it over her head.

'St Christopher,' he said. 'He's going to have a lot of explaining to do. You have him. You have the kind of trust which works with him.'

'Where will you go now?' she asked.

He glanced at her with surprise.

'It's not where will I go, but where will you go. I'm gone, presumably. I'm there, if you like. And believe me, it is the oddest feeling!'

His talk did not surprise Rose. Nearly all the talk she had heard during her twenty years had been dark or elliptical and about people and places she had never seen. She poured some more tea for each of them. She was wondering why she had never sat by the wall like this before and drunk tea, and looked up at the hills.

'Of course, that is the most interesting climb,' said the boy, following her gaze, and he pointed to the head of the combe at the

Longstone. 'I was up there yesterday and I wouldn't mind having another look. I went to Winsford first. The stone there has *Carataci Nepus* carved on it but I like it best when the stone says nothing. Like Ozymandias's tomb. The Longstone says nothing - and thus it says everything, and you can take your pick. Let's go and see it.'

'Now?' asked Rose in alarm.

'Of course now,' said the young man. 'You've done the washing, haven't you? And sworn at the dog. Come on!'

He took her hand and pulled her to her feet. As they climbed up the moor through the bracken, picking their way across the bog and sending sheep off the path in sudden flurries of concern, he noticed how Rose stared everywhere but ahead. He let her do this until they were near the final rise of the hill and then said,

'Don't! I can't bear it. It isn't coming to meet us, you know. It can't. It's stuck in the ground. You can get the same illusion from a tree or a house, only because it is a tree or a house you keep it in its place, so to speak. But the Longstone, that's different. It makes no sense so you give it legs. Can't you see it's a monument and can't you get all the wonder you need out of that?'

They reached the Longstone and he told her of its possibilities, the boundary mark of a forgotten kingdom, a memorial to one of King Arthur's friends, a Bronze Age altar or just an ornament to decorate the hill. They leaned against it and looked out at the vast view.

'The world,' said the boy, 'it really was something...'

Rose recognized the merest bat's squeak note of her own incoherent regret and took the boy's hand in her own. He looked surprised and pleased. He put his arms round her and they stood facing each other and softly touching along the entire length of their bodies, with his head bent above hers and his face resting against her hair.

'Poor Rose,' he said. 'You can hardly call this love-making - and it isn't adultery by a long chalk! But it's something. Everything must be better because of it.'

'I - I like you,' she said.

'I'm pleased to hear it. Nothing could be more reassuring for a -

for a chap in my circumstances!'

'You're laughing at me. Everybody laughs.'

'Nonsense. Don't be so sorry for yourself. I'm laughing at me.'

She looked up at him and he tilted her head back gently and kissed her with elaborate purity on the forehead.

'There,' he said, 'I believe that is how one has to do it now.'

The rest of the day passed quickly. For the first time since she had entered it as Jaunty's wife, Rose felt that the cottage was hers. The sense of ownership amused her. She began by opening all the windows - they rushed up on their sashcords with amazed shrieks - and then she swept up and scrubbed until the brick floor looked as though it had been made out of pale fresh butter. Now and then, as she worked, she glanced out at the bend of the lane, seeing the hand held out in a gesture which was half-wave and half-salute as the boy vanished. He had gone - she had watched him go so deliberately - yet he had not gone. There was no loss. This was why she had claimed Fernside and had been able to look up at Grosbesk and Winbarrow and find them glorious.

Her new-found serenity looked like abandoning her, however, when she saw the dog, at first a bobbing speck, then a ravening wolf leaping over the wall, then a big stupid joyous creature slobbering against her fearful hands and thumping his tail. She bent down and gave him a little pat and then a hug. Then, though quite when and how it happened she couldn't tell, she was dozing in Jaunty's chair and the dog, protected from the damp floor by an old coat, was sleeping too, with his head on her small bare feet.

Jaunty, returning about half past six, saw them through the window, saw the flowers; the acorn cords of the blinds dancing about in the fresh warm Atlantic air. He climbed back into the lorry, drove up to the iron mountain and began to unload. The noise woke Rose and she and the dog came out to watch. Nothing was said. Jaunty heaved and tugged at his spoils, which were mostly old gas-stoves he had purchased from the local corporation.

'That's about it,' he said at last.

The lorry was empty. He stood in the back of it holding a glittering painted abstraction of bars and spokes, all bent and crushed as though it had been tinfoil in a child's hand.

'It's - it's a bike...' said Rose.

Jaunty swung it so that it fell on his special heap of 'done for' things by the side of the linhay.

'Got it from the police station,' he said. 'Belonged to that feller who was killed in the smash-up at Gretton a couple of weeks ago. Bloody fool. Come on, Rose gel, git the kettle on. Here, you!' - to the dog - how'd you manage to slip your collar? We'll soon cure them tricks...'

'He's coming with us,' said Rose quietly.

Jaunty stared at the girl, then the three of them walked slowly into Fernside.

And the Green Grass
Grew All Around

Seventeen is the age of longing, if there is ever such a thing, and when I was seventeen I longed to be accepted by Mrs Carron-Wilson more than anything else in the world. By being 'accepted' I mean to have gone to all her little, glittering, impromptu parties and not to have to endure the particular brand of flawless reservation which blunted her conversation when she remembered to speak to me.

'Stephen!' she would exclaim in the voice she saved up for me, and I hated her unimpeded view of my innocence. Her small, well-shaped eyes would crinkle with what I learned later was real affection, only then I could hardly bear to look at them and found myself studying instead the bumpy paint on her laughing mouth. She never used this voice for her own sons, although Euen and Godfrey were younger than myself. If anything she became even more adult when speaking to them, as if they and herself existed in a more magnificent intellectual sphere than the rest of us, which I realize now they did.

Euen was fifteen and Godfrey was sixteen. They were like a pair of precocious Tudor youths, small, dark and with some iridescent quality about them which cut them off, not only from my comprehension but from my epoch. They smiled very freely and with, to me, still in my last year at my public school, an almost scandalous lack of inhibition, showing their very clean but rather crammed teeth and setting their faces into masks of classical enjoyment. Neither had been to school in the ordinary way. Euen had entered himself for a term here and a term there as the fancy took him, including six months at the Anchors Away School near Loch Duirinish, where all the character-building antics, plus the cold, had left him weak with laughter and a tendency for pneumonia. Godfrey was eventually going up to Trinity. He had a way of standing near me as I got deeper and deeper into some argument or other, his hand stroking his narrow body through a gap in his grubby shirt, his head twisted whimsically away from me, and then saying when I had faltered to a stop, 'So *that* is what you believe!' And immediately my carefully erected ideas would collapse like a heap of badly balanced junk.

Yet I liked Godfrey and Euen, though even if I had not I would have endured far more than their unique brand of mockery to be near Mrs Carron-Wilson. She was in her mid-forties then. Considering everything – considering chiefly the state of her house, the threadbare carpets mapped all over with paraffin-stain islands, the custard-coloured walls burdened to the wainscoting with Ginners, Bevans, Steers, Tonks's and Brangwyns; the meandering archipelagos of little tables, each with its distinctive afforestation of bottles, handcraft equipment and used plates; the grotesquely elegant looking-glasses which pitted one's image with a silvery eczema, and whose frames writhed their rococo stalks through a dusty harvest of curling 'At Home' cards, and the preponderance of divans which crowded the rooms, some of them heaped with runs of magazines, one of them usually revealing Euen or Godfrey sound asleep in the middle of the day – Mrs Carron-Wilson maintained an astonishing chic.

Her figure had a restrained opulence. She seemed to be remembering the fact that she wasn't very tall all the time because she moved with a rather exciting erectness which tilted her full breasts and caused tremulous shadows to flicker over the planes of her thickening flanks. Her head, with its triumphant plume of dyed creamy-ivory hair making a dramatic contrast to her careful sun-tan, was held back as though in constant expectation of interesting news or an embrace. 'Rather avid,' my father once described it. 'No, no, Gilbert!' my mother had protested. 'Not darling C-W!'

And that is how she was known, by my family and everyone else in the village. By rights the Carron-Wilsons should have been both anathema and an enigma to us; instead, by some hidden power which they surprisingly possessed, they dominated our moral as well as our cultural climate. She had been – was still – the wife of J. L. Wilson the novelist. All his early books were dedicated to her, although when I hunted these old novels out and read their inscriptions – 'For Blanche, who made it possible' etc. – they didn't seem to connect with C-W, Euen, Godfrey and Mallards Point, the ramshackle house which was for me the entrance to the fuller life. None of us had ever seen J. L. Wilson and it had never been explained why he had left C-W or why she had left him.

Mallards Point was a nice house, even beautiful in its way, but the Carron-Wilsons treated it as they treated everything else, with just a hint of disdain. It was cottagey Queen Anne, chunky where it should have shown elegance and strength and stiff where it should have been symmetrical. It was in the most fearful disorder. The doors didn't fit and none of them would lock, the warped shutters in the drawing-room were permanently half-closed and they swung across the tall windows like crippled fans. There was a bath with a furry green bottom and a rubber ball for a plug, and a bookcase in the lavatory. The garden, a long thin one, ran down to our little river and was private in a way I knew no other garden to be. It was, needless to say, a wilderness of unkempt grass, scarcely traceable paths and shapeless shrubs. It had a distinction of the utmost charm. When Euen and Godfrey were small C-W had attended a local sale and bought the horses and cocks from an ancient roundabout. The carnival *élan* of these creeper-bound creatures, weathered of all paint, their combs or nostrils flaring above the tangled beds, lent the garden a magic almost indescribable.

What strikes me now, looking back on those days, was the marvellous availability of it all. We came and went as we chose. We were always welcome it seemed. Why? 'We' included my parents, my father always a trifle drunk, my mother skilfully persuading others as well as herself that he was not; the rector, old Doctor Gould and his receptionist Miss Follet ('Receptionist! - the Greeks couldn't have done better,' my father had remarked coarsely); the Misses Nightingale who wrote detective stories under the name of Ben Carver, Sir John and Lady Tinnington, and a dozen other faces from the neighbourhood. There was no deliberate effort to entertain us.

When their own lifeless cottages became too much for them, people strolled to Mallards Point as they might have strolled along to a club had they been in town.

It never occurred to me then, as it frequently does now, how Mrs Carron-Wilson could put up with us. There was every indication that she had known the real thing - indeed, was the real thing. Yet she listened to our gabble about books and plays with apparent interest. It was only when we talked 'county' or chattered about ordinary country things that a distinct look of weariness, and sometimes an undisguised and unrepentant sourness would cloud her normally too-forgiving face. It occurred to me one day that she hated the country, actually loathed it, and it took me some little time to recover my feelings for her as being anti-country was just a trifle worse than being anti-God in our set. It was odd that she should prefer our half-baked views on Dorothy Richardson or Stanley Spencer to our lively, informed comment on what was going on around us. Yet she did and I loved her because of it, though it took me some practice to acquire her heresy.

This made a subtle change in our relationship. Now that I was committed, as it were, to her intellectual freedom, now that I had rejected all the rules and regulations, I wanted some acknowledgement from her to prove to myself that I was different from the rest. When it never came I was bewildered. Mrs Carron-Wilson merely went on being kind to me. 'Euen's in the garden,' she would say, and, 'Godfrey's just gone to the Post Office on his bicycle. He won't be long. Is your father coming this evening?' And so, in about half a dozen sentences rattled off in her breathy, kindly voice, she refused my allegiance.

'I should like to know what C-W really thinks of me,' I said to Euen one day.

'Fishing?' he suggested, his small, Renaissance head tilted mockingly to one side. 'Well, I'll tell you. She thinks you're a clean-limbed-young-Englishman and getting more so every day. Pure Henty.'

'She didn't say that.'

'The last bit? No, she didn't. But you are, aren't you? Well, *look* at you!'

'I don't happen to spend my time looking at myself,' I said.

'It wouldn't alter my opinion of you if you did. I am reading the memoirs of Cellini and I wouldn't be able to do that if Cellini hadn't taken a very long look at himself.'

'I'm not Cellini,' I said oafishly. Euen could reduce me to feeling big and stupid in a matter of minutes.

'True. "My glass shall not persuade me I am old..." '

'Oh, shut up!'

'That, presumably, is the conclusion to all enlightened argument in your jolly decent school.'

'I think you're mad - you're all mad.'

'And you want to be, but you can't quite manage it?' said Euen with cruel percipience. Then he jumped up from the dusty, book-strewn sofa with that sudden switch to a demonstrative affection I found even more petrifying than his malice, and with a contrite look on his face. 'I didn't mean that, Stephen.'

'Oh, yes you did!'

The unnatural roar of my voice and the slam of the rickety door fell like a safety curtain between us, and I picked my way through the muddled rooms of Mallards Point with the detachment of one who has seen a good drama and who now has to face the facts of ordinary life outside the theatre. Mrs Carron-Wilson was scratching mud off her shoes with a twig in the porch, her brightly painted mouth screwed up with distaste. I edged past her as she sat on the top step. There were pale orange freckles on the back of her neck and a crescent of astonishingly white and naked flesh was visible between the sun-tanned skin and the collar of her frock.

'Goodbye,' I said. My voice, I thought, held the right note of valedictory regret mixed with icy purpose. I was leaving Mallards Point for good. But Mrs Carron-Wilson did not appear to notice. The mud came out of the welt of her shoe like a black worm.

'Don't forget about tonight, Stephen. And make your father come.'

'I can't. . . he can't. .'

'Oh, not *again!* You tell him when he's "better" that he's a bore. He won't like that but that is what he is. Tell him I don't love him. What was it Willie Maugham used to tell me about drunks. . . I can't remember. Never mind. It'll come to me when I'm not trying to think. Isn't Fen mud quite the most foul mud there is! There's something about it in one of Mary Butts' stories, something about Ely being hidden in it like a jewel in a toad's head. Except Ely isn't hidden, is it? It sticks up for miles, thank goodness. Let's go over and listen to them singing Taverner next week. It will be good for us and good for them.'

I felt myself choking. 'Goodbye,' I repeated unsteadily. There suddenly seemed so much more to say goodbye to.

She then looked up at me for the first time. 'Goodbye,' she said. Her small eyes were vivid with a mixture of resignation, bravura and courage, and I realized that people had said goodbye to her before.

'For three whole hours!' I laughed jerkily and bent down and touched the top of her head with my lips. Her hair smelt of rain-water and vinegar. When I reached the gate she called out:

'Never mind about telling your father what I said.'

And forgiveness stretched between us in the still afternoon air like a garland.

When I got back to Mallards Point at a little after six Euen and Godfrey had left for Cambridge in the local bus. I recalled now that something had been mentioned about their going to see a film and I felt relieved that they weren't to be present. Lady Tinnington was in the drawing-room. She'd emptied all the flowers from the vases on to pages from The Times and was busy re-arranging them. Her birdy legs in their knitted stockings twinkled as she trotted in and out of the kitchen trailing bits of chicken-wire and jugs of clean water. The only other people present were the Nightingale sisters. They sat together on the sofa, beaming and happy. They had brought their latest joint effort detective story for Mrs Carron-Wilson and it nestled in their heap of discarded voile scarfs on the table before them. It was bright yellow and was lettered, *This is Death, Ducky*, another great suspense story by Ben Carver. They giggled when they saw me looking at it and then C-W came in and we all began to laugh our congratulations. The Misses Nightingale flushed with genuine modesty. Neither of them had ever quite recovered from the miracle of being able to make close on a thousand a year from such an activity. They pushed up their spectacles and dabbed away at their good-natured, colourless eyes with scratchy handkerchiefs. They were twins and spent all the time when they weren't being Ben Carver bottling fruit for the Women's Institute shop in Ely.

Lady Tinnington finished the flowers and we sat there, the five of us, drinking sherry and talking about Cambridge, and I remember C-W saying, as though it was a kind of social duty on her part, 'I must get Gwen Raverat over. She's such good value.' I had noticed that none of the celebrities with whom Mrs Carron-Wilson spiced her conversation had ever arrived at Mallards Point, so I just smiled when the others cried, 'Lovely!' and 'Oh, *do...*'

She bent forward to pick up the detective story and when she settled back again there was a white flash near the hem of her skirt. I thought it was her slip but when the whiteness persisted in burning against the edge of my vision I stole another rapid glance. Blood pounded in my temples and my fingers seemed to terminate in little islands of delicious, feathery pain. The accidentally exposed inside flesh of her thigh faded away into a rich darkness, like the flesh on the legs of Rembrandt's 'Woman Bathing'. Then she moved to pass the novel on to Lady Tinnington and her clothes fell into place. I brought my eyes up to her face, convinced that she must know, only to see that she was unusually relaxed and easy. A ghostly air of girlishness hung about her, defying the comfortable proportions of her somewhat elaborate dress - it had occurred to me before how rarely she wore country clothes. She gave me the slightly roguish look one might give a child and I was mildly affronted. It did not belong to the new role she was about to play in my life. I stretched until my feet made an untidy masculine muddle in front of the half circle of chairs. I was glad I was sprawling, big, ungainly, fair. Euen's repeated remark now seemed a great compliment. I was at the gate of the marvellous adult world and it should be no idiot pick-up who would guide me through, but Mrs Carron-Wilson. In the Decameron and in the *Romance of the Rose* generous matrons were always rewarded with the love of gallant striplings.

I felt I had to convey the approaching change in our relationship at once.

'But it's a gorgeous title, darling!' she was exclaiming.

'No it's not. It's terrible. You know it is,' Miss Connie Nightingale was protesting. 'But of course we don't choose them ourselves. *They* do.'

'They have a young man who does nothing else,' said Miss Nancy Nightingale.

'Well, you're still very clever anyway - both of you. Gloriously clever -don't you think so, Stephen?'

I nodded and entangled her in a challenging stare. She returned this with a silently enquiring interest, then, when it made no sense to her, she dropped her eyes and gave the faintest of faint shrugs. I realized that she thought I was hoping to include her in some unspoken mockery of the Nightingales. I blushed and at that moment she looked at me again, as though wanting me to understand that she hadn't meant to snub me. Her small, slightly discoloured teeth were set in the phantom of a smile and for the first time I was struck by the curious amount of gold in her eyes, and that it was this which gave her her touch of animality. I tried to pass through this controlled blaze into the wild awareness behind it. She wrinkled her nose at me and immediately we were both back in our hateful schoolboy-sensible woman positions.

'I don't know why you are all so wonderfully sweet to me,' she said, holding out her stout little arms to include Lady Tinnington, who, unable to sit still for more than five minutes at a time, was busily turning out a revolving bookcase. 'The awful thing about it is, I never read your thrillers - it's no good pretending. But I know they're good. Jimmy Agate and everybody says so. It's just that I've got a blind spot where whodunits are concerned. I'm missing somewhere.'

'Don't explain. We all love you just the same - don't we, Stephen?' Miss Connie's cosy Wind-in-the-Willows face beamed at me.

I hesitated, then I said, *'A sine qua non.'*

Mrs Carron-Wilson gave a rushing, breathless laugh. 'Oh, I hope not. Love should never "go without saying", as it were, or be without its qualifications. Really, Stephen!'

I felt I had made some headway, though goodness knows why. I was plunged into a dream in which her hard little hands were on my body and was dragged back by a friendly, despairing squeezing of my arm and her voice crying:

'Look at him - he hasn't heard a word I've been saying. Now I shall have to start all over again. Molly' (this was Lady Tinnington) 'has let her lodge to a genius. He'll be our *douanier.* They'll be here directly, I've asked them up for drinks.'

'Them?' I said.

'There's a Mrs Douanier. She's going to take standard one in the village school. She'll be worthy, I'm afraid, but we must all be nice to her because of *him.'*

'They just arrived at the house one morning,' explained Lady Tinnington from the carpet, 'and asked was the lodge empty? I said yes it was and had been for heaven knows how long, but that it had light and water and things, and he thought it would do but she couldn't make up her mind. Anyway, they've taken it - they moved in last Thursday. He hasn't got a job, I've just learnt.'

'But he's a poet, Molly, a kind of Clare figure.'

'Oh, I hope not!'

'Well W. H. Davies then.'

'That's almost as bad. I'm not worrying about the rent, if that is what you're thinking, C-W, I'm worrying about *her*.'

'I know she's having a baby. He told me when I met him in the lodge garden. But later on she's going to provide the bread and butter so that he can devote himself to writing. I think it's wonderful, considering the -well - kind of people they are.'

Lady Tinnington banged the dust from a few more books and then she said, 'There's a good bit of ground there. At least they won't want for fruit and vegetables.'

'But he's not fit to garden, Molly! His back hurts when it bends. He told me it did.'

And then she jumped up, ran to the french window and began to wave. 'Hoorah! they have found the right house.' She smoothed her dress over her plump hips and went outside to meet them. No sooner had she disappeared than Lady Tinnington said hurriedly, 'This is going to be awkward. She doesn't understand, bless her. He's a layabout – you've only got to look at him. Oh dear, how horrible I am to say these things. I ought to let you make your own judgment...'

When Mrs Carron-Wilson returned she was leading by the hand a prim, quiet-looking woman of about thirty whose advanced pregnancy was clumsily exaggerated by the lumpy folds of a ginger tweed overcoat. She wore a tammy and big, round, silver-rimmed spectacles. Behind the spectacles her eyes strained forward in a mixture of watery perplexity and myopia. There was so great a degree of dullness about her that it drew from one the same kind of dutiful consideration as if she had been physically afflicted, blind or something. We all began to stretch out our hands to her and, like a figure in an Indian temple dance, she turned her hands away from us and locked them loosely above her great belly. She smiled insipidly and blinked. She didn't speak. Behind her was a tall, thin youngish man whose slender legs seemed fixed in a malachite base until he began to shuffle forward, when the dark shine became an enormous pair of well-polished workman's boots, obviously too large for him and uncomfortable. In spite of the mild summery evening he was wrapped up in a melton overcoat, its neck opening showing a neat V of white silk. He was grinning broadly, his lips turned back over a full set of strong brown teeth. It was a grin of foolhardy self-confidence. It stated, blandly and bravely, that he was going to brazen it out in our little community. Here comes the poet, his staring eyes declared. He had too much hair, thick hanks of dark brown hair rolling back from his brow in oily convolutions and a frizzy scrub of yellowish-red hair whose slightly indecent quality puzzled me at first, until all at once I realized that his beard had a pubic texture, as did his little matted eyebrows. I could see that he thought our flutter of concern was for him.

'Don't get up! Don't get up!' he insisted, flapping his hand. Then, seeing Lady Tinnington, 'Hullo-hullo-hullo! Who have we here?'

'Now whom haven't you met?' said C-W, and then began to laugh off the introductions in her infectious way. 'This is Miss Nancy Nightingale and this is Miss Constance Nightingale - oh, and this is Stephen. Mr Turp, Mrs Turp,' she finished.

The inevitable catechism followed. Where had they lived, would they like this village did they think? And a hundred other questions. The greatest care was taken not to let them see what we were all wondering, which was what they would live on. Mrs Turp sat near the bookcase and the fat swollen egg of her stomach fascinated me. It was the first time I had really noticed a pregnant woman and now I was able to look at one with an inquisitive detachment and without pity, for I found Mrs Turp herself stupid and despicable. She never uttered a word. She blinked and smiled and shook her head at the sherry. There were ragged patches of brown pigmentation here and there under the flaccid white skin of her face, making it look rather grubby. This, and her Eton-cropped hair, and the square shoulders of her ginger coat, made her slightly monstrous, a travestied youth above the breast-line and a fertility goddess below it. Her bare legs above her ankle socks were polished by the sun.

It was absurd to hear the Nightingales, when they spoke to Mr Turp, going out of their way not to wound a sensitivity which did not exist.

'Then you think that society's obligation towards the artist is a thousand times greater than the artist's obligation towards society?' Miss Nancy was saying. 'I see,' she added.

'I certainly think that,' said Mr Turp in his flat Midlands voice. 'I'm an artist and I'm a victim of the system. If society doesn't help me it closes my mouth, and if you close a poet's mouth you murder him.'

'How "help"?' asked Molly Tinnington from the carpet.

Mr Turp hesitated. Two long, sherry-flushed ribs of flesh shone below his cheek-bones and the rest of his face was hot and sticky. His eyes were gaudily blue and danced about in their moist sockets.

'Mr Turp means patronage perhaps?' said Miss Connie Nightingale.

'Does he? Is it patronage that you mean, Mr Turp?' Lady Tinnington asked. She was suddenly tortured about their rent for the lodge. Was twelve and six a week beyond them? Had she asked too much? Was poetry going to suffer because of it - or that poor baby?

It was C-W who finally had to discover what everybody in the room wanted to know.

'What *do* you live on actually, Michael?' she asked.

The reverberation set up by the blunt question and the Christian name was still tingling in our ears when Mrs Turp spoke for the first time.

'On me,' she said simply.

I looked at Mr Turp, expecting to see the indignant reaction of a puppet, or to watch him turn pale with fear or redder than he already was with anger, only to see him looking amused - even pleased. Then the Cambridge bus squealed to a standstill outside and Euen and Godfrey raced into the room. In the confusion C-W's *savoir-faire* collapsed completely. She was seized with a violent fit of *rire etouffé* and as Euen and Godfrey succumbed in languorous sprawls on the sofa cushions she fled from the room.

'It's the coffee!' I said, running after her. 'I'll give a hand. It must be boiled away.'

She was standing with her back to the Welsh dresser and shaking with the laughter which still had not managed to force its way out of her and as I passed, grinning a good deal myself, she put out her hand and clung to me for support. We rocked together in a sweet conspiracy of mockery. The peculiar tension of the evening: vanished and the curious feeling that our standards had been debased and made to look pretentious disappeared.

'Do you know what?' I murmured in her ear, which was just

beneath my chin.

'No. What?'

'I think he's the end.'

She stopped the gentle cosy rocking and said, 'No, no. You mustn't say that. Anyway, it's not just them I'm laughing at but all of us. I suddenly saw all our faces. So solemn! Well, at least he's nice to look at.'

'Nice?'

'Uh-huh. A nice red fox with his head in the hen-run.'

She brushed the crook of her little finger up under her lashes to brush the tears from her mascara, a little feminine movement of hers which I always found overwhelmingly endearing. Her other hand still rested lightly on my arm just above the wrist. From her hair rose the fresh rain-water and vinegar smell, its innocence in flagrant conflict with the scent she was wearing. Stooping quickly, I kissed her but my mouth slipped on her soft powdery skin and my determined second kiss landed harmlessly near her eye. The rest of my kisses were a confusion as her head twisted and turned and the gold flickered in her half-closed eyes. It was a muddle of faces and breathing and my disappointment was intense. Then an almost paralysing degree of consciousness returned as the hand she had laid against my waist ran between my jacket and my shirt. She gave a little gasp and hugged me and for a second her firm round body touched mine all the way down. There was a scalding sensation as the lively, scratchy fingers trailed across my buttocks and raced along my thigh, and then we were each yards away from one another, driven apart by some hateful sanity. The place where her breasts had crushed against my shirt-front felt cold and neglected, and I knew that I desired C-W as much as I had once wanted her to desire me. None of this took much more than a minute.

When she said, 'We'll use those pink cups Euen won at the fair last year,' her voice was steady and normal – not even tinged with that post-*contretemps* note of wistful regret. Yet I knew that what had happened was hurting her and would continue to hurt her for as long as she believed she had hurt me.

'And let's have that tray we got from the Omega Workshop,' she said.

We returned to the confused babble of the drawing-room. The Misses Nightingale had seized hold of each other's wrists and were staring at the time. Lady Tinnington was fiddling with the wireless, and gaudy bellows of Walton's *Belshazzar's Feast* broke in upon the talk. Euen and Godfrey were squashed up on the window seat and chattering softly in mutually amused voices, though what about it was impossible to tell. They had turned themselves into an island - a favourite trick of theirs. Mrs Turp, her spectacles shimmering in the lamplight, sat and stared into a void. I could hear Mr Turp talking loudly and indistinctly above the general hubbub. He had taken off the melton overcoat at last, though not the scarf, which hung with ecclesiastic nicety in two snowy parallels over his frowsty jacket. C-W pressed into this uproar, vaguely and dreamily, and I followed with the coffee tray. Her speckled golden shoulders and arms, and her languorous movements reflected a cat-like repose and *douceur*, each a strange repudiation of her normal vivacity. I felt half-suffocated with lust, desire and love, as well as elated that I constituted for her at least one of these things. It didn't seem to matter which. I edged in front to hand round the cups. When it came to her cup I steadied myself to meet her gaze. To my astonishment her eyes were fixed on Michael Turp as he half sat, half squatted in the tub chair, his long, straight legs rushing out of it in two shiny serge peninsulas.

'Christianity has failed. Do *you* know why it has failed?' he shouted at Lady Tinnington. 'Well, I'll tell you. It has failed because it has substituted the cup of blood for the pillar of blood.'

He lurched back, immensely pleased with himself.

'That sounds very much like the kind of remark D .H. Lawrence told me,' said Lady Tinnington. 'Only he put those kinds of remarks into his books, not into his conversation.' Her tone was crushing. She wasn't certain that what she had said was true but she felt she had to beat her way out of the vulgarity of the evening somehow.

'Bravo!' said C-W, though not at Lady Tinnington's statement, which she affected not to have heard, but at Mr Turp's epigram. And from that moment, and during the weeks that followed, we each had to fight for our friendship with C-W. Even my father fought. I had not reckoned on his affection for the evenings at Mallards Point. 'Damn layabout!' he snuffled. 'Only time when you can get C-W alone these days is when he's in Ely drawin' the dole. Too good-hearted, that's what she is. Feller takes advantage y'know.'

As for myself I sincerely believed that I was heartbroken and acted accordingly. I mooned around her and carefully worked out little ways in which we might come into seemingly accidental physical contact. But the old free and easy intimacy had vanished for myself as well as for the others. Meanwhile, C-W concentrated on the great task of launching her protégé. She was deliberately mysterious about his work. 'We would see,' she said. Eventually, under Lady Tinnington's blunt insistence, a sheaf of grubby ruled paper pinned together by one of J. L. Wilson's bulldog clips was handed to us. Silently, amazedly, we passed them round the room. The poems were scrawled in large uneven pencilled letters. They were formless, badly spelt and frequently indecent. They left one a trifle frightened and speechless.

'They're only the roughs of course,' C-W told us. There was no hint of apology or explanation in her voice. She folded them carefully and replaced them in her bureau. As we walked down the lane - she was on her way to the Turps' lodge - she drew me aside and said:

'Stephen dear, there's something I've been meaning to tell you. The boys are off to Cornwall tomorrow as you know. So - well, what I mean is, don't feel that you have to waste your summer holiday by entertaining us old fogies at Mallards Point. It's nice for us, of course, but it must often be ghastly dull for you.'

'When will they be back?' I asked, not really caring but unable to think of anything else to say. I felt ashamed and humiliated.

'The twenty-eighth, as usual.'

We came to the lodge and through the open window I could see Mrs Turp, static and motionless. She didn't even look up when C-W called, 'Coo-ee!'

For more than a fortnight I kicked my heels round the village, playing tennis at the rectory, rowing with my father and bicycling along the tedious black Fenland roads in the August heat. Two days before Euen and Godfrey returned from their holiday I went for a long walk and came back along the road which led past Mallards Point, and rather than risk being seen I strolled along the field path which ran parallel with the garden wall, and led to the river. I thought I would climb the wall, at the bottom, cross the tangled garden and make my way home across the park. The sun was brassy and nothing moved except the heat mist on the distant water-meadows. When I was within a few yards of the river I climbed the orange brick wall. Espaliered pears and apricots had run riot and made a dense fringe above the parapet. I sat among the pear leaves with my feet dangling in the brown cool branches and looking down into the dear, familiar garden, noting the creeper-bound fair horses and cockerels, the peeling white greenhouse and the uncut lawns. I wondered if C-W's battered punt was still moored to its willow. To see the water I had to stand up on the wall and keep my balance by clinging to the twigs.

Swaying unsteadily, I peered through the ripening fruit into the still and mysterious depths of a Giorgione. The river was a hard metallic aquamarine and the punt was soldered to it by the intense blackish gold sunlight. Rushes were stacked at its fringe like green weapons. They cast long stabbing shadows on the bank. Two figures lying on the bank had their heads in the darkest of these shadows and their white, nerveless nakedness sprawling on the grass had a tragic quality, like the torsos of lovers who had been discovered and decapitated. The man had a delicate marbled refinement, his limbs were long and slender and very white. A watch glittered on his wrist. He was smoking and one pale arm rose and fell. The woman had wandered into the Giorgione mystery by mistake. She was one of Rubens' crushed-raspberry-and-milk Sabines. Her rich shapeless flesh was heaped on the ground and in the ruthless sunlight demanded pity.

Suddenly the youth propped himself up on his elbow. The effect of Mr Turp's mottled bearded head on the pure classical shoulders was grotesque. He was angry and his flat voice reverberated in the motionless afternoon. I slipped from the wall into the neighbouring field, my heart beating wildly.

'What do you mean "it can't go on"?'

C-W's voice hovered between common sense and sentiment in the way I had always found enchanting.

'You know exactly what I mean, Michael. I don't have to go over everything again. The boys are coming home on Thursday, and well, the holidays are over. Let's leave it like that.'

'Let's leave it like that, eh!' He imitated her speech. 'Let's leave it that you've had your bit of fun and I can go to hell!'

There was a defensive argument by C-W which I couldn't catch and then I heard her cry out, 'Michael, oh, Michael!'

But although I knew she was alone and weeping by the water I didn't go to her because her tears had no relevance for me. Though I did go to Mallards Point the following week-end. We were all present except the poet, his wife and my father, who was poorly.

'I must get Rose Macaulay to come down,' said C-W. 'She's *such* good value…'

The Shadows of the Living

The activity, both inside and outside Springwaters, had been immense. Springwaters, because the source of the broad, short, sluggish Bourton river literally sprang from the rough pasture just behind the house. Faulkner had watched all the preparations with his usual oblique gaze, keeping them at bay, as it were, and not allowing them his full interest.

He was in the study doing the farm accounts but the door was ajar and he could see all the to-ing and fro-ing; Sophie heaving the furniture about and Mrs Blanch helping her. They were making a space in the library so that seventeen clergymen, including a bishop and an archdeacon, might robe. Through a series of doorways like those in a Velasquez, Faulkner was able to see the darting movement in the Great Hall as the village ladies spread an enormous parish tea.

'What can I do?' he had offered.

Sophie had not needed to consider the question. 'You can keep out of the way, that's what you can do.'

The upheaval was bothering him, he realized. There was something overreaching about it; a sense of going too far. Some kind of misjudgement, not so much of the occasion but of the person who was central to it. Once, he had got as far as the 'field of operation', as Sophie called it, to suggest some kind of calming-down in all the preparations. It was, after all, the induction of the new rector, not a hunt ball they were about. But the women wove around him, like ants round a stone, impervious to everything except their tasks and burdens. So now he ran his fat old-fashioned Parker up and down the feed bills, trying to concentrate, trying, too, to take the day in his stride. After all, parsons came and went, and Mr Deenman would be no exception.

Staring straight ahead, Faulkner saw the familiar heart of the village, the huge shapeless green, its little paths busy with people, its surround of lanes glittering with cars and vans. The embryonic river trickled through it and children sailed over it on the swings which he and Sophie had given to commemorate the Festival of Britain. What had somebody said - quoted - when looking at the same scene from the Hall? 'And all shall be well, and all manner of things shall be well.' Well he certainly hoped so! Church and Hall shone towards each other in the late April light, as they had done for centuries.

A figure dramatically appeared on the top of the tower and soon the patronal flag hurled on the wind, a vivid cross on a white field, a scaffold as a matter of fact, thought Faulkner, surprising himself. A peculiar stomach-fluttering wax smell drifted through the room. 'Blasted polishing and cleaning!' he grumbled to the sleeping dog. 'What's it all about, eh? You tell me, boy!' It's about God, he thought morosely. It's either about God or it's about nothing. The alternatives see-sawed in his subconscious. If I believe, then *what* do I believe? he wondered. 'Sophie!' he shouted.

She put her head round the door.

'Sophie, I was thinking, something has happened to us, hasn't it? To us and to our world. God isn't here as He was, well, when grandfather was here, is He? It's the truth, isn't it? It should make us scared or sad, yet it doesn't. Think how big God was when the men built the church and how little He is when you cut sandwiches for Terence!' Terence was the Bishop.

'I refuse to think anything of the sort,' said Sophie. 'You look a bit pale; are you all right?'

'I'm O.K. It's that damn floor polish. It seems to upset me.'

'Darling, nobody has been polishing anything, and don't complain. Why don't you pack those accounts in if you don't feel like it? Go and do something in the garden for an hour - you've got time before lunch.'

'I'm your tiresome little boy, aren't I?'

'You're my dear old boy,' she said, kissing his thinning hair.

The gules and martlets and lozenges in the armorial window were caught in sunlight and spattered the pair of them with gaudy shadows. A few minutes later, Faulkner was happily walking through the orchard, noting the swollen buds and disturbing the finches. The smell of wax persisted but it no longer upset him. On the contrary, it seemed to lift and strengthen him. And when the first tentative sounds of the practice peal broke from the church tower he felt a return of ease which was almost as good as a return of certainty. What a relief! How could he have explained to Sophie - to anyone - that there had been moments during the past month when he had heard (although that was too strong and definite a word, maybe) the tumult of a destroying force making its relentless way towards the village, and seen wisps of smoky darkness, and had known the taste of substances which drew the lips back from the tongue in gagging refusal? Strolling back to the house, he heard the pips for the World at One and Mrs Blanch calling, 'Colonel! - her Ladyship says "Lunch and hurry!" '

Sitting with the two women at the great scrubbed kitchen table, Faulkner ate quickly, as though solid food could fill what pockets of emptiness might remain within him. He thought, as he frequently did, though without rancour, of that enviable thing in most people's eyes, his inheritance, and how much better his life would have been without it. All the rooms and acres and farms, and the duties which festooned them, the local bench, the committees and, of course, the church. He and Sophie were museum-keepers, both in the metaphysical as well as in the material sense. Lumbered! He might, with a bit of conniving, heave the house and its contents into the lap of the National Trust but he could scarcely shed his duties. Not at his age. But he wished that life had provided him with more than merely a decent response to social obligations. It would have been nice to have been clever like Sophie, or really good like Mrs Blanch. The trouble was, he never did have much imagination.

He rose and freed a butterfly which was beating its wings against a pane. A gust of over-hot air burst at him through the momentarily open window. He almost said, 'It's going to be a scorcher,' then remembered the date, the fourteenth of April. A jet from the nearby American air-base screamed across the garden, spinning a rope of smoke behind it.

Both Bishop and clergy arrived promptly at 2.30. Mattock, the new young constable, fussed their cars over the cattle-grid into the park. Most of the cars stopped just inside the gates to let wives and other passengers get out and walk across the green to the church. Faulkner met everybody on the terrace, drawing them through the hall in the courteous way which seemed to make his house their property for the time they were there. His hospitality was his special genius, though he had no knowledge of this.

The little Bishop was merry. For someone who slaved fifteen hours a day at an administrator's desk, such functions as introducing a new priest to one of these beautiful time-lost country places lying in the wilds of his diocese came more into the category of recreation than work. He wandered happily from group to group. The response to him, Faulkner observed, was a pleasure verging on radiance. The older clergy seemed to lose their staleness when he chattered to them. As for the young men, they noticeably gained in spiritual confidence or authority. Or something. Faulkner watched with a mixture of embarrassment and longing. God flickered in his brain like a neon sign, one minute with total definition, the next without form and substance.

The Bishop, looking at his watch, said, 'Not a sign of him yet, Colonel! I hope that old bus of his hasn't had a breakdown.'

Faulkner's confusion was obvious.

'Your new Rector, Colonel - remember?' said the Bishop with mock severity.

Mr Deenman: it was true, the curious, unsettling appointee had clean gone from Faulkner's mind. 'The man of the moment!' he smiled – 'And me forgetting him!' The gaunt untidy figure rushed into his consciousness; the odd harsh voice, so compelling yet so difficult to understand at times, suddenly filled his ears. Deenman had been the Bishop's nomination after a year had passed without another soul applying for the living. The Bishop was speaking to him again, although now his words contained an underlying seriousness.

'You won't forget him, I'm sure, Colonel.' He was really saying, 'Deenman is a lonely, wifeless man who is going to need a bit of unobtrusive help and encouragement.'

'He'll be all right, Terence. Never fear.'

Why did the Bishop insist on their calling him by his Christian name and yet continue to address him as Colonel?

'I expect he's gone straight to the church,' said the Bishop. 'We may as well go too, I think. We can wait at the back until he turns up.'

The impressive little procession, headed by the blacksmith's teenage son carrying a tall brass cross he had made for his apprenticeship exams, wound its way darkly over the green, Faulkner and the other churchwarden attending the Bishop with wands and solemn steps. Cars were lined up in rows round the churchyard wall and the dead seemed to be slickly wrapped in tinfoil. It was what Faulkner called a good turn-out. Except that the bellringing bothered him by its resonance. He thought that it was probably something to do with the wind – although he had never known such nerve-touching sounds before. Each bell seemed to skilfully slide away from its true note and produce a deliberate travesty of what was expected. The clashing was being built up to some sort of climax. Faulkner's bewilderment changed to anger. As the procession entered the churchyard, the last vestige of shape vanished from the peal and a chaotic shaft of percussive noise took over. 'What the hell. . . ?' He turned a half-apologetic face to the Bishop, only to glimpse the serene smile and the silver flash of the crozier. Faulkner's worried glance passed on to Robarts, the people's warden. Robarts was a ringer and had been a tower-captain in his day. But the old shepherd was shambling forward in his usual manner, his features as expressionless as he could make them. You couldn't get anything out of Robarts, thought Faulkner, even if the world was coming to an end. Which was what it sounded like.

They were about to enter the porch when the huge old 1950's Humber which Faulkner had last seen when Dr Deenman had arrived at the Hall for his interview, and smothered in what appeared to be an entire winter's mud, lurched into view and shook itself to a standstill at the very entrance to the churchyard. He's not going to leave the thing there! Faulkner thought incredulously. Right bang in the way!

The procession had stopped and in a few seconds, bowing in that strangely excessive way of his, Mr Deenman strode through it to his place at the front of the nave. No 'good afternoons'. Just a gaunt dipping of the large head in its crushed and dusty Canterbury cap. No smile. Once inside the church, however, Mr Deenman's odd rushing confidence seemed to desert him; the huge strides slowed down and the tall solitary figure passed through the dense congregation with an awe which silenced the whispering. The first notes of the introit, piercingly grave, added to the drama. Nerves, thought Faulkner, rather relieved. Deenman's behaviour up to this moment was beginning to overwhelm him. He saw the new Rector's glance pass from object to object in the chancel. It was as though he were checking an inventory, making sure that everything remained as he had left it.

Scarcely moving his head, Mr Deenman's gaze fell on carved angels and devils, the Mothers' Union banner and all the other ornaments and fittings, while the altar candles blazed in his spectacles, filling the dark eyes with reflected fire. Faulkner remembered now that this was the first time Deenman had seen the church. He recalled how surprised he had been - even a little hurt - when, at the interview, he had offered to show him over it and the new Rector had said, 'No, not now. Not yet.' Adding stiffly, 'I thank you.' 'He talks rather old-fashioned-like,' 'Shepherd' Robarts had said approvingly.

The induction went faultlessly, the clever Bishop manipulating the best instincts of the laity. Tolerance and love were manifest. The ancient revolutionary argument of Christ's philosophy was heard plain and clear. Mr Deenman played his part to perfection and emerged as an undeniably holy man. He was led by the churchwardens to the door, the font, the lectern and the altar in turn, and making great promises all the way. Finally, he was taken to his rectorial stall, this being the first in a row of magnificent fifteenth-century misericords on the right of the chancel. A curious hesitation occurred at this point, a flight of confidence not unlike that which had affected him when he had first entered the building. He almost sat in the correct seat, then slipped quietly into that next to it. The archdeacon, who was still holding his hand, grinned and insisted on the official stall, and Deenman accepted it, though so gingerly, Faulkner had remarked to Sophie afterwards, 'You'd have thought it was the hot seat!' While they sang the *Te Deum*, Mr Deenman remained hunched in his place, his eyes fixed on the great painted oak angels roosting in the roof. The time then came for him to make the customary brief speech of thanks. The first few sentences were conventional enough, although Faulkner was once again struck by the rich, rough voice with its unplaceable accent. It was only necessary to say a few polite words. It was obvious that the new Rector realized this but that he also was struggling with a compunction to add something personal. This obviously got the better of him for, to the controlled astonishment of the packed church, he replaced his cap and began to preach. The magnificently spoken words were crammed together in complicated phrases which were often hard to follow, though the reason for the outburst was plain enough - accusation. Wrath. Faulkner listened, fascinated but made slightly sick, as one listens to a gale.

'What is this that Peter said?' demanded the new Rector. 'Wash both feet, hands and head? Verily to open the matter clearly unto you, by these hands are understood *opera hominis* - the works and deeds of man! For the hands are the principal instruments whereby man does his work and labour.'

Here Mr Deenman held up his hands which Faulkner saw with distaste were extremely dirty, brown and strong but with blackened, broken nails.

'Therefore by the hands are understood words and deeds. . .' The Rector was now staring at the hands of the people in the front pews, his look passing from one to the other, rather like an officer at an army inspection. When he reached Faulkner, he spoke straight at him and pointing. 'These thy evil works must be washed clean by penance ere thou go to the great maundy of God, or that thou receive thy Maker!' And he swung round to the altar.

'He can't mean that he is going to refuse me Communion!' thought Faulkner. 'Why? What on earth have I done? What the hell is he getting at? The man must be mad!' He looked at the Bishop for support but he sat on his uncomfortably carved chair with all his usual implacable sweetness.

'And not only thy hands, thy works, but also thy head,' continued the Rector, 'whereby is understanding of all thy five senses, thy five wits... There is thy sight, thy hearing, thy smelling, thy tasting and thy touching. These senses otherwise called thy five wits must also be by penance washed!' Leaning over the partition made by the sawn-off stump of the rood, he looked into Faulkner's amazed face and said, almost conversationally, *Thy hands, thy hands that did it, they must be by penance washed...'*

He now turned to the assembled clergy in the choir, then to the long rows of politely listening faces in the nave, and said simply, his hand indicating the apparent peacefulness of the scene, *'Haec requies mea.* This was my rest. This was my place of quiet. I was to be happy here as long as I lived. But what followed? *Nulla requies* - no rest...'

A few minutes later, everybody was strolling across the green to the parish tea which had been laid out in the Hall, while the bells rang with perfect precision. Mr Deenman was shuffling along with the other clergy and carrying his surplice over his arm. Sophie saw that it had a large tear near the hem.

'You know that we're expecting you for dinner tonight, Rector!' she cried. She wanted to add, but who is going to get your meals and look after you in the future? How are you going to manage in that big old rectory? 'He's going to be a bit of a problem', she whispered to Faulkner. 'Darling, are you all right? Is it your funny tummy?'

A boy flying a kite was so absorbed that he seemed unaware of the surge of churchgoers. 'I won't let you go, I won't let you go,' he was muttering over and over to himself as he clung to the string of the desperately straining pink shape.

A few weeks later Faulkner bumped up the Rectory drive with some papers for Mr Deenman's signature. The barren-looking house with its curtainless, ogling black windows no longer worried him. The new Rector had made himself comfortable in a two-roomed den adjacent to the kitchen and simply ignored the rest of the building. A massive table, a few books, his clothes on hangers dangling from the picture-rail, a stiff little iron bed standing on a square of brown drugget and a prie-dieu with a padded kneeler appeared to be his total household goods. After his initial shock, Faulkner found himself rather approving this austerity. Why should a nuclear age parson be obliged to set himself up in Victorian domestic style? He glanced around and, seeing that a spade and barrow had been left in the courtyard, wandered off in search of Mr Deenman, now and then shouting, 'Rector!' The neglect in the garden really did rather upset him. It worried him to see the untouched lawns and weedy beds. Yet he was determined not to criticise. Things had been easier since he had made up his mind to accept the Rector as he was. 'Just let him get on with things in his own way,' Sophie had said. 'He is so *good*— everybody says so.'

Following the sound made by a machine, Faulkner came across the Rector just beyond where the formal garden ran into a large rough ridge of ground, dense with grass and gorse, and treacherous on the north side with a blackthorn hedge. He had cleared some of the scrub with a scythe and was now trying to plough the clearing with a rotavator. In spite of the modern machine with its cheerful green paint and shining gadgets, there was something in the bowed, fatalistic attitude of its operator which suggested to Faulkner a scene he had witnessed in France, a solitary peasant, chipping away in a vast Norman field with a short-handled hoe, who had seemed to him the essence of everlasting human toil.

The Rector was dressed in old battledress trousers held up with a wide leather belt, a flannel shirt and his clerical collar. The rotavator was either jammed or the Rector did not understand the working of it, for after a yard or two's straight ploughing it seized the initiative and swung the heavy figure round in a mad uncontrolled arc, churning up haphazard scraps of root and gravel. When Faulkner hurried over and switched the thing off, the Rector looked as if he had reached breaking point. His hands trembled and he was almost in tears.

'My dear man, why wear yourself out on this dreadful old bit of ground? It's part of the glebe but nobody has touched it in my lifetime. It's just a donkey acre. If you *must* have it ploughed, then I'll ask Arnold to bring a tractor up and see what can be done. Though take my word – it's useless.' (Why was the silly ass fooling around up here anyway when there was a beautiful bit of kitchen garden simply begging to be dug?)

'Perhaps you're right,' said Mr Deenman. He was making a great effort to recover his dignity, or maybe (thought Faulkner) simply not to show anger and frustration. 'It seems a pity, that's all. Not to mention having to give up part of my vocation!' He gave one of his rare smiles.

'Oh come now, Rector! We don't expect you to farm as well as preach!'

'You don't?' Mr Deenman was plainly astonished.

'Why, no,' replied Faulkner uncertainly. What was the chap driving at? He changed the subject. 'Sophie says I'm to bring you back to supper.'

'And I am to bring you back to God.'

For a moment Faulkner could scarcely believe his ears. To 'get at him' here, out in the garden, to swing the conversation over like that – it was the limit! All his suppressed dislike of the priest rushed to the surface; he could taste its putrescence in his mouth, it burned like acid in the corneas of his eyes, it soaked out of his palms and glutted his stomach. His loathing of Deenman was blind and desperate, like the loathing he had had for a rat which would not die, *would not die*, though he had beaten his walking-stick into it in a paroxysm of revulsion. He had died, for an entire abyss-like minute, but the rat had dragged its frightful wounds away. Deenman was touching him! Jesu. . . Jesu..

'I thought you were going to catch your foot on that stump. I shall have to dig it out. We'll go over to the church and say the office, then have tea. Call it a day.'

'What office?'

'I'm not certain. Perhaps you'd like to choose – it's the Feast of St Alban.' He fumbled in the pocket on the front of the battledress trousers and withdrew a Bible. 'That's right – Ezra. They are laying the foundations of the temple. "The people could not discern the noise of the shout of joy from the noise of the weeping. . . "Well, that's life for you.'

'I think I should go home,' said Faulkner. 'I told Sophie I wouldn't be long.'

'You won't be long - I can promise you that.'

'Perhaps I should have said that I'm not very good at this sort of thing - saying offices and all that. I'm just a once-a-weeker I'm afraid.'

'Don't worry,' answered the Rector. 'None of us is very good at it. Here, half a sec, I'll get my cassock.'

Again Faulkner noticed the double language, as if two time-divided colloquialisms had joined each other. Then he remembered that Mr Deenman knew endless unusual things about the Reformation, odd little scraps of social information, customs and the like. He had conducted a party of local historians round the cathedral and Faulkner and Sophie, dutifully trailing in his wake, had been amazed.

The Rector returned from the house with the cassock untidily flung on him and attempting to fasten its many buttons as he half-walked, half-ran to where Faulkner waited. His movements, too, were contradictory, alternating as they did between clumsiness and grace. The cassock heaved around the thick body, a horrible garment, Faulkner decided. Looked as though it had been slept in, or under. Yet it was plain that the Rector assumed it with a sense of honour.

They left the Land Rover in the drive and walked to the church. Mrs Howe, cleaning the altar brass, looked up and said, 'Rector, Colonel.' The building, as usual, was freezing cold and smelled cosily of vermin. Faulkner imagined Mrs Howe going home to tell her family about him being on his knees on a Wednesday afternoon and her husband carrying the news to the pub that evening.

The Rector, after giving the dismantled altar a stare, turned into the Faulkner chapel and plunged before the gaudy tomb of a Robert Faulkner who had died in 1641. An aquamarine light from the east window bathed the alabaster face.

'All that will have to be shifted,' said the Rector conversationally. 'He's in the altar space.'

He spread his books on a chair and knelt. Faulkner crouched a little to his right. Mrs Howe watched with an expressionless face, her hands continuing to polish at a tremendous rate. For a while the Rector muttered his way through Evensong and Faulkner managed to say the responses. The devotion soon became something normal and ordinary, and his cool English worship gave way to an uninhibited contact with God. As the service proceeded he rationalized all the difficulties which had arisen between himself and the new Rector. They stemmed, surely, from their degrees of belief. The Rector was God-possessed, while he was, well, God-acquainted. He tried to pray. Not to say words but to break through the decent Anglican formula and reach God's ear. A silence. A universe of flint. Sentences which not only fell short of their target but which returned to him like spit in the wind. He was soiled by his own prayer. It didn't work for him and, if he was honest, it had never worked. Being Robert Cosgrave Faulkner, J.P., T.D., hadn't worked either. His life was trivial. It was trivial because it was nothing more than a packet of unexamined gestures. The gesture he made towards heaven was the worst. God was so sick of it that he had sent him a slight coronary (over a year ago now and no further effect) and he had sent him Mr Deenman. It was time the Rector rose from his knees. Faulkner felt giddy. He was also quite unmistakably aware of a rank odour coming from the cassock and that the bulging shape which pushed through the broken boot in front of him was Mr Deenman's bare foot.

As if conscious of Faulkner's doubt, the Rector half-turned in his direction and whispered, 'We are like women who have a longing to eat coals and lime and filth. We are fed with honour and ease and wealth, yet the gospel waxeth loathsome and unpleasant in our taste, so how can we feed others with what we cannot fancy ourselves?'

Faulkner leaned forward until the large ear with its whorl of red hair was almost touching his mouth and said, slowly and distinctly,

'They burnt the parson of this parish. They burnt him on the green. It was a long time ago. His name was Daneman -John Daneman.'

'Blessed John Daneman?'

'I don't care about that. *But I think you ought to know.*'

Mr Deenman said, 'My strength hath been my ruin and my fall my stay. I was in danger, like a chased bird. Yet who would wish to remain in a misshapen or ruined nesting hole?'

'*I think you should go.*'

'Where should the frighted child hide his head, but in the bosom of his loving father?'

Faulkner got to his feet. His head throbbed and there was an ache in his eyes which made the late afternoon sun unbearable. He half-dragged the Rector to the varnished board containing the list of the incumbents and jabbed at a name about halfway down, 'John Daneman - suffered 1554.'

'And it wasn't Bloody Mary,' said Faulkner. 'It was the village. They did it off their own bat, on the green. That green!' And he pointed through the open door at the endlessly swinging children and the bus crawling to a stop and women with prams and three old men waiting for death on the Jubilee seat. He saw the slight greying of the Rector's swarthy face, and was satisfied. 'So I think you ought to go,' he repeated.

'I think I should, too,' said Mr Deenman. 'That is, if I'm to tidy up in the garden and get changed for this evening. Please do thank Lady Sophie for her invitation - it really is most kind.'

Faulkner walked back to the Rectory in order to pick up the Land Rover. Neither of them spoke. Mr Deenman was strolling in a concentrated sort of way, eyes on the ground, arms folded and when people said, 'Good afternoon', Faulkner was obliged to reply for both of them. The air made him feel better every minute.

As the year wore away, Mr Deenman came less and less to the Hall. It was not so much a question of his refusing invitations as something implicit in his manner which forbade Sophie to offer them. She was rather pleased about this. It meant that the Rector's way of life was a deliberately chosen independent thing and not in need of her carefully concealed props. Faulkner, on the other hand, felt oddly affronted by such independence. But both of them, like the rest of the village, got used to the unkempt Rectory and to the sight of the massive figure bent over a book in an uncurtained room or futilely slaving away in the garden. Doors and gates were never shut, and a naked bulb was often seen burning throughout the night. The services were taken with a mixture of stillness and commotion. The congregation seemed to have adapted itself to the passionate tirades which occasionally broke into an otherwise conventional sermon, though for Faulkner it was like waiting for a bomb to go off, disappointing when it did not, terrifying when it did.

Once or twice he had sounded the local opinion regarding the Rectory. Decently, of course - the Hall had always been a place where the gossip stopped. To his astonishment, he discovered a good deal of admiration for the grubby clergyman. 'He's a funny old bugger all right, but he'll give anybody a hand,' was the verdict at the pub. This was praise.

But one Saturday in September, Faulkner took the letters to the post and fancied he saw a very different reaction. It was a hot day but summer was ebbing nonetheless. The baked elms, their green fronds fading into ultramarine shadows, had no illusions about it and rustled with dissolution. The harvest had been snatched up by mechanical grabbers before anyone had realized there had been a harvest and from the high land surrounding the village, already stripped down for the plough, there came a warm and mocking wind which spelt no good. Or so Faulkner believed. He wasn't well; there was no longer the faintest doubt about it. It was not what his doctor said but what he himself knew. Because there was no pain or discomfort, the unusual thing which was happening to him - he had never before had actual, unmistakable illness, the state which alters life or ends it - was novel - almost luxurious. It was the feeling of pure sorrow which he found so acceptable, an acknowledgment of his own personal grief for something within himself which he could not name. He and Sophie had had a holiday in Crete, enjoyed a good summer, in fact. But it was the intensification of the rather ordinary views within walking distance of the Hall which had fascinated him ever since they had returned. A group of trees, a pasture, the home woods which he must have seen countless times now burst against his vision in a climax of beauty. At such moments he was praying, though he never knew it.

It was while he was taking one of these last-of-summer walks that he passed by the field where the village football team was playing a visiting side, and that he saw amongst the gaggle of spectators the awkward figure of the Rector. The match ended just as Faulkner was approaching and players and spectators swirled around the tall clergyman, who smiled and nodded. To Faulkner's surprise (to his satisfaction, he was inwardly bound to confess) these nods and smiles were returned by hostile glances or at the best indifference. It gave Faulkner a curious thrill to see the hurt on Mr Deenman's face when this happened. An overpowering emotion caught at him; the kind of blood-triumph which used to sweep him across the hunting-field in his youth leaped in him with a forcefulness he had long forgotten. What he remembered was Mr Deenman's remark - 'I was in danger, like a chased bird' - and he saw a great squawking crow, winged and unable to soar, tumbling desperately over the furrows and himself in pursuit of it. 'Get him, sir! . . . Get him, sir!' the villagers were howling. The footballers and their girls began to drift homewards, Mr Deenman with them. Faulkner could hear the distinctive voice but not the words. Now and then there was laughter, and at the gate, raised arms. Waves? 'I must get back too,' thought Faulkner. Sophie had arranged for the whole houseparty to go to the Boulez concert at Cheltenham.

They were still having tea in the garden when he returned.

'These constitutionals of his, they really do wonders for him,' said Sophie. 'Just look at him! - he looks fit to kill!'

The days which followed were extraordinarily full. The activities which Faulkner and Sophie had put off on account of their long holiday – five weeks – and the harvest, crowded one upon the other. This busyness did not make life run fast, as it is supposed to do, but expanded it. London meetings, a Northumberland shoot, an unusual amount of time at his club and the like, took him for a while out of the direct village orbit. Mrs Blanch's descriptions of what had been going on in his absence left him only politely interested. The truth was that when he was away from home he no longer felt or glimpsed the end approaching. On the other hand, nothing that he did outside the village gave him the extreme, almost ecstatic, happiness which he now drew from this familiar place. It had to be gradually, deliciously enjoyed: every hour with it was like a bite of the cherry and the time would come when he had devoured it all and he would no longer exist. This remained inconceivable.

'Let's go away again after Christmas, Sophie.'

'Marvellous! Where?'

The way she agreed to his every whim bothered him. She might have wrangled as she usually did; it would make things more normal. She never had possessed subtlety, only a big dull good heart. She had bored the passion out of their marriage.

'I don't know yet. Somewhere warm.'

After tea he walked to the post office and was kept waiting while a huddle of boys bought fireworks and Guy Fawkes masks. A few large leaves had trodden into the shop and the sweet smell of decay from the lanes and gardens infiltrated the cluttered room.

'Days drawin' in, sir - Colonel,' said the postmaster.

'They must,' replied Faulkner. He had not meant to sound either gnomic or vague but at that moment he had witnessed something very strange. The boys who had bought the masks had just got them on when the Rector passed. Waggling their heads and laughing, they were flattered by his elaborate fright, eyes rounded, mouth horrified. But Faulkner, hidden behind racks of groceries, was able to see a spasm of true terror take hold of Mr Deenman and shake him as if he were in the maw of a fiend. His own heart thudding with excitement, he greeted the Rector and accompanied him on the way home. He took the path which led to the waste at the back of the green and it was as he thought. A huge pile of faggots, straw, cardboard boxes, old tyres and other rubbish stood waiting for the fifth.

'I - I didn't think I had better come this way, if you don't mind,' said Mr Deenman.

'Then you know this way?'

'No-yes, of course I know it.'

'Of course you do.'

Faulkner heard the fear and could smell the disgusting evidence of it.

'It's all pretty barbarous, don't you think?' said the Rector.

'I don't know...' considered Faulkner. 'Old customs and all that. Fire cleanses, you know.'

'Well, it certainly will in this instance,' said the Rector, pointing at the heap of rubbish.

Joking, thought Faulkner. Nervous reaction. He was about to destroy Mr Deenman's confidence with a further threat when he felt his arm taken and himself led rapidly away from the bonfire. A voice inside him shrieked with loathing at the contact but the words - if words they were -vanished in the harsh talk. And what a freak the man was! Scuffed boots, old army trousers, stink and hair everywhere! Christ! they would have known what to do with him in the regiment in the old days!

Some children arrived, their arms filled with sticks. 'Remember! Remember!' they cried.

'We cannot forget, can we, Rector? Ever.'

Mr Deenman made one of his strange lunging movements, head swivelling forward on a powerful neck, trunk twisted to the side but legs somehow immobilized. It was the trapped gesture which Faulkner found so exciting. When it came to the point the Rector was not the kind of quarry which ever got away. In such a fix, it was natural that he should roar. The words erupted over Faulkner but, expected as they were, their force rocked him.

'You do what you do, not for our Saviour, but for sport. You are like Leviathan in the sea without a hook in his nostrils, a Behemoth without a bridle. I know thy ways. I see thy painlusting arm. Smoke always goes before fire, to declare that fire is in kindling, and a sickness before the tempest to tell that the storm is in breeding. You mouth Christ while you play the hobgoblin. You parade virtue while you lurk under a hollow vault. You sent me out of this dear world as a cinder in His dear Name. It was your pleasure -your pleasure only. My flame was by the hour, yours shall be by the eternal clock. I am ash but you are anathema!'

Suddenly, the Rector's voice changed, his body regained its normal gaunt height and he asked, 'How long?'

'Three days - Thursday.'

'Just after All Souls?'

'I suppose it is; I hadn't thought about it.'

'You poor creature,' said the Rector gently.

'I?' Faulkner was genuinely astonished.

Mr Deenman just smiled. 'We part here, don't we?'

'He's taking it pretty well,' Faulkner thought, watching the confident figure stride away into the dusk.

The fifth was a full day for both of them. Sophie's day for the Bench and his for the County Council. Then they both had to be together in Tewkesbury for a meeting about forestry, as well as do some shopping. Sophie insisted on doing the driving, saying that she liked it, though Faulkner knew that this was one more of her none too subtle ploys to make him ease-up. It was ridiculous really. He felt so strong, at least in that sense. The weather was perfection. A spell of sunshine was coming to a close and the hint of a drastic change - gales, even early snow showers had been mentioned in the television bulletins - made the last lavishly summery hours precious.

Sophie, when they had collected everything, had some tea and delivered a boot-full of iris roots to her cousins in Kingham - trailed home, as she described it. Faulkner, normally a bad passenger, sat docilely beside her, watching the yellow-glaring trees, the small massive stone houses and the ancient white road. He imagined his ancestors, nearly five hundred years of them according to the local historians, using this same path whenever they journeyed west. Not that he was often given to such ideas. Of course it was something - even in 1970 - to be a Faulkner, but family in this sense had never meant much to him. Partly because he was rather a dud at history, he supposed. 'You'll have to ask my wife,' he said when people enquired about the great-something-grandfather who had fought with Monmouth or written 'The Testament of Huntsmen'. Once, when his father had been alive, some Catholic priests had arrived to collect information about the Faulkner who had signed the warrant sending Father Daneman to the stake. They were so embarrassed that it amused his father. When the old man had said, 'Other days, other ways,' they looked a bit offended, as though time had nothing to do with it. All the same, Faulkner continued to wish that he had not been born in this kind of estate-prison, that he had been free, as most men are, to go and do what he liked where he liked. No arms, no armour. Nothing of that kind left over to anchor him.

A pale rocket tongued its way up the sky and feebly burst. 'Oh, look!' cried Sophie. 'I'd forgotten. How pretty.'

'They should have waited until it was dark.'

'Do you remember our fireworks parties, darling? When was the last -when Rodger was young, I suppose.'

'Rodger's twenty-first.'

'Of course. What ages ago! We're getting on - do you realize that?'

He did not reply. She chattered on, driving slowly but well, pointing at obvious things, missing things which really interested him, being Sophie. A top-drawer Earth Mother.

More sporadic fireworks went off, mostly a long way away, odd flashes and sparks neutered by the westering sun. 'Pretty'! They filled him with sorrow. It was about six-twenty when they reached home.

Half an hour later, while Sophie was in the bath and Mrs Blanch was laying the table, he heard the first shouts. He hurried from the house at once, taking the path through the kitchen garden which came out near to the piece of rough ground where they had built the bonfire. Other people were scurrying in the same direction. He could hear their quick tread, their urgent voices, even at times their breathing. Above this confused, thick but modulated sound rose the howls of imprisoned dogs, also other massively fretful noises which he took to be panic in the factory farms.

A homing bomber, a cross of lights, passed to the American airfield, adding its throb to the uproar. A group of men ran from the pub and the main road was ablaze with cars and motor-cycles. Isolated bangs gave the turmoil a curious stateliness, like minute guns announcing some great solemnity.

Faulkner could see the unlit bonfire now, tall as a house and immensely ritualistic. The crowd already gathered round it was restless but at the same time restrained. Children twittered in the darkness like disturbed birds. A bull, scenting danger, began a regular bellowing on some unseen field; the row created a brief mirth, then a crude acceptance. Faulkner pushed his way to the bonfire and touched it with his foot. He was near to worship, to love maybe, something overwhelmingly exultant, like a coming to life.

He looked at his watch. Seven-thirty. Then at two young man standing slightly apart.

'Right. Let's go and get him.'

The taller of the young men stared at Faulkner and then at his friend.

'We can't start without the Rector, can we?'

Faulkner's playful words produced a cautious grin.

'He'll come when he's ready, I expect, Colonel,' answered Mamby, the thresher's son. He continued to look at Faulkner uneasily, his fingers playing with a medallion which hung from his neck.

'He'll come when we tell him to. Come on.'

Followed by the couple, Faulkner saw the gleamingly curious eyes of the crowd and felt the heavy expectancy.

'Not long now, eh!' he called out to a group of women, some with small children in their arms. The women replied with shrill, hooting laughs.

As usual, the naked light burned in the uncurtained Rectory window and, in spite of the sudden drop in the temperature, the front door stood half open. Faulkner walked boldly up to the window and saw Mr Deenman. He was praying. He knelt at the prie-dieu with his hands clasped in the most extraordinary manner, on the top of his bowed head, the fingers making a tense arch above the wild grey hair. He was wearing his cassock and was very still. Mamby and his companion were clearly shocked and after the first glance into the room backed away.

'We'll give him another couple of minutes,' said Faulkner. 'Do the right thing, what!'

The boys scarcely heard him. They had retreated to the overgrown lawn and did not know what to do. Faulkner remained at the window, taking in every detail of the scene, the neat bed, the teapot and cups on the scrubbed table, the letters waiting to be posted, the open book -Teilhard de Something - he couldn't quite see. Also *The Times* open at the Court page and a sleeping cat. Mr Deenman himself was motionless. Faulkner looked once more at his watch then strode into the house.

'Daneman - we're ready.'

His hand grasped the cassock and shook it. Mr Deenman rocked slightly then toppled crazily from the prie-dieu. The young men heard the confusion and rushed forward. They saw the body of the Rector sprawling on the floor, the eyes fixed in terror and a great bare white leg exposed by his disordered robe. And at the same moment there was a boom! as the bonfire was ignited and a long, wailing roar of relief.

'Christ, oh Christ. . .' murmured the boy with the medallion.

It seemed extraordinary that on November 12th, the day of the funeral, the garden should be full of roses. The mild autumn had produced a massive second flowering. The flagged terrace was drenched in their scent. The Bishop trailed up and down after Sophie, listening to her rose talk and thinking about the service he had just taken. Faulkner had driven straight back to an interrupted farming conference at Oxford. What a tower of strength the man was!

'I hear the Colonel did everything that could be done.'

Sophie snipped a fat, dew-logged Zéphivine Dreuhin with her secateur. 'Well, you know what Robert is,' she answered loyally. 'He's only sorry that he got there too late . . .

The Common Soldiery

I don't remember how old I was, nine, perhaps only eight. Certainly not ten, because that was when we moved to Cumberland and everything was different. And not six either, because nothing happened at all when I was six. I once asked my Aunt Dulcie - who you may remember was the daughter of General Hardell and so not my proper aunt, but the sister of my father's best friend and the obvious person to take charge of me after my father's death - 'Aunt Dulcie, what happened when I was *six*?' And she said, in her hollow voice that was like a clergyman's, 'Why, child, nothing - nothing at all!'

She may have been right. She herself was an expert at separating time from experience. It all came about because of what she saw at Tambura in 1884. 'There were things done that day,' I once heard her tell Mrs Foley-Foley, the rector's wife, 'that you wouldn't credit. . . ' She then stopped abruptly, seeing me in the room, and her amber beads cracked warningly. 'Go into the garden, little boy,' said Mrs Foley-Foley, who was burning with curiosity. And she bent down to frighten me.

So I never really knew. I thought of the most awful thing it would be possible to witness and decided that it was the war-canoe in *Coral Island* which was launched on a ramp of living men, the sharp keel riding over their bursting breasts. For a whole year I believed that this was what Aunt Dulcie had seen - except that the ramp was made of soldiers from the *Illustrated London News* with brave, glassy eyes and sturdy legs bandaged with puttees. There wasn't a sound as the canoe carved its way over their bodies. Only the clink of their medals. But whatever it was, it must have been strange to make her spend every day wrapped in a carriage-rug, playing bezique with callers.

I was allowed to be present on these afternoons, so long as I absorbed the close inanimation of all the thousand trifles in the room. If I failed in the smallest degree, Aunt Dulcie would look up from the cards and say, 'Six-of-clubs-can't-you-sit!' So I sat, sometimes for hours, in a balsa-wood copy of the coronation chair which was really a commode and had a china bowl where the Stone of Destiny should be. Sometimes I counted, silently, the trophies nailed to the walls, four clubs, nine assagai spread out like a cruel fan, a spear. . . a Crusader sword.. . a pair of duelling pistols. But more often I turned the pages of *Portraits of Illustrious Ladies*, silently again, because any rustling made Mrs Foley-Foley - 'it was strange, she didn't know why' - suffer. Or I played solitaire with hands sweaty with fear that one of the whorled marbles would leap from the board and go raking over the floor.

Also I liked to just sit and listen to Aunt Dulcie talk. She had a brilliant, artificial way of speaking and sometimes in the middle of a fascinating story she would change quickly to bad French or Italian. It was not long before I realized that Mrs Foley-Foley was often as uninformed by these tactics as was I, for whose sake they were employed. It made her exceedingly angry, because until that moment her bottom lip had hung forward in expectation like the shiny lip of a little jug. To have the denouement dashed away in my Aunt's French, spoken, I am told, in the high Paris manner, infuriated her. Her wrath would then be directed to me. She would stand up suddenly, scattering her hand of cards. Leaning over me until her gold chains, warm from her bosom, dripped on to my skin and I was almost stifled with the smell of cachous and felt flowers, she would say, 'Go into the garden, little boy.'

Mr Foley-Foley gave me lessons in the mornings. I used to walk to the rectory, which was only just across a little meadow, at nine o'clock and stay there until luncheon. I never saw Mrs Foley-Foley on these occasions and the mornings existed for me as entities outside the limits of the day - little complete days on their own. Mr Foley-Foley taught me Latin, Greek, nature-study, arithmetic and the Collect for each day. I sat beside him at along, bare table. Fixed on the wall over our heads was an oar with a brass plate let into it. Sometimes Mr Foley-Foley would stare at this with infinite regret. The fireplace was decorated with stone heads like those in the church and on the mantel there were three Oxford Marmalade jars full of spills, very beautifully made from pages of *The Times*. I never saw Mr Foley-Foley use one of his spills. The walls of the study were quite covered with paintings of mountains framed in nobbly, stick-like frames which lapped at the corners to make the sacred sign. There was nothing on the floor and in winter we had no fire and when Mr Foley-Foley said: 'Right! Warm-up!' we used both to lean back from our books and hoot into our palms. Mr Foley-Foley was very kind to me and I liked him. He once gave me some port when it was very cold. He put the bottle away quickly, but not before I had seen its label, *Sacratincta*. That afternoon when my Aunt said: 'Well, Leonard, and what happened today?' I stopped turning the pages of *Portraits of Illustrious Ladies* and answered casually: 'After nature-study we had Communion.'

I enjoyed my life and was amazed when visitors, in tones usually employed for the bereaved, spoke of the deprivations I must suffer because of the absence of other children. Other children were my greatest dread. I wished for nothing more than to take my place in my Aunt Dulcie's drawing-room and let its fetid peace soothe the prospective terrors of October when I was to be sent away to school. The drawing-room was endlessly diverting. Its ugliness was complete. Among all its crammed commitments there was scarcely a redemptive line. There was, too, a fearful masculinity in its glossy tables with their bulbous, calf-like legs and the earth-brown curtains swagged coarsely like tarpaulins about a saluting base. The piano and the Chicago organ were heavy with battle trinkets. Aunt Dulcie poked the fire with the sword with which General Hardell had scarred so many dark skins and she sharpened her pencils over an upturned shako. There were countless photographs of smirking subalterns languidly posing on residency lawns. Fly-spotted mounts hugged the fading gardens of Cawnpore and Allahabad and spread their protection round unremembered terraces and shrubberies faintly enlivened with gangling Englishmen.

'Who is this one?' I asked before the game was made taboo because my Aunt grew weary of it.

'Captain Merrydew.'

'And this one?'

'Captain Fraser-Porter.'

'And him - the one propped-up on his elbow at the end of the row?'

'Mr Lovering. He lived in the big house you can just see through the trees.'

'What sort of trees are they?'

'What *kind* of trees - Good heavens, child, how should I know!'

'Who is that gentleman?'

'Which?'

'The young one with the smiling face.'

'This one? Here?' She bent and stared into the closed, still world of the photograph until her reflected features made a base upon which the faces of the straddling cavalry group swam uncertainly in a biscuit-brown montage. 'Mr Tooley,' she said.

'I don't mean Mr Tooley,' I said in a superior voice. 'I know him. I mean the nice one who is standing over there, away from the others. Him!' I pressed my finger over his face and left a smudge.

My Aunt crouched forward again and then drew back quickly.

'I don't know,' she said.

'You don't *know*?'

'Of course not! Why should I? He is just one of the men - the common soldiery, you understand?'

'Oh,' I replied.

For some reason she found this provocative and ordered me from the room.

On another occasion I annoyed her by asking questions about the *Portraits of illustrious Ladies.* They had finished playing bezique after the knave of diamonds and the queen of spades had once more unerringly found their ways to my Aunt's hand (she always played to win), and Mrs Foley-Foley was pouring tea. I think that my behaviour on this occasion put the idea of Mildred into their minds for the first time. It began quite innocently. I asked 'Who is that?'

'Mrs Norton,' said my Aunt.

'And this?' The heavy folio cracked ominously from my inability to hold up so heavy a volume.

'Lady Caroline Lamb - support the spine with your other hand; you're breaking it!'

'And this?' I said, ignoring her - I felt that I had to do this as a protest because of the way Mrs Foley-Foley was staring at me.

'Lady Blessington: be-good-enough-to-do-as-I-say, Leonard!'

There was a flattering tension in the room. Mrs Foley-Foley and the tea-pot were atrophied in a gesture from a Ptolemaic frieze.

'Did you know her?' I asked rudely. There was a brisk retort of splitting buckram. Defiant herself, my Aunt found the quality insupportable in others. Her eyes glittered grimly and she clattered her ornaments.

'No. Take hold of the book with both hands!'

For answer I tried to turn a page without putting the book down. There was a reckless crackle of dry paste and disintegrating gauze. With huge daring I said: 'I thought you knew everybody in pictures,' and then, with what I considered was dazzling wit, 'except the common soldiery.'

There was a livid pause during which I remember looking mockingly at Mrs Foley-Foley's absurdly frozen surprise and then a cold, stinging violence crashed down on my ear and ran in numbing streams down my cheek and neck. My Aunt's face was so near, I thought she might bite me. *The Portraits of Illustrious Ladies* fell to the floor and achieved its complete dissolution.

'Pick it up!' hissed my Aunt.

I did so, laboriously shuffling the scattered plates together. My head rang and stung at the same time and my humiliation was like a fountain spurting through me and threatening to show itself in torrents even more shameful than tears. Mrs Foley-Foley was not to be left out at such a reckoning. Although her hands clenched enviously at the blow, her deprivation gained some comfort from the severity she was able to put into her voice. Rising at the side of my Aunt, she snatched the book from me. 'Now leave the room - *this instant!*' she said.

About a week later Mrs Foley-Foley brought Mildred Hemp to the house for my Aunt's approval.

I hated Mildred Hemp at sight. Every repulsion I knew existed for me in the coarse erubescent limbs and the small, stubborn eyes. She was about sixteen, I suppose, big and strong, with a nard-like shine on her hands and face and a mop of dull, kinky hair of which she was inordinately vain. ' 'S natural,' she said, burying her blunt fingers in it the first day we met. She walked with that rather ursine padding with which old village women get themselves from the bus to home and I resented going for long, dragging walks at her side. Her job was to keep me out between luncheon and tea, my tea at six; not *theirs* at four. If she had been the reverse of all the things that she undoubtedly was – lazy, grubby, artful – this fact would have been enough to make me loathe her. When I saw her lurching along ahead and heard her constant 'come *on*' and knew that it was she who kept me from the delicious intimacy of the drawing-room, and the deft, soapy shuffling of playing-cards, my Aunt's extraordinary conversation - even Mrs Foley-Foley's malicious glances I could have wept. How I envied Captain Merrydew and Captain Fraser-Porter their maple frames so comfortably reflecting the tea-things. Like the poet's unravished bride, I saw them 'for ever panting' - were they not straight from epic chukkers in meadows pungent with frangi-pani? There was no doubt that they were for ever young. I saw the adult world as an exquisite state and resented with all my heart the long wait before I could take my place in it.

Mildred's treatment of me was capricious. She either ignored me or drew me into a stifling intimacy which I found alarming. She seemed armoured with an almost impenetrable stupidity, but sometimes a quite casual word on my part would have an astonishing effect. She would stop, her mouth would gape as she found speech and her little dark eyes would settle on my face like insects. She looked like this when I tackled her about botany.

Like the majority of country people, Mildred had only the sketchiest ideas about flowers. For her they had social standards which no degree of beauty could override. 'Them old common things!' she said once to my starry armful of bull-daisies. But the blowsiest rose would send her into sycophantic raptures. As soon as I realized the extent of her ignorance I grew boastful. It was my passion for catechism again, but this time with myself answering the questions.

'What's that?' I demanded.

'That old hedge stuff?' stalled Mildred.

'It's bergamot,' I said scornfully. 'And this?'

Mildred shrank. ' 'S unlucky.'

' 'S not,' I mocked. ' 'S henbane. Well then,' I plagued, 'you know what this is. .

' 'Rhinums,' answered Mildred smugly. 'Here, give it to me.'

I broke a flower off and laid it in her hand. She looked round furtively. Across the lawn the drawing-room windows shone dark as freshly split coal. There wasn't a sign or a movement.

'Look,' said Mildred. The velvety orifice of the flower gaped in the vice of her scrubby fingers.

'Well?'

'You can put your finger in,' said Mildred.

'Well . . . ?' I repeated, bewildered by her whispering.

'Go on,' said Mildred. 'Don't you want to put your finger in?'

I did so and the flower closed gently about its tip.

'It's only a snapdragon,' I said, mystified.

'A what?'

'Snapdragon - stupid! Snap, snap, snap, snap!' I shouted boisterously, setting the little polleny maw at her nose.

'That ain't what we call them,' said Mildred, slapping my hand away. 'Let's have a fight shall us! See who's the strongest!' She seized me in her arms.

'No! No!' I yelled, struggling wildly. She let me go at once.

'You're a sissy,' she said. 'I'll tell your Auntie you kicked me you see if I don't.'

So August dragged on. In the mornings Mr Foley-Foley and the beautiful bare, scrubbed study with green apples nodding and dabbing against the windows; in the afternoons, Mildred and long hours in the garden or hot, complacent walks. My Aunt conceded little to the seasons. A few flowers might find their way inside, but otherwise her drawing-room was the same, winter and summer. The windows were never opened, even on the most stifling days, and the inimitable pourri, a subtle blend of wine-lees, damp books, upholstery and Osborne biscuits, was never dispelled. Unbeknown to my Aunt, who never came down before luncheon, I made a regular pilgrimage to the drawing-room every morning before setting off to the rectory. One morning, as I had just got settled in the coronation chair, I was horrified to see her emerge from the thick curtains at the window. Her face was full of a secret excitement and she kicked her skirts out rather jauntily before her as she crossed the floor. She wore her usual haphazard powder, but more frugally and her skin gleamed under its dust, a warm, translucent mauve. She sang softly - Terry-terryterry... di-di-di, dada! in a narrow, etiolated voice and at the same time displayed the outlandish finery of her dentures.

Her mood was infectious. Instead of feeling apprehensive at being discovered in the drawing-room, I caught at her gaiety and felt gloriously happy too.

'Won't you be late for Mr Foley-Foley?' she said.

'When am I going to school?' I parried.

'Soon. In October. You'll not like it a bit - but there! - if we all did what we liked!'

'You do,' I said grudgingly.

She stopped her spritely parade up and down the room and gave me her rather frightening stare. 'At least it might do something for your manners,' she said.

'I'm sorry, Aunt Dulcie.' I had no wish to be toppled from my vantage point. 'Why were you singing?' I asked very politely.

'Is Mildred going to take you for a nice long walk today? What will you talk about, do you suppose? Tell me!'

'Nothing,' I muttered sulkily.

'Gracious!' she cried, picking up *The Times* and running her reddened nail down the front page, 'Arthur Paget's dead. Terry-terrrryderrrry-dadada-didi. . .' She cracked the paper like a whip.

'I expect he was a great friend,' I said in my most grown-up tone.

'*Quite* a friend,' said my Aunt.

I was flattered that she had not descended to the appropriate voice for little boys. '*Quite* a friend.' She might have been speaking to Mrs Foley-Foley. This was a height, I felt, that must be consolidated. I thought carefully before I answered. 'In the midst of life,' I said, 'we are in death.'

My Aunt stopped rustling the newspaper. She stared hard for a second and then threw back her head and uttered a burst of jagged mirth. I was appalled. She recovered at once and pointing to the photograph of an officer on the piano, with a high, tightly-frogged tunic, said: 'That's him.' The contemplation of his fair young face suddenly saddened her. 'Seventy-two,' she mused, 'now you wouldn't call that old, would you? - Not in these days, I mean!'

'Not a bit,' I replied, gratified by her indulgent tone.

'Terry-deeerry-derrrry... didid-da-di-da. . . 'she sang, sweeping the curtains back and drowning the room in sunshine. Outside, the rectory meadow was prinked with tents, and the sky, made doubly blue by the fluttering canvas freshness, was pricked with pennants. Myriad figures passed and repassed, long-shadowed in the morning sunshine on the dark lanes that threaded the mushroom brightness. Bunting strained, metal glittered and through the sealed window came the faint uproar of many voices laced with the silvery scream of a bugle.

'Soldiers!' I cried.

My Aunt at once assumed an indifference.

'*What* a nuisance!' she said. 'They must be the Cashelary Boys - I heard that they were coming.'

'The Cashel . . .

'The Duke of Tipperary's Horse - they're gunners - no great shakes - they let 'em through at Malakal.'

She said no more and we both looked out of the window at the brave scene. I watched her overtly, but she didn't seem to mind.

Excitement danced in the hooded kernels of her eyes. Her lips were pressed outwards in a narrow bridge. I saw she was lost in a dream, a fantasy supported by all the might of the ghostly young men of the photographs, of the discarded trappings, the medals and the shako with its broken plume. Her head nodded as though she heard again the malicious chatter of the memsahibs and the rhythmic clack of fans from stifling billiard-rooms where the monosyllabic males distracted their exile. For too long, she seemed to imply, it had been the brave music of a *distant* drum! For too many years, the sluggish descent from her bedroom to her card-table at a very late hour. But this morning it was different! This morning she had responded, fresh as Pippa - to reveille!

I crept away, leaving her still staring at the rows of neat canvas bells and pavilions, her stiff, straight back framed in the maroon bobbles of the curtains.

'The old bitch,' said Mildred.

'I shall tell her!'

'I wouldn't put it past you...'

'I don't want to go for a walk, anyway.'

'That makes two of us,' said Mildred.

'What?'

'You should say, "pardon".'

'They're gunners,' I informed her distantly. 'The Cashelary Boys.'

'My uncle was in the Beds,' said Mildred.

We trudged on angrily and had gone about a mile when Mildred stopped suddenly and said: 'I don't feel up to much.'

'You mean you're ill?' I asked dubiously. Her little eyes were brilliant, her hair kinked out ebulliently, her cheeks were polished and, I noticed, fresh and well-scrubbed. When my Aunt was ill she fell back in her chair like an engraved bone.

'They never did pity me,' said Mildred, patting her face abstractedly. 'I shall feel better when I've had a lay down.'

'But where . . . ?' I was vaguely alarmed.

'You go home and tell your Auntie,' said Mildred in a faint voice.

'But what's going to happen to you?'

'I'm going home too - it's a short cut.' She indicated a little path leading down to the village.

'I'd better come with you,' I said, feeling suddenly important. 'Oh no you don't!' said Mildred with surprising energy and then, remembering her sickness, 'You just clear off home - that's a good boy. Go home and tell your Auntie - you'll be all right - it isn't far...'

'Tell her what?'

'Tell her I'm queer, of course!'

'Will you be coming tomorrow?'

She looked at me with surprise. 'Of course, silly. I shan't be queer tomorrow!'

I left her after a last incredulous stare and began to walk back the way we came.

I didn't go home; I went to the camp. Half the village had done the same and the rectory meadow was like a fairground with rather stern sideshows. The guns huddled together in twos and threes, some in neat pits in which their carriages had dragged muddy crescents. The soldiers mainly ignored the visitors and except for a few of the vainer sort who assumed wistful, narcissistic attitudes when they thought they were being noticed, the general feeling was that of a beach where a thousand bodies can produce nothing more than a disinterested intimacy. There was an all-over smell of washing-up water, a stale foodiness mixed up with the odour of sour, bruised grass. A bugler practiced incessantly behind a wagon, sending streams of short, morose little notes out on the languorous afternoon. I shuffled along slowly with the crowd, peering covertly into gaping tents and intensely aware of the burnt, bland, lineless faces of the men as they looked up from their endless polishing of brass and leather. The cookhouse surprised me with its vastness; its acre of canvas pavilioning yards and yards of spindly tables set out in preparation for a brutal banquet. I even penetrated to the confessional isolation of the latrines, but by accident, and hurried away when I glimpsed the soldier sitting there, his face pure and distant as the Buddha's as he looked out at the opposite hills with vacant eyes. And all the while I was searching for the magic world of Captain Fraser-Porter and Mr

Tooley and their dashing milieu of polo-scores, crested bookplates and tripod dressing-tables cluttered with manly trinkets; silver card-cases, studs, cigar-cutters and heaps of loose change where sovereigns jostled rupees. I was searching, too, for Mildred.

It was Mildred whom I found. She was standing in a curious three-sided canvas box, rather like a screen when both leaves are brought round rectangularly. It was, I suppose, a diptych against the wind in which to set-up an artillery-board. It had been set-up this time round a slender tree. Mildred leaned against the tree and one of the soldier's arms encircled this as well as her. She was caught between the rough bark and his body in an attitude of apathetic obedience - almost indifference. Above his trembling shoulder, she stared back at me, transfixed with surprise, yet oddly without alarm. Her mouth was gently parted, her face paler than I had ever seen it before and her little piggy eyes had shrunk to points of fire. The soldier rocked against her like a big baby. He didn't see me. It was all a second or two. No more. Then I was running down the meadow, faster and faster, out into the lane and, with a wild thankfulness, into my Aunt's garden.

I raced in, through the kitchen door, along the passages, into the hall, and only at the drawing-room did I stop to get my breath. My Aunt and Mrs Foley-Foley, a pole-screen apart, were taking tea by the fire. The room was deliciously hot and stuffy, with the flames reflected jauntily in all the bright odds and ends. It might have been December. The curtains were hardly parted and let in the smallest light. Neither moved when I entered and took up my old position in the coronation chair. For a terrible moment I was tempted to shock them by shouting out all I had seen, to splinter their politeness with a rude barrage of words. As though offering me this opportunity, a choice of 'now let's hear *everything* - or nothing, ever', my Aunt and Mrs Foley-Foley paused and grew crisp and still until they looked like Chinese ladies with cards for fans. I sat in an agony of suspense with my breath coming in short, jerking bursts. But gradually the room distilled its familiar calm over me. Deliberately, like a catalogue, I noticed all the well-known things, the furniture, the weapons and, at last, the photographs. There they all were, their easy figures making white barriers across the Cawnpore lawns. All except one. And he stood alone. Now I knew the reason for his segregation. And how right! I was glad. How could he be considered in the same breath as Captain Fraser-Porter, Mr Tooley or Captain Merrydew! I turned from him angrily and tugged a large book from the library rack. It was called, *With a Colour-box in Tuscany*. It had tissue paper over the pictures. I turned them reverently, My action broke the stillness.

'Eh bien, enfin? cried my Aunt. Turning to Mrs Foley-Foley she continued, her voice loud and gay: "So," she said, "*Il me donne grand plaisir à faire votre connaissance. . . Je vous en prie presenter au Monsieur le Capitaine.. .* "Imagine!'

Here Be Dragons

Miss Appletide met the dragon when she was sheltering from the rain in Bessarabia. For a minute or two neither of them spoke, the dragon chiefly for historic reasons and Mary Appletide because she thought the rain might be only a shower, and so casual an extension of her acquaintanceship might only serve to complicate life. When one is an inveterate traveller, as Mary Appletide was, there are cogent reasons for being prudent at all times, not least among dragons. But this proved to be no shower.

'I fear I am disturbing you,' she remarked as the downpour continued.

'Not at all,' answered the dragon. As it spoke a suspicion of charred breath filtered in her direction. That she had noticed it was evident by her flinching, a reflex action she would have given much for the dragon not to have seen. She was a very polite woman.

'I am sorry,' she said.

'So am I,' replied the dragon, this time taking care to hold a scaly paw in front of his mouth. 'You see it's so long since I spoke to a soul!'

'How do you occupy yourself?' asked Miss Appletide.

'I read, much of the night, and go south in the winter.'

'Ah! I see you are an admirer of Mr Eliot.'

'I really prefer Mr Henry James,' said the dragon.

'He is just Henry James now,' said Miss Appletide.

The dragon received this news with great sadness. It lolled back mournfully so that Miss Appletide heard its scales crunch on the rocky floor like old discarded scabbards.

'Are you English?' it enquired at length. 'If so, perhaps you can tell me why you all make such a ridiculous fuss over that young George Something-or-other who fought my uncle? Don't be the least embarrassed to say what you think. We none of us cared for the uncle, but he was harmless in himself and it has always seemed to me that you rather overdo the George business.'

Miss Appletide was torn between patriotism and alarm. 'Well-' she said uncertainly, 'although I hardly like to remind you of it, the dra– your uncle was terrible in his demand for virgins, or girls, as we call them these days.'

'He *was* a misogynist,' admitted the dragon.

'I can see that you are far too intelligent to hold such views,' replied Miss Appletide in a voice made flattering by apprehension.

'What views I possess are decreed by age and not by emotion,' said the dragon candidly.

'You must have seen a lot of changes,' said Miss Appletide, who was glad to change the subject.

'More than most,' answered the dragon with complacency. 'I am very, very old.'

It moved dolorously in the cave. Miss Appletide could see its eyes spilling sadly in their horny sockets like wet gold and the ridge of sharp eruptions running down its back like a relief map of the Pennine Chain. Its sides quivered with an ancient breath like a pair of crippled bellows. It was a dragon in dotage and a creature deserving pity. Miss Appletide certainly felt sorry for it. Her sympathy, allied to that extreme ambitiousness which all true travellers possess, brought the most audacious idea into her head.

'I wonder,' she said, 'if I might make a suggestion?' Without waiting for the dragon to reply she went on, 'I am at present staying at the Hotel Lupescu at Chisinau, but in a week I hope to return to London. I could, if you would like it, make arrangements for you to come with me.'

'And what should I do when I get there?'

'Well,' answered Miss Appletide lamely, 'you could -' she was going to say 'visit the Zoo', but something warned her that this was quite the wrong answer. She tried to think of all the things a dragon might like to see in London and found them surprisingly few. 'You could see Hay Hill,' she concluded vaguely.

'If there's anything I loathe more than another, it's allegory. Fairy-tales, if you like. They've dogged me all my life. I should hate Hay

Hill!'

The rain continued to fall in blinding sheets, barring the entrance to the cave with a drenching flood.

'Well, there are other things,' Miss Appletide was going to say: ' "Bertram Mills" Circus – the Changing of the Guard...' But everything she thought of seemed fraught with danger.

'Such as?' asked the dragon.

'People,' said Miss Appletide, recollecting suddenly how well on the whole she herself had got on with the dragon. 'Dedicated individuals like Professor Julian Huxley, Mr E. M. Forster and the Rector of All Souls, Langham Place these, I feel sure, would love to meet you!'

An air of foreboding filled the cave, partly due to the rain, the steady roar of which was making it more and more difficult to speak without shouting, and partly due to a thoughtful fog which seemed to spread: from the dragon's corner. A terrible suspicion was spreading its tentacles in the dragon's mind. That there wasn't an ounce of truth in the suspicion made it no less real. This woman was actually urging him to visit a country where dragons were as abhorrent as the plague! A country which had spent the best part of a millennium equating dragons with evil! A country which encouraged plaster statues of his uncle's murderer! And here was this woman trying to lure him to England.

If only he wasn't so old! He remembered the fierce golden flames which once jagged from his nostrils like swords, and his claws which once pulled the very rocks apart. Now he was 983, weak, and a mockery, and this woman would return to England and boast how she had faced a dragon in its den and kept it at bay! They would fête her, believe her lies, canonize her even! You could never be sure with the English. They worshipped the oddest gods. Give me, prayed the dragon, a little strength again! Just this once! Like a tickle of spring on a dark January day, it felt the centuries wilt before a secret warmth seeping up inside its horny breast. At first it could hardly believe that its prayer was actually being answered. As though to convince itself, it gave a little surreptitious puff against its paw and was rewarded with a smell of scorching.

Miss Appletide stood looking out into the rain. A smug kindliness surrounded her. The dragon watched her with hatred. They would love him in London, would they! In London where his poor uncle was still prodded to death in a thousand purple windows by that awful George! So that was where she would take him! In triumph, no doubt. Well, he would see.

'Are you a virgin?' it enquired.

Miss Appletide was flummoxed at once. The dragon was not only saying the most extraordinary things, but saying them right in her ear. She could feel its breath, an unwelcome reek, at the nape of her neck.

'Am I a *spinster?*' she corrected. 'Yes, I am.'

It was the last thing she said.

Everything a Man Needs

Margery Nethersole had confidence, self-assurance, call it what you will. Her poise was obvious and challenging, and people and arguments less poised, although not necessarily wrong, collapsed at her approach. Sheer presence allowed her to win usually half the battle, occasionally all of it. It was something, of course, which one would get used to after fifty-odd years and Margery had got used to it. When life was rough, she was shining and smooth, like a lighthouse in a gale. She had always been called reliable and now that springy grey curls advanced across the still mainly chestnut masses of her hair her role of wise woman increased. The demand for her services on committees and in personal difficulties grew. There was no problem, great or small, on which she withheld her advice. Her method was to beam a powerful common sense on every complexity, with the result that she scarred not a few lives whose terrors called for a less drastic approach. In any case, people never blamed her when her *mana*, as she liked to call it, didn't work; they blamed themselves for lack of faith or for not understanding her instructions. And so her name remained the natural conjunctive to any emergency in central Suffolk.

A problem shared is a problem halved was one of Margery's favourite axioms and all round Ipswich there could be seen faces entirely concerned with these half-problems on the one hand, and the fact that Mrs Nethersole knew the whole secret on the other. To do her justice, there was no need for this latter anxiety. Information where she was concerned was a strictly one-way traffic. She collected confidences as other people collected rare or strange objects and was congenitally incapable of giving them away. Experiences and confessions were packed inside her like shale, an instant stoniness fossilizing them the minute she received them. It was strange that there were those who doubted her discretion, though less strange, perhaps, that those whom she had helped should hate her, as one sometimes hates a seducer. 'You can tell me *anything*,' Margery would say, fumbling in her bag for a Goldflake and coughing comfortably, and, amazingly enough, people did. They talked, she listened. If she saw herself as anything it was as the local sin-eater, but a growing number of people saw her as a kind of walking file in which, in a moment of madness, they had thrust their reputations. An inescapable O.B.E. for social services did nothing to lessen the fact that she was human and one victim of her charity had a recurring dream in which Margery appeared as a piggy-bank from which he could only regain what was once his alone with a knife.

Only one person understood Margery's secretiveness and this was Perpetua Cranmer, her friend-housekeeper since before the war. They had actually met on Abdication Day in the Charing Cross Hotel, recognizing in each other the peculiar happiness which follows a blessed release.

'I thought it was for the King,' said Perpetua, indicating Margery's black.

'Heavens, no!' smiled Margery. 'It's for Alfred. Or was. But I'm wearing it today because it suits me.'

'Alfred?'

'My husband.'

'Oh, I am sorry. Was it a happy release?'

'I expect so. It is usually reckoned to be, isn't it?'

'I didn't wear black for Mummy,' said Perpetua. 'She asked me not to - to save the money, you know.'

'Do go on,' said Margery.

'I shouldn't be telling you all this. It is such an imposition. I mean you don't know me...'

'But I do know you,' said Margery. 'Besides, it helps to talk and you can say things to a stranger which you cannot say to even the dearest friend.'

'How understanding you are,' said Perpetua, and she then told all there was to know about herself, which was very little. She then ordered more hot water and invited Margery's confidences in return.

'But I wouldn't dream of boring you with them,' cried Margery. And she never did. They had shared Penault Fayre, their house on the edge of Ipswich, for thirty years and all this time the only things which Perpetua had been able to discover about her friend had been such odds and ends as had accidentally sagged into view, like the hem of the oyster silk slip which Margery inevitably wore under her tweeds. Naturally, Alfred provided the greatest mystery. Who was he. . . *who*?

'He worked in Dunbury, Fife and Loman's.'

'A solicitor?'

'Just. He died before he began really to earn.'

'He must have been young?'

'Oh, he was - we both were.'

'He must have been, well, more than just a solicitor,' persisted Perpetua. She had lived with Margery for years before daring to hold this conversation. At first she had imagined that the subject filled her friend with pain but there was soon plenty of evidence to prove that this wasn't so.

'He was just a young man,' said Margery. 'They're all much of a muchness, you know!'

Perpetua refused to believe this, but having no evidence to support an argument, she broke a cotton indignantly against her teeth. She wanted to say, "an ordinary photograph would tell me all I need to know. Your wedding picture, Marge." But years of reserve prohibited any reasonable discussion of the subject and Perpetua was left, more often than not, with a miserably embarrassing flush induced by a special look, half-playful and entirely too knowing, which her friend turned on her when she stumbled into talk about men. Sometimes she thought of Alfred with Margery - no, she didn't mean just that, but simply the two of them, young and companionate. And Alfred sitting for his finals. Fancy having to do that the year one died! Time heals, they say, and time had healed the place where Alfred had been in Margery's life so totally that there wasn't a sign left of his existence. Not a snapshot nor a collar-stud. Perpetua had looked, not once but scores of times, turning over the papers and oddments in Margery's desk and hoping to see his signature. Margery bore his name of course, and no wonder, for else she would have had to revert to Miss

Cart.

'He was part of you,' said Perpetua accusingly. She was suddenly Alfred's champion, his remembrancer.

'Don't be too sure of that!'

'Oh?'

But Margery was not to be drawn. She stood up, banging threads and fluff from her thick skirt with the hand upon which Alfred's rings glittered feebly.

'Come on, Perp. Get the booze out - and stop ferreting.'

They drank their sherry like medicine and then went into the kitchen to begin the dinner. The kitchen was warm and lofty, with a scarlet rug in front of the Aga and a buttoned Victorian armchair full of sleeping kittens. Old wooden cream platters were heaped with withered Cox's Orange Pippins and flaking ropes of onions swung from bacon hooks. There were endless labelled canisters, all of them containing what they said they did, and in generous quantities. A *jardinière*, besides its usual burden of plants, held a load of freshly made marmalade and a torpid cat. Crates of beer and wine lay under the dresser and a huge straw-coloured table whose pale sweet grain eddied in the lamplight stretched itself purely across the scrubbed brick floor.

'Mmmm!' murmured Perpetua appreciatively, entering her kingdom.

'We live well, is that what you mean?' asked Margery. Her friend thought she noticed a change of inflexion; some clouding or maybe brightening in Mrs Nethersole's voice, causing it to sound like the voice of a stranger. The eyes, too, while retaining both their customary shape and expression, contained some new intelligence which Perpetua could not fathom. Surprisingly, it occurred to her that the sensible, practical front had slipped and that she was looking at a revealed, an exposed Margery. It was the merest momentary displacement, rather like when one of their colour slides went crooked into the projector and brought the garden out flaring like Africa on the screen.

'As some kind of compensation, perhaps?'

The non-typical sharpness of this brought the familiar Margery hurriedly into focus.

'Maybe. But we don't have to go into it. After all, we are not the usual kind of women who, er, share, are we .

It was more a statement than a question.

'No, we are not,' said Perpetua so distinctly as to make it clear that, this hitherto tacit fact having been uttered, there was no need ever to mention the subject again. She was stripping a chicory head leaf by leaf and now she rejoiced in the mutual silky coolness of her fingers and the plant. Behind her, she could hear Margery laying the table, bonking down their heavy silver on the spotless wood, chinking glasses, sounding slapdash but achieving perfection. Order! I love it! That was what Margery said - this, in fact, was her creed. Alfred, the marriage, it had all been tidied away. Order. This was all it was. Perpetua had pondered that it might be so before but now it convinced her. She could have hugged Margery, except they never hugged. Or touched. Or even shook hands. Order. Sweet, immaculate order. Feeling happy, she leaned over and switched on the kitchen wireless. It was the same instrument on which they had listened to Churchill and ITMA. A group thumped away. Shopping around she found an announcer offering selections from *The King and I*.

'That's better,' cried Margery, 'let's have some real music!' She had finished laying the table and was crouched over a big Boot's diary on the dresser, checking over tomorrow's engagements. The Bench in the morning. School governors at two. Then nothing until six, which was Library Committee. One got a fairly clear day like that sometimes; she wondered what she would do. Perpetua, glancing round at her, saw only the stalwartness, the large beam and the contradictorily small, pretty feet. Margery's face was in the shadows. It hung down over the page, the faintly swarthy flesh pulling away from the bone and creating soft fresh planes. Her mouth in this absorbed, leaning forward stance was pouched and greedy like a child's. Her thick lustreless hair swung out in fat scimitars which hid her earrings. Body at this moment was definitely one thing, and mind, indicated by the ballpoint with which Margery was scrawling in further appointments, another. Bare neck and arms flowed out of sight with great richness. Something in the very reality of such an ignored corporeal wealth proclaimed an unlooked for and unthinkable defeat of an intelligence which had hoarded it so matter-of-factly. There was no surface tremor, no discomfort as it is so curiously called. Nothing to suggest to Margery or to anybody else that she would act as indomitably out of character as in it.

Two days later Margery returned from Ipswich with a pile of shopping which included some garment or other, judging by the softness. Breathing heavily and carefully, like a singer, she whipped it open and tossed what it contained over to Perpetua, who caught it with a little scream of pain.

'Sorry, I forgot. Men's shirts are always full of pins.'

Perpetua spread the shirt on her lap with one hand and sucked her finger. The heavy salty taste of blood filled her mouth. The small, decided injury, the shirt and Margery's ordinary face left her feeling more stupid than astonished.

'I just went in and bought it,' said Margery like a teacher chivvying a child in the direction of the required answer.

'Compulsion. . . perhaps?' asked Perpetua in an attempt to say what she imagined Margery would have said had she done such a thing.

Margery laughed (her safe old laugh). 'I didn't lift it, love. I went into Whithers and asked for a man's shirt, size fifteen, and bought it.'

Subsequent action and its sharp corollaries stem from a small moment when conspirators decide to see eye to eye. Perpetua did not say 'Why?' She said, 'Whithers - isn't that the outfitters near the bus station? They don't know you there.'

'That's right, they don't.'

A long pause while Perpetua's blood flowed, disgustingly filling her nail.

'It's for Alfred?'

'Alfred's dead, isn't he?'

Teacher was back again.

'Oh, I don't know!' said Perpetua crossly. 'Who then?'

'That is exactly what we have to decide. Who and what, though chiefly who.'

Perpetua's tight, waxy face relaxed.

'Oh, Marge, it's a game!'

'If it is, I've had my turn,' said Margery.

Perpetua thought hard, like when she played Scrabble. Her first move would show at once whether she understood the rules. 'I'll put it in his room shall I?' she said.

'Whose room?'

'Thomas's.'

This time she scarcely had to think at all.

'Thomas's room will do,' said Margery, adding, 'Only knock before you barge in.'

Perpetua hesitated then left the kitchen and went upstairs. The bedroom doors were shut all round the landing, her door, Margery's door, the bathroom, the guest-room. He wouldn't be in the guest-room if he actually lived with them, would he? There were two more spares. She chose the first.

'He was out,' she announced, returning slightly puffed.

'Never mind,' said Margery. 'He won't always be.'

About a week later, Perpetua went into the spare room to air it and noticed the shirt lying on the bed. It was slightly damp and the room itself ached with its sealed uselessness. The curtains were faded on the folds and the leather buttons on the rolled-up mattress were curled and crinkled like perished flowers. There was a thin, pervasive smell which she could not name. It was the smell of poverty. At first she only put the shirt in a drawer, opened the windows and laid the mattress flat. Then came sheets and pillows; a great Turkestan rug for a bedspread and the duelling prints from the top of the stairs where they could not be seen. Hangers in the wardrobe. A lamp. Some books. She was like a child playing houses and dashing off to fetch a thing the moment she thought of it. She was putting the finishing touches when Margery arrived. She was carrying something in her hand and appeared more surprised to see Perpetua than the transformed room. She laid it on the dressing-table.

'What is it?'

'Shaving soap.'

Perpetua's face set up a desperate fluttering, like a bird on the point of being dispatched. Making a room comfortable in one's own house, that was one thing, but to buy shirts and shaving soap... Then Margery looked at her with that steadying, special look which was full of the wise, broad view of things, and which she usually reserved for youths she was about to sentence to three years' Borstal training, and Perpetua understood. She opened the little drawer under the looking-glass and displayed her father's set of razors, seven in a blue velvet case, one for each day of the week.

'Very thoughtful, dear,' said Margery, 'except a young man of twenty-four is bound to use a safety.'

Not long after this, perhaps not more than a month, Thomas was safely confined within the margins of a game. The actual rules remained implicit, mostly because both Margery and Perpetua disliked the idea that they were playing to rule, although it was hard to see how else they could play at the moment. Besides, the excitement came only in moments of over-play. Breathless after such a moment, and with a little creeper of veins suddenly appearing on the sides of her emphatic white nose, Perpetua would exclaim, 'What a couple of fools!' Meaning the two of them with whatever it was delivered to the room, which stayed damp and strictly uninhabited so far as it was concerned. During this time, each of them learned the great importance of the casual move. After all, Thomas was not a doll to be shaped and stuffed and attired, although it was his clothes which presented his first great test of faith. Their cost. It was scarcely credible. The Oxfam baby thrust at Margery with his broomstick legs and, with an urgency not entirely despicable, her car called for an exchange. There was money in the bank but there were also priorities.

Perpetua thought she was just being logical when she declared, 'If he is - you know what I mean, Marge - *if* he is, he would come first. Naturally.'

Margery flew at her.

'If? If?'

Perpetua flinched and then had a brainwave.

'I know! He can have some jeans and pullovers from Marks and Sparks.'

'Who can?'

'Tom. You know, that young man we've got upstairs. Also, we'll have to get him a record-player and a motorbike and...'

'You've made your point, Perpetua. Tom or Thomas, we don't get him for nothing, is that it?'

Perpetua did not answer. She was staring at her friend with the large faded eyes in which the vitality came and went like a faulty street sign. 'Marge,' she whispered, 'I've got to know something. Thom. . . as, is he... 'Her brain began to throw out words for Thomas and one of them rolled straight off her tongue. '*Is he a gigolo?*'

There was a second when it looked as though Margery's stern hand would strike Perpetua. Instead, her head bent down and down until her face was so close to Perpetua's that all she could see was a pouch of powdered fur. The pouch was open and through the crimson slit she was screaming at Perpetua under her breath, a sound so thin with temper that it hardly had the strength to be heard. She imagined something like 'dirty bitch', except who could believe that Margery would say words like that? Yet Margery had got to be made upright and audible again. The slap set Perpetua's hand stinging as if she had pushed it into nettles and all her fingers had left a birthmark-pink negative on Margery's cheek. There was lots of life in Perpetua's eyes now and a wonderful energy in her painful hand. She would have liked to have slapped Margery again and only kept herself from doing so with great difficulty. After falling back in a chair in a frumpish sitting position, Margery rose, looked at her watch and went out to the garage. The car crunched round under the window and, whether out of saintliness or habit, Margery toot-tooted. The pink fingers on her face had turned into a kind of dahlia.

She drove to Hunter's right in the middle of the town and bought a two-piece suit off the hook. Her behaviour was superb. She was refusing to cheat, even when there was no one to watch her. She took her time. She did not say it was for her nephew, nor did she flinch when the proprietor, who was a colleague on the Library Committee, bustled over to give her his special attention. From her handbag she took a card on which were the sizes of an eleven stone man which she had copied from the Ideal Weight Chart in a colour supplement.

'He really is stock!' remarked the assistant. 'They're usually just stocky when they think they're stock, but he's stock, your friend - husband, madam.'

She went on buying, shoes, socks, pyjamas, underwear, just one of everything. The proprietor passed and repassed with professional indifference. The assistant now and then ran his tongue along the edge of his top teeth. When she had finished he stuck down the packages with Scotch tape on which was printed 'Everything a man needs.'

'There, everything,' he said.

She drove home and Perpetua helped her put the clothes away in Thomas's room. They worked silently in an atmosphere which was stifling at first but which later grew more and more lax, until by the time they returned to the warm drawing-room their peace had reached the stage of a delicious nervelessness. In the midst of tea, Perpetua, thinking of the pale colours, the fresh blues and greys, said,

'He's fair then?'

Margery nodded and answered, 'Is that all right?'

'Oh, perfectly,' said Perpetua. 'Marvellous,' she added.

'All so excellently fair!'

'Is that a quotation?'

'Coleridge,' said Margery. Swallowing a mouthful of cake and staring at Perpetua with eyes which said, nosey-parker-there-won't-be-any-peace-until-I-tell-you, she murmured, 'Alfred was small and dark.'

'None of Thomas's things would have fitted him, then?'

'No,' answered Margery. Her voice rose and broke on the word. It seemed to fill her with tumultuous relief. The cruel double-vision of the past few weeks (of which she had bravely not complained to a single soul) vanished as she spoke this resolute syllable and she was back once more to the big plain outline which constituted her usual view of life. Could it be the Change? If it was, she did not intend to tell Perpetua. And even if some such logical excuse for her recent behaviour was not forthcoming, what was there to get upset about? She thought she had been using her imagination in helping others but it was obvious now that some other faculty had been involved all these years and that imagination, or whatever one liked to call it, had been suppressed, causing it to burst out now. These and other arguments for her conduct raced through her mind while, at the same time, she heard her tongue carrying on a reasonable conversation with Perpetua. She had frankly changed the subject and was describing that morning's embarrassment when Dr Cleary's wife had appeared before her for shoplifting, but Perpetua's huffiness and displeasure could be felt long before Margery got to the part about the court's civilized attitude to the tragedy.

'What's wrong?' she demanded, halting the recital and similarly bringing the analyses, all various, of why she should have gone into the village shop, of all places, and bought a dozen handkerchiefs initialled T, to a standstill.

'I know what you're getting at,' said Perpetua. 'I'm not a fool. But just speak for yourself that's all!'

'I'm speaking about poor Mrs Cleary.'

'Are you - are you sure?'

It was on the tip of Margery's tongue to have the matter settled there and then, but this seemed too harsh in view of what had happened. What had happened? A psychiatrist or a parson could offer a thesis if they were asked, no doubt, but what was the use of this when she had the answer within herself and only needed the courage to exhume it! She had been off her chump and old Perp had been damned decent about it. She'd find out why if it meant digging down to Australia! Excelsior! She leaned over and patted her friend on the knee. 'Don't worry, it's all right!' Her big smile ruled everything. 'It's all right. .'

In her room that night she delved into what she supposed would be termed her subconscious. It was a process or deed which she found quite repulsive but she did it gladly, knowing now that she did it for others. A banana-like moon dangled outside the window, picking out the furniture with its feeble mocking light. Now, what is it all about? Margery asked herself. It was 16 April, 1936, wasn't it? Yes. Why should you be so certain of this - because it was the day after. . . (Yes, go on) after Alfred's funeral. (Doesn't that explain it? Who behaves normally after their husband's funeral; you were not yourself.) I *was* myself, my dreadful, dreadful self! (Nonsense!) No nonsense about it; I obliterated him. (But men don't live on in their 'effects', as the law describes them. You could have given his clothes to a tramp - plenty of tramps in 1936 but they would have gone just the same. Why are you accusing yourself?) I'm not accusing myself, I'm seeing myself. (You looked a bit daft, that was all. I looked. . . I looked wicked. . . (Oh, for God's sake!) I *did!*

'Did you call?' asked Perpetua through the closed door.

'Goodnight.'

'Goodnight...!'

Then it was the day after Alfred's funeral and she was in the semi-detached in Reading, opening windows at first to get rid of the stench of the wreaths and then opening Alfred's wardrobe, and his chest of drawers, and his stud-box, and his Minty bookcase, where his school prizes were only separated from Roman Law by a run of Sappers, and then she was carting all this stuff into the garden in order to get it out of the house. There was a mountain of it. She had to run backwards and forwards half the day before Alfred was out, all out. Marrying her and then dying! Dying all the time they were married and then - dead. And all this stuff to hide his flimsiness: golf clubs, and fishing rods, and the Hilary term photograph with Alfred fourteenth along in the back row, and, help! one of those B.S.A. bicycles with a laced-up chain case - what on earth was she to do with that? Oh, the horror of seeing his suits in flames and his braces jumping in the heat like snakes. His shoes sizzled like meat and his umbrella burned like a martyr, cloth first then ribs. The explosion of his watch in the incandescent glory which such mediocre possessions had so strangely created really did mark the end of Alfred. It was beautiful, poetic!

Margery had told herself at the time. Although it could not have been, for else how could she have spent thirty years repenting her bonfire? She now forced herself to recall every memorable minute of it with such completeness and totality that she was left charred and ashen herself. Poor Alfred! He had made her put it all back. Had haunted her, she supposed. She tried to think of him, of what he looked like, but all she could see were a pair of rather stubby hands and heavy shaving shadow. Pig! she told herself. She must sleep now. Tomorrow she must talk to Perpetua.

Her intention had been an honest confrontation, a clean break, but these were checked by the daring of Perpetua's latest move. She had picked up the letters from the mat in the usual way and was waiting for Margery to sit down at the breakfast-table before sorting them out. Margery sat, her relief smothered in foreboding. The bulk of the letters were for her, as usual. Two were for her friend but there were two more, and these Perpetua placed against the toast-rack. Her brow was shiny with achievement and a pulse throbbed busily in her naked throat.

'Oh, no!'

Margery's despair sounded like wonder to Perpetua; that was the way she was thinking. 'Of course, I had to give him a surname first,' she said.

The letters were circulars from *Reader's Digest*, and the National Gardens Scheme, and they were addressed to Thomas Home, Esq., Penault Fayre, Flint Drive, Ipswich.

'But what the hell will the postman think?'

'Its pronounced Hume.'

'Perp, concentrate!' Margery's disappointment was making her shout. 'What are they going to say at the Post Office when they sort my letters and then, er, his?'

'What does Mrs Ellis say when you buy all the pipe tobacco?'

'He is going to give up smoking,' said Margery meanly. And we are going to give Thomas up, she longed to add, but she needed time to explain all this and she had to be in the centre of the town by nine-thirty. I'll tell her tonight, she thought. She was sitting in the car and rubbing a space in the dust on the windscreen with Kleenex when Perpetua's pleading face appeared.

'Smoking is one of his few pleasures,' she said accusingly.

Margery did her best to see beyond the mask - it must be mask, surely? - Perpetua was a bit withdrawn, as they called it, but she wasn't daffy. Nothing showed. It was Perpetua's ordinary bare morning face before she covered it up with cosmetics.

'But the expense, darling. .'

'He can afford it. You seem to forget he earns two thousand a year.'

'At twenty-four?'

'Yes. It's great, isn't it! He's going a long way, that boy. You'll see!'

'I must get on, too,' said Margery, tugging at the choke.

'What am I going to do?' she asked the Golly mascot bobbing against the window. 'I don't know what to do!' She felt ponderous and stupid. This feeling reminded her of her childhood and the dismal realization of being too big to join the game. She drove past the old part of the cemetery where the gravestones staggered about like bad teeth. That was what Alfred's grave was like she imagined. She had not been near it since the day of the funeral, although she had got them to put up a cross. She could be a sentimental old hypocrite and go and see it, she supposed. Perpetua needn't know. And, anyway, it would get her away from the house. The idea hardened into an intention. The uproar in her head died down. The policeman on traffic control saluted her trimly and received her commending nod. I acknowledge you, too, Alfred, she thought. I do - Guide's honour!

That evening she explained her plan with deliberate vagueness to Perpetua.

'Just a couple of days in Berkshire, you know. Take the car, look around...'

'Visit old haunts?' added Perpetua. 'Oh, I don't mind, I've got lots to do. I'm out all Saturday evening, anyway. They're doing The Knack at the Rep. Thomas is going to be away too.'

'Is he?' said Margery with automatic interest. She could have bitten off her tongue. She heard Perpetua telling her, with incredible elaboration and conviction, how Thomas was going bird-watching at Minsmere and how pleased he was with his new field-glasses.

'How much were they?' she asked shakily.

'It's no use having a cheap pair,' countered Perpetua.

'How much?'

Perpetua was offended. 'You'd better ask Thomas.'

'Listen - listen! You've got to listen. There isn't a Thomas. Do you understand? *No Thomas*. He doesn't exist, he didn't exist. Ever.'

'I understand all too well,' answered Perpetua coldly. 'You decide when people exist and when they don't - or even if they ever did. Like your husband.'

Margery felt the raw blush eating its way up her neck and across her face, making her ridiculous and hideous. It was the 'your husband', the implacable relationship between Alfred and herself. Perpetua saw the ugly blood-flooded skin and was immediately shocked and contrite. She couldn't apologize: her lips twitched soundlessly. But her eyes were strained with regret and her hand flew out to Margery's like a cold white bird and held it awkwardly. Margery squeezed it. How were you to know where the most naked nerve lay? She was telling her friend in this rare contact. She went upstairs to pack. What on earth did one wear for a night in Reading? She would drive out to the Downs afterwards or perhaps to Windsor and look at the Castle. When she got home on Sunday she would set to work on the whole problem, even if it meant talking to Dr Healey.

The drive down was easy, miraculously easy, taking her a little under four and half hours to reach April 1936. For the dim road took the same twists to the cemetery and the weathercock on the chapel spire caught her eye just as it had then. The evergreen smell and the sharp gravel under foot were identical. Countless little numbers on tabs shaped like the ace of clubs sprouted in the grass, making her think, as she had then, in big, sad, obvious and satisfying terms of mortality. She made her way instinctively, pride refusing to let her inquire at the office as to the whereabouts of the grave. She remembered it as being a long way and she also recalled passing a remarkable stone, a kind of undertaker's Rock of Ages which looked as though it weighed a ton. And there it was, only riven. Or something had happened to it. It was fallen on its back with its wet base stuck with snails for all to see. Other monuments were cavorting themselves with equal abandon. They had toppled and cracked or simply gaped, as at the Resurrection. And suddenly the cemetery was not silent any more but was full of struggling, gesticulating men, talking and writing things down. Bewildered, her heart thudding, Margery walked through their midst to Alfred's grave. His cross had snapped off and the marble wound shone frostily in the sun. A fringe of sour grass hid Alfred's name. She knelt and pulled it up by the roots.

'Alfred Nethersole,' she read. Said. Many times. The men clambering about near her drew back. They included two policemen and a photographer. It's all right, Alfred, thought Margery, they think I'm praying, I expect. But I'm apologizing. I'm sorry. She tried to remember Alfred's face and a vacant splodgy horrible thing wordlessly introduced itself. She saw for the first time the extent of her destruction. Pity struck her like a brand.

'Alfred!'

A policeman and a workman were leading her to a seat. They guided her feet round scattered lumps of granite and through crushed flowers. She could hear the larks singing against a babble of indignation.

'What happened?' she asked.

'Vandals,' said the policeman shortly.

'Must want a job!' said the workman. 'I mean desecrating the dead, what could be worse than that?'

Perpetua began to dress for the theatre at six. Margery always laughed at this 'dressing' which wasn't dressing in fact but a glorified fixing and arranging of Perpetua's ordinary quiet clothes, and the addition of a gold bangle and a fob watch, plus her mother's rings. 'All for Ipswich!' she would mock, only kindly. What she failed to realize was the importance to Perpetua of what preceded the dressing, her spoiling, as she liked to describe it to herself. She bathed and did her nails and pumiced the little depilated patches on her legs. She took her time to fix her well and carefully dyed hair - tinted, she called it - in a clever facsimile of Katherine Mansfield's fringe and chignon. They could have been sisters, somebody once said years and years ago. But mostly she sank into a leisurely and unconceited appraisal of her own flesh. Its contours beneath the blanched, glowless skin had an arrested, immaculate quality. The immutability made her so grateful. None of the taken-for-granted things had happened to it. Women of her age - fifty-three - resigned themselves to appendicitis scars, Caesarean puckers, limp breasts and livid groups of vaccination marks but she was untouched. She wore a sleeveless navy-blue sheath and her three-strand pearls. She felt - it was one of her favourite words - svelte.

The novelty of being alone at Penault Fayre pleased her. She walked about trimly in her high court shoes putting out lights and checking the heating gauges. A mackintosh hanging in the hall made her think, 'Thomas!' Her cool and certain feeling at once left her and a troubled exciting sensation took its place. Her eyes widened and her hand reached for her necklace in a swift guarded gesture. She could feel her breasts against her bare arm; they disturbed her by their new sense of obvious largeness and warmth. She was no longer svelte, with its concomitant reassurances of grace and restraint, she was perspiring freely and her suspender-belt seemed to drag and claw at her legs. Thomas's room was dank - it was always dank, whatever one did to it. It was on the sad side of the house. She opened the lower sash and the early spring-night smell came pouring in. A pair of tangerine-coloured pyjamas lay on the bed. She tucked them under the pillow to keep them from getting damp. The open book on the bedside table was Born Free. She closed it, marking the place with an envelope. At the bottom of the long drive, just before she turned to walk up the lane to the bus-stop, she glanced back and thought how lonely the house looked and yet how rarely she left it. 'I don't touch it, somehow,' she told herself. 'But Thomas does - he's there all the time, even when he is at Minsmere. I know it and Margery knows it...'

The Rep let her down - or she let it down, what did it matter, the fact was that what she had come for and what she was offered bore no relationship in her mind - and this was a habit it tended to repeat. She felt stupid sitting in the front stalls with a group of mostly middle-aged women with blued hair and powdered necks, and watching a boy and a girl in jeans bickering on a mattress. She had 'gone to the theatre'. Such an action suggested some kind of magic and beauty in return for her money but the girl, who was grubby and plain, was shrilling, 'Rape! Rape! Rape!' like an ululating native. At least Margery wouldn't be waiting with the Horlick's all ready and a 'I can't think why you go if you don't like it' and her own mean answer of 'If I stop going to the Rep I wouldn't go anywhere!' She smiled her way through the departing regulars in the foyer and got a taxi. The short drive home was the biggest treat of the evening. Instead of Horlick's, she gave herself a whisky, then made up the Aga. A hint of the happiness she had felt earlier on returned. It was a joy and a privilege, as her mother would have said, to have a real home. Not a flat or one of those estate developer's boxes but Penault Fayre on its tree-swathed hill with its rich Victorian decorations and silence.

Silence. That was because of no Margery and thus perfectly understandable. And no Thomas. Only herself. She filled a hot-water bottle and went upstairs. Owly was calling - she must tell Margery. Pussies were sound asleep. That *daft* play - and after all those marvellous reviews she had read! There was a scraping noise and then a creak. She listened intently and heard it again. Thomas's window! She had left it open. With the zip of her dress open at the side to reveal a long petal-like slash in the tight silk, she hurried next door.

The light blazed before she touched the switch. She saw the pyjamas first, more and more of them until their waving brilliance seemed to fill the room, and then the door slammed behind her and her head was being thrust back into the choking folds of the dressing-gown hanging against it. 'Thomas! Thomas! Thomas!' she shrieked against a barrier of gagging wool. What was the use? she asked herself, just as she thought she would faint. Who could hear? Then her face was free and she was panting and gulping in the close stale air, and words, like a whispered shout, were beating against her ear.

'How did you know? How did you find out? Who told you? *Who told you?*'

'Thomas. . .' she gasped weakly.

'You heard it on telly, didn't you? Didn't you?'

Oddly enough, the blow steadied her. She struggled up from the floor with an elaborate knowledge of what she was doing. She heard Thomas say, 'I'm sorry about that, missus, but you asked for it and you got it.' She could see his face now, fair and damp and rather tired. His hair stood up in a ferocious spike and his blue eyes maintained a constant vivid motion. He was nearly pretty but hard. 'Now, missus,' he was saying.

'Miss - Miss Cranmer.'

'Listen, old doll, how'd you find out? Tell me.'

'This is Thomas's room and so you are Thomas.'

The blue eyes ceased their mad dancing and became fixed and still. She returned their flat concentration and repeated, 'You-are-Thomas. Aren't you?'

'I see,' he said, his voice quiet and drifting now. 'I'm Thomas and this is my room, is that it? Let's get things right. Is that it? Is it?'

She nodded, relieved. She had subsided into a crouched sitting position at the foot of the bed.

'And what happens in Thomas's room, eh? I bet you haven't seen Thomas lately, have you?' He laughed. His mouth with its wet red flesh and fine teeth hanging over her had the richness of a cave. The laugh stopped abruptly and her head was being forced to look down at something which lay in the palm of Thomas's hand. It was one of her father's razors. It was open and rocked lazily to and fro against the life-line. 'Just so you realize,' Thomas told her. 'Because I've got to eat and if you touch the phone or call out. . .' and he drew the blade in a flashing little arc just above her pearls. What would Margery do? She wondered. She knew what Margery would say - something sensible.

'Get back into bed,' she said. 'You're getting cold.'

'Or cool, perhaps. Like you, eh?'

He put the dressing-gown on and then the slippers. The clothes pulled him together somehow.

'Are you an American?' she asked. His accent slipped about and worried her, the voice avoiding identity, as it were.

He looked vaguely pleased and said, 'Lead the way, lady,' like a Hollywood gunman.

She broke two eggs into the pan. 'Go on until I say when,' he murmured, standing close behind her. She broke another and he said, 'When.' She also cooked some bacon and fried bread. The greasy breakfast smell in the middle of the night - it was only a little after eleven, actually, but the twin sensations of strain and ordinary behaviour reminded Perpetua of the war, which always went on most after bedtime - revolted her. She had to make a great effort not to be sick. The heat from the Aga met her in waves and she gripped the rail unsteadily. When he first touched her she thought it must be to stop her from falling. Then she felt the hand inside her dress, rapid, searching.

'Don't,' she breathed.

'Not now - later? Is that what you mean?'

She remained rigid, hardly able to create a pulse-beat. That this could - would - *must* happen to her was unbelievable. Had never entered her thoughts. She must protest, explain. He had to understand! She turned and shook her head soundlessly. He kissed her and wiped his mouth on his cuff.'

'Say thank you,' he said. '*Say thank you!*'

'Thank you.'

She watched him eat. The eggs disappeared in halves and afterwards he ate a lot more bread and a whole pile of fruit. Perpetua had never seen anyone eat so in her life before; it was animal but it wasn't ugly. The cats had woken up and sat blinking and detached. He threw them scraps and they ignored them.

'This is a nice loving house,' he said, 'a real nice loving house.'

She sat staring, sometimes at the young man, sometimes at the grain ridges of the table, wondering what to say. Now and again he caught her look and once he winked, an incredibly coarse gesture in the context of his rather blank good looks. She picked up his plate and carried it to the sink. She had fastened her dress and now she began to wash up with mechanical efficiency. He sat watching her with languid patience but when she turned to the Aga with a damp cloth, he dragged it from her hand and said,

'Uh-uh! That's enough.'

She flew at him. Her hands thumped against his chest, making his laughter jerky and breathless. 'No-no-no-no-no!' she was shouting, just like somebody she had heard recently. It was the heroine in the play. He caught both her wrists at last and held her away from him, easily and conceitedly, without apparent effort. Speaking quietly and in a natural Midlands voice, his mouth parted in a deliberately sweet smile, he said, 'Listen, doll. Who came into Thomas's room stinking of scent and whisky with her dress all undone? But never mind *that*. Who is stupid enough to let a scared old girl go charging off to the neighbours? - that is what we have to consider.'

'I wouldn't betray you, Thomas.'

'You won't get the chance to, doll.'

Grasping her shoulder with one hand, he switched off the lights and, in a dream, she accompanied him up the stairs and into the spare room. He transferred the key and locked the door. Then he pulled off the dressing-gown and slid into bed. 'I leave at six,' he said. 'What are you going to do?'

Perpetua stood looking down at him, quite motionless. She was conscious of the cold stippling the skin on her arms and of a sour distinctive smell from which there was no escape. Disturbed birds scuttered in the guttering outside. The young man breathed with a profound regularity and depth which suggested near-sleep; it was nearly one o'clock. I can't just stand here, she thought. I can't just stand in this room for five hours! Her fear had gone and she now felt the incredulous annoyance of someone who had lost the last train and for whom there was no other choice but to sit on a bench until it was light. Her unbelief communicated itself to the young man and he grinned. Then he put an arm outside the bedclothes and patted the space by his side. Total refusal seemed to make her enormous. She thought she must look absurd, horrible, and bent forward in a mixed gesture of attempted recovery and extenuation. His hand reached out and grasped her arm.

'You can't stand there all night, can you now?' he said.

She shook her head. She couldn't. For one thing there was the terrible light bulb swooping out of the ceiling and almost hypnotizing her with its harsh filament, though most of all there was the cold. There was, too, her draining will-power which was reducing her reactions to a puppet's responses. This could not be happening to her, *it could not*, thus how could she greatly care? She switched off the light and lay beside him. All the landmarks of her conscious identity were obscured. She was crashing through a black and fantastic forest where tense and unwanted sensations were thrust upon her. Her hair was torn and pressed across her face and sometimes she was eating it. There was invasion and outrage and sometimes the most ordinary conversation as though nothing had happened - was happening - at all. For instance he said, 'I shall have to change sides, my arm has gone to sleep,' and she said, 'I'll put the hot-water bottle on the floor; that'll give us more room.' The birds chuck-chucked and clawed the eaves the whole time. The room wasn't properly dark because the grey night seeped through the comfortless unlined curtains. She could see her pearls, phosphorescent on the dressing-table, and her stockings, pale as dust. She could not sleep - wouldn't ever sleep again - but he slept. He hissed faintly and sadly and occasionally caught his breath in a muted sob like a baby. The hours dawdled by, taking every second of their time and with them wandered the vast unwanted leisure of her thoughts. No recollection of any happening in her life occurred to her without a full-scale analysis becoming attached to it. Margery appeared and reappeared in her relentlessly exposed confidence as a great shutter, a wall, a dense hedge, a swooping baton commanding her occasionally ranging free-notes to cease. There was no longer anything to feel grateful for. She ate, breathed, that was all. So did a maggot.

Cocks were crowing now. How medieval that sounded and who ever listened? The morning lay deserts of time away and so far without a hint of an horizon. Where their bodies touched there was careless moist agreement, the kind of humanity which the flesh itself took for granted. Not because of this but because her tumbling dreams made her uneasy, she dragged herself up into a sitting position, saw, incredibly, her breasts like suns and snuggled down again. She could see him lying in profile with his lips slightly parted and silver spit glittering as he whispered his way through sleep. He smelled, acrid, institutional. Where had she noticed this odour before? In a class-room? No, in Nissen huts during the war. That was it. During the war and during the year she spent in the W.A.A.F. before Margery got her out with 'pull'.

'What are you doing?' he asked without moving, without opening his eyes.

'Only getting comfortable.'

'I was asleep.'

'I'm sorry.'

'You keep on being sorry, don't you? Life is just life. You don't change it or stop it by being sorry.' His eyes were still closed. The mouth was hardly enough awake to frame the words.

'I'm sorry. . .' she began before she could stop herself.

He giggled, turned to her and pulled her against him.

'There you go.'

'Are you never sorry then?'

There was a pause this time, not his usual snap response. 'Not now - not yet, is what I mean. But I will be. I mean you can't live and sit still, and if you live you make things happen. Funny things sometimes. Good things and bad things.'

'You're quite a philosopher,' she said without irony. Yet the remark displeased him. He turned from her abruptly and even in the uncertain glaucous haze of earliest morning, with the things in the room mere hulks of darkness, she caught the look on his face as a hardening of the mouth and eyes thinned the expression down to the mean and glinting one she had seen in the kitchen. But now, instead of fear, she felt pity. She patted his shoulder and then his hair. Awkwardly.

'Go to sleep,' he said. 'You got what you wanted, didn't you?'

Incredibly, she did sleep. The merciless images chasing one after the other through her brain tore away into blankness like a fractured film. She awoke to the inconsiderate sound of the bath running and of drawers being opened and slammed shut. He was robbing, of course. She clutched her hands together and felt the rings. Her necklace and her watch lay where she had left them. What was it then?

'What are you looking for?' she called.

'Blades.'

'They're here - in the little drawer under the mirror.'

He chatted while he dressed.

'You'll be on that buzzer to them the minute I've gone, won't you, doll?'

'The . . . police?'

'The police,' he mimicked. He was pulling clothes out of the wardrobe, feeling the material of the suit, choosing socks. She might not have been present. 'And then,' he said, 'when you've told them all they'll want to know, you will be a very interesting lady in the neighbourhood. You think about that, doll. Think of the look on the beak's face!'

'Where will you go?' she asked.

'Harwich, maybe: get a boat.' He put on the jacket and turned to face her. 'There now, how do I look? More like Thomas?' He looked transformed.

'Things could be better for you if you got abroad.'

'A new start?' he mocked. 'But better than never making a start, eh? Poor old doll!'

Her eyes filled with tears. She lay there letting them roll to the sides of her upturned face. She had not removed her make-up and scraps of it still adhered to her skin with cruel irrelevance.

'Poor old doll. . .' he repeated thoughtfully, staring down at her. He left the room and returned with her handbag. He must have noticed it lying on the dresser last night, she told herself. 'Now I am sorry about this,' he said, handing it to her, 'but we can't spoil the sailor for a ha'p'orth of tar, can we?' She gave him five pounds. 'I'd better have a spot of loose, too,' he said. 'For the bus.'

'There's some silver in the baker's jar on the dresser.'

'Thanks.'

She looked past him, deliberately not seeing him.

'I did ask,' he reminded her. 'I asked, you asked... for what was there for the asking.'

'Go away-*go!*'

She heard the back door bang and hurried to the window. He was swinging down the drive. After a few yards she saw him stop, glance back at the house and shake his head incredulously. She went into the bathroom. There was water everywhere, grey suddy water in the primrose basin and still steaming water in the bath itself. Blobs of shaving soap spattered the floor. Her immediate thought was to clear everything up before Margery returned - in time for lunch, she said. What was she going to tell her when she discovered that the clothes had gone? What was she going to tell her anyway? Would Margery go to the police? In a way she was the police. Her imagination reeling, Perpetua began to clean and tidy, at first with a certain plodding efficiency but after a little while with an unnatural rush which made her clumsy and confused. Soon she was running about the place, frenziedly putting it to rights. She was brought to a halt, not by the actual surprise, but by the harsh confirmation of the bundle which lay under the bed. The shoes were worn down at the heel and the trousers and jacket of thick grey flannel were each stencilled on the inside with 'Thomas, J.N.' and his prison number. There was a striped, collarless shirt and a pair of grey socks with reddish sweat-stained soles. She carried them into the garden, holding them away from her. Her face was now dragged into a knot of hysterical loathing. That it was of herself merely intensified the revulsion. She envied the brilliant simplicity with which the foul things and the foolish things, the prison uniform and what was left of 'Thomas', pulverized in the flames. The bed-clothes roared their purification and blazed thankfully in a tent of light. When it was over, when the room was stripped and it and her strength had been crushed, Perpetua crouched in it. Her mother's rings itched on her scorched hands and ashes powdered her brow. She wasn't weeping when Margery found her. Just sitting still and thinking that there was no substance in her life to burn anyway.

Margery looked at the smuts, looked at the hollow spaces and then saw the murderous smoke blowing outside in the garden.

'Alfred . . . Alfred . . .' she said.

A Wedding in the Family

Perhaps I haven't mentioned it, but Aunt had a sister who lived with her for pretty near a lifetime and then quite suddenly got married. She was fifty-one on her actual wedding day. Aunt, I suppose, must have been all of sixty and my Uncle Jake some age in between. Anyway, they all seemed to have been on the earth since historical times to me.

The sister who got herself married so unexpectedly was called May - never Aunt May, just May. Later on I came to realize that it is trifles like that which keep people young. Folk used to say, 'They're lucky to have each other' - meaning Aunt and May - and my uncle always called the younger of the two 'the gal'.

May was a good name for her. She was a very large woman, fat, firm and shining. There was a glory about her. She seemed to smile all over and she sailed about Aunt's small house in an almost visible aura of love. She wore quantities of starched white lace which scratched my skin when she kissed me, yet never scratched hers. Her skin was pale and perfect. The only thing I ever saw remotely like it was the statue to Lady Louise Lavenham in church. Although May never wore scent and most certainly not powder, and only washed her black-gold hair in vinegar-water, she always smelled like summer. She was a great hugger and kisser and when she swung me in her arms, I could feel the laughter bubbling through her body before it poured out in delicate cascades of sound, like the rector's wife practising the trilly bits in 'Where the bee sucks, there suck I'.

Everybody said that May was useless. 'What'll she do when poor Aunt's gone?' they said dismally. '*Pore thing!*' they said. May danced twice a year, once at Christmas and once at the Horky. She wore more starched lace than ever for these occasions and with the slender figures of the men careening against her bulwark off whiteness, she was like a tall rigged tea-ship in comparison with the bouncy barge-like hulks of the other female dancers. May always danced every dance and Aunt never danced at all. When people saw May dancing they always spoke about all the things she *couldn't* do, such as pickling and gophering. They recollected how she had once filled the font with cow-mumble because she had thought it pretty - cow mumble, that common ol' stuff and unlucky anyway! They said they felt sorry for Aunt and thought she would get her reward in Heaven. I never heard Aunt reply one way or the other to this kind of talk. Aunt never doubted that she was a cut above the ordinary kind - which indeed was true. 'Never explain yourself, Toby,' she used to say.

But to come back to May. One day my uncle and I went to tea at the Bullace House and found everything arranged suspiciously 'extra special'. There were tongs in the sugar and a plumcake a foot across. May was heaped up on the sofa like a mountain of blossom. The mountain turned into a snowdrift when she hugged me. All through tea she laughed extravagantly at all we said - as well as managing to eat four pieces of plumcake with her beautiful little teeth, which looked quite useless. After tea there was the sort of silence which occurs when people are plucking up courage to say something earth-shaking, and then May romped me into her huge lap and cried:

'I know one little boy who isn't going to say no to a brand-new uncle!' Immediately Aunt burst into small, choking, pig-like noises which I never associated with grief until I saw a single fat tear slip down her smooth cheek like hot candle-wax.

'There, there, Aunt' comforted my uncle. 'It's in the natural order of things, ain't it, my dear? The young birds flyin' up out o' the nest...'

I looked across at May, who was just half a century old, and saw the happiness glimmering in her eyes.

'Considering,' she said, 'that Mr Bence's farm is only on the other side o' the hoss-pond I don't know why folk have to take on as though I were off to a missionary-land!'

On the way home I heard my uncle muttering to himself, 'It's a master-funny bit - I mean it ain't even as if the gal had got a mite o' money...' The wedding was unique in many ways, but particularly in the way it transformed the Bullace House into a summer dream. It was the hottest day that June and the long trestles had been carted up from the parish hall and set up in hollow squares in the orchard. Aunt had starched all her best linen sheets, turning them into luxurious tablecloths which sank down into the new grass, so that they were all spattered at the hems with buttercup pollen. Late pear-blossom blew across the hams like pink snow and my uncle had decorated the wine-casks with garlands of rambler buds. We had to be at the Bullace House at four in the morning to prepare all this and although we worked frantically until almost midday, when we had to change for church, there was never a sight or sound of May. Once, about ten, Mr Bence - he wasn't my uncle yet - rode by, but with a carefully averted gaze, which Aunt said was quite right because to catch a glimpse of his bride before the ceremony was about the worst thing that could happen to any man. Mr Bence looked old to me, and I said so, causing Aunt to shriek, '*Old*, Toby? What on earth do you mean, boy? Tom Bence and me set in school together!'

Then twelve o'clock struck. The lane in front of the Bullace House was jammed with the four cabs hired for the occasion and the be-ribboned Victoria hood was down and roses and sweet williams had been tucked into its folds. The horses had branches of elderberry looped up in their harness to keep off the flies. I was dressed in a white sailor suit and striped cotton socks, and my hair had been slicked down with water into a crescent over my eyes. I took my seat in the first cab with Aunt and then we all bowled off under the beech trees to church, Aunt dipping and swaying with the springs.

I don't think I have ever seen so many people in church, before or since. Old Mrs Crosbie sat at the organ and played variations on 'By cool Siloam's shady rill'. It was the saddest thing. All the candles were alight on the altar and the altar itself was all swamped in lumpy gold and white embroideries, some of which Aunt had helped to make. Then, suddenly, there was a scampering noise at the end of the church and Mrs Crosbie gave a great jerk. Pressing her feet down with all her might she plunged into the Wedding March from *Lohengrin*. The noise was enough to have split the slender painted pipes.

And then May appeared. Her veil fell in tumbled swags of white tulle over the brim of a soaring cartwheel hat and drifted in wisps about her majestic shoulders. Her left hand was locked in the crook of my Uncle Jake's arm and her right hand and all the front of her billowing dress was obliterated in a smother of smilax and roses. Smiling beatifically, she gave no sign that she was exerting every scrap of her not inconsiderable strength to prevent my uncle from galloping up the aisle. This exhilarating procession had been rehearsed in her imagination too long and too often for her to be bullied out of a single moment of it now.

I saw Mr Bence, stiff as a poker near the pulpit, shudder slightly and then take a peep over his left shoulder, and I saw the look of horror mixed with intense delight which confused his features. When I mentioned this to my uncle later, he said, 'Aye, boy, that would be the sort o' look a man would have when he realized that he had sown the wind and reaped the whirlwind...'

It was when the bridal procession was making its way out of the porch that I saw the sadness sweep over Aunt. She bore up until May and Mr Bence had clambered into the rectory Victoria, then she trundled forward on her stout legs and tugged wildly at the door-handle. 'There's a mort of room for me on the other seat,' she was saying excitedly. It took my uncle to make her see sense, but she drove back to the Bullace House in the first hired cab without saying another word.

We stayed on at the wedding breakfast until the hot sun sank out of sight and the blue summer evening crept in under the apple trees and turned the ruined tables into white and silver islands. My Cousin Patsy Kettle was made to sing 'The Lady and the Rook-boy' for the very last time and Aunt was seen, gliding about in her best dress, as she locked up the hens. The roses had tumbled off the barrels and lay all crushed in the trampled grass. The barrels had been renewed time and time again, and still nobody went home. May sprawled in a wicker-work chair with her huge hat on her knee. Mr Bence leant over her, his small mottled face within a fraction of her marvellous hair. They were each smiling small private smiles which the other couldn't see.

Old Mrs Crosbie and several other ladies clacked round my uncle. I saw the two Miss Boggises, a pair of skinny sisters my uncle had never been able to abide. The thinner of the two Miss Boggises was staring up at my uncle as though he were a vision. Her eyes glittered and her normally long pale nose was the richest poppy red.

'What I say, Jake, is that May ought to be a lesson to us single folk not to reject our portion of happiness here below,' she shrilled. 'Who knows it ain't flyin' in the face of the Lord to live selfish lonely lives when we might be nurturing one another?'

When my uncle did not reply the thinner Miss Boggis gave her sister a nudge and then played her trump card. 'Don't forget, Jake,' she said, 'May is three year older than we and *she* can't cook a turnip mash...'

My uncle swayed very gently. There was confetti and petals in the brim of his hat. Gradually, through the rich miasma left behind by the day's welter of music and wine, it dawned on him that he was being proposed to. A cornered stag could not have shown greater terror. He swivelled blindly and then, with myself trotting sleepily beside him, he began to crash his way through Aunt's dense orchard and head towards home.

'Toby,' he bawled, 'never be the last man to leave a weddin'. For one thing it ain't polite, and for another, you're likely to land yourself with bad company for the rest o' your born days!'

The Right Day to Kill a Pike

On the day my uncle and I set off to kill the pike there seemed to be nothing moving, nothing breathing and nothing living in all the world. There are such days in every month, though this particular day had come in February. I recognized it the minute I opened my eyes. The sun wasn't shining, the wind wasn't blowing, it wasn't dark and yet it wasn't light, and all the trees looked black and dead.

I hung out of the window above the naked rose branches and shouted across to the bullocks in the low pasture. I thought they might gallop across the frozen grass towards the house, which they sometimes did, and so bring a little action to the static universe. But they, too, were afflicted with the prevailing moodiness and did not budge.

My uncle was making tea in the kitchen when I came down, a favourite task of his and one which usually involved a lot of encouraging conversation with the kettle - 'Come on, Suky! Boil a bit, you ol' divil! Wake up there! . . . Git on - bubble!' and a great deal more of such talk. But on this particular morning he was silent. He set the cups out sadly, and when he only put three heaped spoonfuls of sugar into his own I knew that something was troubling him, for he wasn't a man to deny himself in the ordinary way of things. He walked over to the door and looked out, and shook his great head mournfully.

'It's the waitin' time come round agin, Toby,' he said sombrely. 'The winter's gone before the spring had time to git here...'

'It's winter until the twenty-first of March,' I said. I was eleven and full of facts.

'They only say that for convenience sake,' replied my uncle. 'And don't you be so riddy with y' learnin' at this time of the mornin'.'

'If it isn't winter and it isn't spring, then what is it?' I demanded.

My uncle looked around the kitchen carefully before answering. He didn't like his housekeeper to know everything. Then he whispered harshly: 'It's the betwixt and betweens, that's what it is, Toby. They're worse than Hallowe'en - a damn sight worse! You mark my words.'

'It's only just a dull old day,' I said.

This made my uncle very wild and he began to leap about the kitchen with his eyes flashing and with his moustache twitching. 'It's more'n that! It's more'n that!' he was shouting. 'It's a mortal funny thing, Toby, that some folks ain't allowed to say an opinion without having other folks arguing the toss with 'em. I tell you, boy, there's a lot can happen on a day like this.'

'What are we going to do about it, then? What can we do, Uncle?'

He plugged his dark, hairy nostrils with snuff before replying. Then he said, speaking with slow deliberation: 'We shall have to kill a pike.'

'As a - a sacrifice . . . ?' I whispered. The idea was so astonishing that I could hardly say the word. 'Like. . . like the ancient Greeks?' I added.

'Learnin', learnin', learnin' - where'll it git you?' was all my uncle said in answer to this.

'Perhaps an old rook would do?' I suggested. There were hundreds and hundreds of rooks wheeling and wailing round the elms all day long. For some reason I hated them.

'No,' said my uncle. 'A rook is bad, but it ain't nearly bad enough. It'll need more than an ol' rook to help the spring along. Now a pike, Toby, is the wickedest criture the good God iver made.'

So, after breakfast, we set off towards the river. My uncle carried all the sections of his bamboo pike rod and an enormous fish basket, and I carried the gaff and a cocoa tin full of spinners. It wasn't a very cold day but both of us were exceptionally well wrapped up because my uncle said, killing a pike was a deed which chilled a man's mortal soul.

We crossed the fields of winter wheat, still smelling faintly of snow. The ditches were churning with flood water and robins sat bold as brass in the creaking hedges. The sky looked low enough to touch and was flint-grey all over, even where it brushed the horizon of the marshes, where it usually had a bar of pale gold. My uncle reckoned that the day could not have looked worse if somebody had thrown an ol' hosscloth over it.

'If I was a prayin' man, Toby,' he said, 'which I ain't, I'd be a settin' in my pew today. But as I don't happen to be a prayin' man I'll kill the ol' pike instead.'

'It could just be a superstition. . . 'I said daringly.

'Oh - ah,' said my uncle. 'Could be that some folk have as many answers as a dog has fleas! But *everything* don't have an answer or there wouldn't be miracles, would there? I suppose you do happen to believe in miracles, Toby?'

'Of course,' I said hastily.

'Then shut your trap,' said my uncle.

We came to the river. Its banks were honeycombed with big, black, squelching hoof-prints where the cattle had crossed. The mud welled up and seeped through the lace-holes of our boots, but my uncle never appeared to notice this and plunged deeper and deeper down the bank with his eyes fixed hypnotically upon the soupy, torrential water. Although he kept up a running monologue of his own when he was fishing, he refused to let me say a word, as he said it scared the fish, and this is something I have noticed among most fishermen who take friends along to watch them fish.

He decided to fish upstream, and made his first cast just beyond the hollow willows, a spot more celebrated for dace than pike. As his line cut the water he became noticeably more cheerful, and even began to hum a few bars of his 'Handsome Recruit' song as he screwed more and more sections of bamboo to his rod. Soon it would be long enough to poke the furious swan brooding on the far bank.

The silvery spinner flashed as it entered the dark water, and I thought of the great pike wounding and devouring each other in the blackness below, their bellies sliding over the weeds and their row upon row of needle-sharp teeth grinding and shining. I imagined their gluttonous fascination with the treacherous spinner until the greediest fish swallowed its last dreadful meal of barbs and hooks. Breathlessly, I waited for the bamboo to sway, for the float to bounce, for the victim's thrashing, gleaming parabola from the troubled water.

But nothing happened.

My uncle shrugged his enormous shoulders and cast again. Then he moved behind the willow, where the water was frighteningly deep, and here he flicked the line into such a skilful arc that the spinner disappeared between two patches of floating straw and sticks - the very spot a pike would choose to lurk in.

But nothing happened.

And so it continued. By elevenses he had fished up as far as old Billy Boggis's mill - and nobody ever went *that* far for pike. By dinner-time he was a good mile down river from where he had started. And not once was there even the suspicion of a pike. Nor anything else, for that matter.

I slunk about on the bank, cold and bored, lunging at sere bulrushes with the gaff. My clothes had stopped being warm and were just heavy, and there was a delicate emptiness where my big breakfast had been. I wanted to go home and make toast by the kitchen fire, draw the curtains and forget all about the pike: to shut it out and pretend that neither it nor the dismal day existed. But an inexplicable loyalty kept me to my uncle's side. In some way I realized that it was a testing time for both of us, and that I mustn't fail him.

He was now bawling things into the river which would have scared a shark, and I sympathised with his anger and began to loathe the slothful pike for their cautiousness and cunning. I no longer felt sorry at the idea of the multi-barbed hook lacerating their horny mouths. In fact, I longed to see a narrow, cruel jaw dragged free of the secret water, and didn't care about the pike's agony. Catching a great pike had become for both of us the most important thing in the world. So important was it that we forgot the reason which had made us go fishing in the first place, or if we hadn't we never mentioned it.

At three o'clock in the afternoon my uncle, snorting like a midge-tormented horse, said that he would walk along the bank as far as the ford, cross the river and fish from the other side. The fact that neither of us had waders didn't seem to occur to him. I didn't dare to mention it. The ford was shallow, but deep enough to cover my uncle's boots; it reached my knees, and I felt it cutting icily through my flesh like a liquid green knife. Nothing I have ever known was as cold as the river was that dismal afternoon.

Speechless with shock, I plunged behind my uncle as he made for a point opposite the willows where we had started out, what now seemed a whole lifetime ago. Slowly and depressingly, as the little daylight there was faded, he cast his line again and again. We were both absolutely silent now. My uncle was fishing mechanically, as though in a dream. He was tired and hungry and frozen, but still his iron wrist made the bamboo rod whistle in the bitter air.

So exhausted was he that when the line began to race off the reel he hardly knew what was happening. In the usual way he was very casual when he got a bite; now he began to shout and jump about with excitement.

'The gaff! The gaff, Toby!' he was hollering, though the fish was still well out in mid-stream.

Then he began to reel-in with trembling hands. I hardly dared to breathe, and prayed that the pike, with its stupendous cunning, wouldn't get free of the hooks, and held the net ready for when my uncle would rake it from the water with the gaff. The brown river was in turmoil. Another minute limped by and then the pike rushed into the net like a suicide.

We said little on the way home. What was there to say? I carried the rod now and my uncle humped the pike in the plaited fish-basket. The gaff swung triumphantly from his button-hole. The look on his face must have been something like that on Tobias's after he had wrestled with the angel. It was nearly dark, and we were crossing the last field when the ineffably delicious and thrilling scent drifted into our consciousness. It was the smell of the newest leaves and the earliest grass. It cleansed the stagnant evening for a moment or two, and then was gone. As it disappeared, a blackbird began to sing in the nut hedge, and although the day was over every living thing seemed to throb with expectancy. My uncle still said nothing, but as the blackbird's song poured across the shadowy field his eyes met mine with a look of self-righteous triumph.

The housekeeper was speechless with anger when we got home and made us both have mustard baths and go to bed immediately after supper.

'Oughter be ashamed of yourself, Jake Kettle!' she screeched at my uncle. 'Takin' that poor dear child out on a day like this and gitten' him mellingitus, I shouldn't wonder! All for the sake of an ol' fish that eats mud!'

And she took the great pike down to the bottom of the garden and slung it on the bumby heap.

The October Bagman

My uncle was a seasonal man. His life was neatly punctuated with pleasant celebrations. Nowadays there is a tendency to live only for the summer, but he took the year as it came, welcoming every little scrap of it.

'Toby,' he shouted, one cool, golden afternoon when we had come into the house with the last of the russets, 'we shall be needing the cask stool in the parlour on Tuesday - and you'd better take the ornaments off the big table.'

I stared from my uncle to the almanack, and from the almanack back to my uncle. The only Tuesday which looked different was the one which said, 'The Feast of St Michael and All Angels'. 'Is it a church day then?' I said.

My uncle looked shocked. In the first place church days for him had very little to do with the Liturgy, being chiefly concerned with more important matters such as oiling the hearse, tarring the vestry roof or putting mousetraps in the organ. None of these things had to be done yet, it seemed. And certainly none of them warranted bringing a wine barrel into the parlour.

'Don't tell me you ain't been a-looking forward to the Bagman, Toby?' he breathed with heavy incredulity. 'Surely you weren't missing out on the Bagman and going straight on to Guy Fawkes?' His clear blue eyes pressed forward with astonishment until they looked as if they might spill from their sockets. And from that moment until the Bagman came he was in a state of considerable tension. Twenty times at least the evening before he flung open the parlour door to see if the barrel was straight. Half a dozen times at least he substituted elderberry for turnip and turnip for wheat, each time carrying the casks as tenderly as if they had been sleeping children in case he shook up the groundsels.

On the great day he rose at six and boomed his holiday song:

'Do not weep for me, Lisette,
Let not grief your beauty stain;
Soon you'll see your Recruit again.
Soon you'll see your Recruit again...'

Then he went into the parlour and changed the wheat for his best honey-wine, hurred on the tumblers and rubbed them on his sleeve, and put a match to the fire. When the Bagman arrived, round about eleven, the parlour was hot and bright and airless, and my uncle was seated in it wearing his rook-shoot hat. The Bagman took *his* hat off - in deference, I suppose, to it not being his parlour. He was a small, straight man with a reddish-black face and a carefully watered cowlick of ginger hair plastered to his forehead. He wore moleskin breeches and several silver rings. He had beautiful yellow eyes like a cat and the unsurprisable expression of one who was pursued by the strangeness of life.

'Toby's grown,' he said. His voice had a wheedle to it.

'Toby's ten,' roared my uncle, who disliked to think of me as a child.

'Deary me,' said the Bagman, and we all sat down, and the Bagman whispered, 'Business first, Jake?'

'Oh - ah. . .' said my uncle in an uninterested voice.

The Bagman left the room in a flash and returned dragging with him what looked like a roll of dirty bedding. It was tied up with three straps and two other straps made a sort of harness for the Bagman's shoulders. When the bundle was released it rolled open for several feet revealing scores of loops and pockets packed tight with scissors, needles, curry-combs, Prayer Books, fishing tackle, hair-pins, pig powders, crucifixes, macassar pomade, fireworks, slate pencils, rat poison, Union Jacks, snuff, keepsake lockets, jack-knives, Old Moore's Almanacks, playing cards and sticky-looking prints of the Royal Family and Joe Chamberlain. And this isn't a fraction of what the bundle contained.

My uncle concealed his violent interest and said, 'I see you're a-trying to get rid of your ol' stock.. .'

The Bagman's golden eyes grew dark with injury. 'You niver sniffed a better snuff'n that you got off me last time, Jake,' he reminded my uncle. 'Why, hearls have taken wildly to that snuff - and harchdeacons.'

My uncle began to shake his head sadly. 'Worst Christmas I iver spent,' he sighed. 'Worst Valentine's too. They thought I'd got the rarest disease seen in these parts since the ol' Queen died. Could only have been the snuff, they said...'

'Thimbles?' said the Bagman hastily.

'Thimbles,' snorted my uncle. 'We ain't got to *thimbles* yet, ha' we, Toby?'

I grinned with embarrassment.

'You need a nice picture now, Jake,' said the Bagman, 'a beautiful print of 'is Majesty to hang over the clock. .'

'You don't happen to have the Duke of Cambridge by you I suppose?' enquired my uncle sweetly. 'Now he's always seemed the right gentleman to hang over a clock...'

The Bagman then began to rummage about in his stock with frantic concentration. 'Tell yer what I *have* got,' he kept on repeating. But my uncle took no notice at all, for at that moment he was squatting by the honey-wine cask and letting the thick yellow liquid trickle down into the tumblers. He passed a glass to the Bagman who said, 'Just to be sociable, Jake,' and then drank nearly all of it in one gulp. The wine and the fire shining on his eyes made them more golden than ever. My uncle drank as he always drank, with small, secretive movements. The wine didn't appear to get any lower than his collar, but ran richly under the skin of his face and neck, burnishing them.

'What you need, Jake, is a halmanack with all the Newmarket fixtures and plenty of prophecies about the end of the world,' said the Bagman. 'You stand in want of pig powders, I shouldn't be surprised...'

'I reckon you ain't a honey-wine man after all,' said my uncle critically. 'Toby, draw a pint of parsnip in that white jug.'

When I returned, it was to find the Bagman swallowing his second

- or it may have been his third glass of honey-wine. My uncle was drinking too, but whereas he got nearer and nearer to looking like a huge darkly purple plum about to burst, the Bagman just went on looking exactly the same as when he came in. My uncle was immensely loquacious and told the Bagman a great many curious things about our neighbours, and the Bagman screwed his golden eyes up into an expression of broadminded forgiveness of human frailty. 'Rum, Jake, rum!' was all he occasionally said. He drank glass after glass of wine and said how very unlike it was of him to do so.

Their conversation now became elaborate and obscure, elaborate so as to fool me and obscure because the things and people they talked about seemed to belong to the olden days. I fidgeted and my uncle roused himself and roared, 'Satan finds work for idle hands to do!' The Bagman said that when he was young a boy who kicked the furniture he was thrashed, and rightly. I crept from the room and ate cold rabbit pie in the kitchen. The kitchen smelled faintly of rotting fruit and of newly pickled walnuts. Michaelmas daisies rustled outside the window and a few last leaves floated down from the horse-chestnut tree near the barn, sailing past me like wispy, shrivelled hands. I went into the orchard and watched the swallows depart in a streaking dark echelon pointing to the east. I felt very sorry for myself. It was unlike my uncle to exclude me from the conversation or from any part of his experience which I chose to be interested in. I stole round to the front of the house and watched them both through the low parlour window. The fire was leaping and raging and gilding everything. The Nottingham lace curtains were heaped against the window panes like snow. The Bagman was wagging a silver-ringed finger at my uncle and neither of them paid any attention to the huge pile of wares filling the polished table. It was too much. I crept back and sat with absolute stillness between them.

The strange thing was, neither of them seemed to notice me. They were lost in talk. Their voices wound in and out round each other's like the sound of a pair of competing fiddlers at a horky. Nothing which happened in Suffolk was of too small a consequence to interest my uncle. And the Bagman was like a human magnet to whom every shred of gossip clung. If all what the Bagman told my uncle was true, then Ipswich was worse than Babylon, and Stowmarket very much worse than Paris. It was as if the Bagman's mind had taken a lesson from his pack and had accumulated a vast stock of tales about everything and every person in the county. When he got to the terrible Peasenhall murder, my uncle, tactfully this time, suggested that I took a message to the rectory about the glebe sheep.

When I got back the Bagman had gone and my uncle was stretched back in the comfort of his chair with a faintly bewildered look on his face. On the table beside him was spread a new leather purse, a watch-chain, Old Moore's Almanack, a pike gaff, all sorts of buttons and a set of darning needles and a big gingery-looking print of Joe Chamberlain. On the mantelpiece were many more things from the Bagman's pack. A little loose change lay near the empty honey-wine barrel.

'Who is the Bagman, uncle?' I asked.

'Who *is* he?'

'Who was he then?' I persisted.

'He was respectable, that's what he was,' said my uncle. His voice was slow and vague and his rook-shoot hat flopped helplessly over one eye. '... they reckon he let drink git the mastery. . .' A mortified look came over him when he saw me looking at his lavish purchases. 'It's a terrible thing, Toby, when a man would sooner have his drink than his sense...'

The Packhorse Path

May had been cold and June had been worse. Now it was July and although the trees were dense with leaves and the grass swept brilliantly against my thighs in the danker corners of the orchard, and although the swan pool was uproarious with shivering youths in the evenings, and the evenings themselves were long and light, there yet remained a little bitterness about everything.

It was summer in name only. I felt cheated and my uncle felt something far worse - a grinding ache in the small of his back which now and then flared up into a quick, sharp pain. Each time it did this he swore very softly and distinctly. It was lumbago, of course.

'It's no good, Toby,' he roared at me after a singularly agonising twinge had bent him over like a jack-knife, 'I shall have to have me back ironed by the old girl from Rendham' - he meant the district nurse, a woman he particularly detested - 'and you'll have to take the sheep over the packhorse path in the morning.'

'All the way?' I asked.

'Oh no,' muttered my uncle sarcastically, 'just half-way. Just take a hundred head of sheep along the packhorse and leave 'em there. Just take them poor, dear creatures out into the wilderness, so to speak, and forsake them. .'

He was still growling like this when I left him, to sleep for the first time in my life in the barn loft. There was no need to do this, but my uncle always slept in the loft before he drove a flock into Ipswich and I thought I would do the same.

Besides, it was a very special night. When I woke up I would be fourteen. But I never quite slept. The darkness fluttered against my bare face like a black wing, and the straw sifted constantly about me as I breathed. All night long the thatch susurrated with a delicate conspiracy of sounds. Ropes hung above my head in tangled swags of chaff and cobwebs, and a single flashing star stared in through a crack where the weather-boards had warped.

I was neither frightened nor at ease and felt a special tenderness for the plough horses in the boxes below me as they lunged against the manger bars in clumsy slumber. Their names were Rose and Gardiner. My uncle had called them after the Peasenhall murderer and his pretty victim. The first cock had hardly shrieked when my uncle's huge head and shoulders thrust themselves up through the hoist-trap. A three-cornered tear of dying moonlight lit up his face.

'Toby!' he muttered.

I flung myself into a sitting position. The straw had impressed itself into my skin, and all down the left side of my body there was a deep pattern of husks and stalks. From what I could see of my uncle, he looked quite recovered.

'You know what today is, Toby?'

'The day you're taking the big flock to Ipswich,' I said daringly.

'Ah!' said my uncle in a much fainter voice. 'If the good Lord'd give me the strength, there'd be nothing I'd like better. I was never afraid of work, Toby!'

This wasn't true, but I said nothing.

'You know what today is?' asked my uncle again.

'It's my birthday. I'm fourteen.'

'Fourteen. . . 'I heard him rumbling as he descended the loft ladder. 'Fourteen and skinny as a mop handle! I took sheep to Ipswich when I was half fourteen!' he yelled. His voice was thick with guilt. He knew that I knew he was better.

'You going to be ironed, Uncle?' I shouted through the hoist window - I could see him hobbling into the house, one enormous hand planted in the middle of his back, his face like a gargoyle with mimed agony. Then I laughed, not at him, but because I felt so happy, and the day smelt of new winds and new flowers, and because Rose and Gardiner were making rapturous blowing noises through their soft muzzles, and I had never felt so well in all my life.

I pulled on my shirt and trousers and slithered down the willow ladder into the harness-room, where my uncle had left me what he called 'traveller's grub'. This was a small Boxford cheese, an awful looking strip of roast beef, a loaf and a stout bottle filled with cold tea. There was also a half sovereign and 'Happy birthday, Toby Kettle' scrawled hugely in the dust on the harness bench.

I packed all the food into a haversack, laced my boots, rushed back to the kitchen and ate my breakfast standing up, shouted up the stairs to my uncle, whose answer was a mournful groan, called the dogs and set out for the fold.

The dogs were wild with joy. They tore through the ripening corn, making long, rippling pathways in the rustling gold which healed a few seconds after they had passed. Each time they returned to me they hurled themselves against my chest, their eyes brimming with ecstasy, their dewy muzzles thrust against my throat.

'Medoc!' I roared in a fatuous imitation of my uncle's bellow. 'Sue! Jumble!'

But it was useless. They, too, felt the rare invasion of the morning as it sped through their senses. They made tawny leaps at fantasy foes and barked hard, one against the other.

We all four rolled about in the soaking weeds at the edge of the field until the tremblingly distant complaint of the sheep penetrated our consciousness. Then we raced off to where they huddled in the still uncertain light, their pale fleeces massed behind the wattles like captured clouds. They streamed out when I dislodged the entrance hurdle. The dogs, all dignity and pomp now, careened up and down the long jogging ranks, keeping them in order, ordaining which way they should go. Medoc led and I walked behind.

The Ipswich sheep-drive was done in two days. Half-way along the packhorse path a set fold had been made. The sheep travelled about ten miles on the first day, then were driven into it for the night. There was also a flimsy little shelter for the shepherd, like the stable in certain old paintings of the nativity. The set fold was just under Tavenham churchyard and once when I had been there with my uncle, I remember waking up and seeing the memorials shining brightly in the starlight.

The flock moved slowly, the bobbing animals all hindering each other. Their fleeces, absorbing the early light, were like shifting snow. At ten we passed the Satan tree - goodness knows why it was called that - but there it was, a rather sinister dead hulk of hornbeam which used to scare me stiff. The tree creaked, the flock swung away from it like a timid regiment and even the intrepid Jumble looked faintly nervous, so perhaps there was something evil in the ruined hornbeam.

It was then that I remembered *her*. She was called Ellie Nineteen and she was a tramp. I had seen her twice, once stalking through the market-day crowds at St Edmundsbury, and once resting in a hedge where she must have been convinced no one could observe her, because her lips moved as she stared into the distance and her big, fine eyes glittered with tears. When I told my uncle he said that she was most likely thinking of the handsome sailor who had broken her heart.

She slept in church porches and no one ever turned her out. They said she must be rich because she never did a hand's turn in the fields like the other tramps. And, anyway, she bought butter in the village shops - butter! All the village people were frightened of her, so they said nothing when she passed because she was all right if you left her alone. But they had said that about the dog my cousin Patsy brought back from Norwich and it had bitten six people, none of whom had spoken to it.

So the lovely day darkened for me. Soon I'd catch a glimpse of her, I knew, dragging her heavy skirts over the acrid yarrows and polleny mosses of the packhorse path, her proud head crowned with its great, shapeless hat and her big, dark eyes fixed on me.

'Good morning, Miss Nineteen,' I said to Jumble. 'How do you do, Mrs Nineteen,' I called out softly to Medoc. But supposing her name wasn't Nineteen? Supposing she thought I was cheeking her - would she chase me with her big stick? 'Good morning, ma'am,' I said with enormous politeness to a motionless lark. I shouted it out -

'Good morning, ma'am' - and then it happened.

'Good morning,' said a voice almost at my elbow, and there she was, leaning against the dwarf maples by the ditch. Her skirts stretched down into the undergrowth and the breeze was pushing up one side of her shady hat. Ellie Nineteen had learnt the secret of stillness and was not unlike a tree. I looked at her as though she were a unicorn, and she looked back at me rather mockingly.

'Lovely day,' I said.

'There's nothing wrong with the day.'

'It's my birthday,' I said, astounding myself.

'Well, we all have 'em!'

And then she strode off down a side track and she never once looked back. I thought the handsome sailor had had enough to put up with and serve her right! But she had smiled when she spoke and there had been a goodness and beauty in the smile which her abrupt words could not eradicate.

All day I thought of that smile. It made me forget her gaunt height and the horrible black stain round the hem of her dress as it trailed, sodden, in the grass. I found myself glancing behind me with constant expectancy. When the guelder and blackberry thickets scuffled with the secret movements of hidden animals, I would turn quickly, thinking it might be Ellie Nineteen. Sometimes I thought I quite distinctly heard the rough, dragging sound of her skirts. I no longer dreaded her - or anything. I was happy again.

The packhorse path had never looked so wonderful. The sun warmed up for the first time in weeks. I took my shirt off, and hoped that my china-white shoulders would soon match my dark arms and neck. I took my boots off, and felt the tentative blades of the cool needle grass slipping between my toes. And the sun, which for weeks had hardly shone, now spun high in the sky like a roasted penny and little streams of sweat ran down the inside of my arms.

I looked up into the blueness and kept thinking of something I had read somewhere - 'this brave o'erhanging firmament, this majestical roof fretted with golden fire'. I was still thinking of these bright words and of that mysterious smile when the little achy lumps began to grow in the back of my legs and the sheep's isolated complaints merged into a general blare of weariness.

It was about eight, I suppose, when we got to the set fold and we were all as tired as it was possible to be without actually falling asleep. Usually the sheep put on a last thankful spurt and raced in, then all one had to do was to fix the two hurdles which formed the gate. But something was different about the fold this time. Long before I could see it properly I sensed that something was wrong.

The sheep knew it too and blared louder than ever. Medoc, who was scouting ahead, kept on returning with furious yelps and bounds. Then I saw that someone - the gippos most likely - had a spite of some sort. Anyway, they had seen fit to push all the hurdles over, so that it wasn't a fold at all, only a muddy acre strewn with fencing, wattles and sticks.

I didn't quite know what to do at first, but felt suddenly dizzy and my eyes stung with that immediate kind of misery which rushes into the heart after a disappointment. All the outside part of the fold was in the dirt with their heavy splays and cast-wheels sticking up in the air. The fold was subdivided with iron wattles, and these were flung about like firewood.

I sat down on a hummock and put my boots on. Then I drove the flock back onto the track and made the dogs stand guard. After that I began to tug away at the hurdles. They were long and heavy, and they swung about crazily when they were touched. I hadn't got half a dozen of them the right way up, and then not joined properly, when I heard her shout.

'Can't you keep your dogs to yourself, boy?'

'Medoc! Jumble!'I yelled. 'Back!'

Ellie Nineteen said no more but just took hold of the far end of each hurdle. Her easy strength lent them balance and they rose almost without effort. Once when I fiddled about with some tying wire she called out, 'Get them up first, child. Do as I say!' She worked with a simple dignity. There was no heaving or tugging or awkward feminine movements.

'Now,' she would command, and the despairing litter of cast iron and sticks gradually became the set fold again. When we got to the wattles, which were very light, I said, 'I think I can manage now.' But all she said was, 'Get a hold, boy, and don't chatter.' At last it was done.

'And one out,' she said, 'to make a gate?'

'You understand sheep,' I replied.

'I understand a lot of things,' she said, 'but I don't understand the sort of fools who send children on a sheep drive!'

'I'm fourteen,' I said indignantly.

'And I'm Nineteen - or so they say.'

'Are you really?' I wanted to ask. But I didn't dare. There wasn't time to say much more just then because the dogs were hustling the sheep through. She helped me seal the fold. I wanted to thank her but didn't know how. I thought of giving her the half-sovereign but I was frightened of her rage - she might think I was being condescending. No one could be angry about food. I spread it out and she watched me. I thought she was probably starving. I chopped the beef in half and offered it to her on the end of my jack-knife. She flipped it into the grass with a brusque wave of her hand.

'Yellow as charlock,' she said.

And then she went to a gorse thicket and soon returned with a big, steaming can. It was matt with smoke-black and swung from a bent wire handle. The smell which came out of it was impossibly glorious. She swayed it like a censer under my nose and laughed.

'The Phasian bird,' she said.

'It smells like pheasant.'

'They are apt to,' she said.

'Is it - is it pheasant?' I asked, guiltily.

'To me, at this moment, it's supper.' She fished the delicious, slippery brown fragments out with twigs. I have never tasted anything so good since. And the quantity! I could feel myself stretching.

'We won't ask each other questions,' she said.

'No,' I agreed.

'Only one thing.'

I looked across at her. She had removed the big, broken hat and her long hair streamed on to her shoulders.

'Folks have to live as they can.'

I sucked the gravy off my fingers and murmured, 'I know.'

'That's all right, then,' said Ellie Nineteen. 'So long as we understand each other!'

I began to nod with fatigue, but not the horrible weariness I had felt earlier on. This was something different, something very special. I heard her picking up the pheasant bones and dropping them into the billycan. Then I heard her begin to trudge down the track towards the church. After a few seconds she returned and bent down and kissed my hair.

'Good night,' I whispered.

'You just keep an eye on them blasted dogs,' she said crossly, 'till I get clear.'

The 'Duck' - this was the pub in Ipswich where all the shepherds went after they had transferred a flock - was packed when I got there. I went only because I thought that my cousin might be there and he could give me a ride home in the dog-cart. I couldn't see a thing at first when I pushed open the door, just a smoky cave solid with jovial bodies, and people calling out, and winking watch-chains, and a vast stuffed pike in a glass case. Then I saw my uncle staring down on me with his innocent-looking watery blue eyes.

'Why,' he said, 'Toby, by all that's holy and good! How did you get on?'

'I thought you couldn't walk,' I said. 'I thought you couldn't stand up straight.'

'The Lord has been good to me,' said uncle, trumpeting into his handkerchief.

'You look very well, Uncle.'

'Ah,' said my uncle, sighing deeply, 'if we was all as well as we *looked*. . . who knows the private sickness o' the human heart!'

And suddenly I thought of Ellie Nineteen, as she trudged off to shelter in the church porch, of her gaunt figure fading out of sight down the packhorse path, and in a small way I understood her grief.

'No one knows,' I said solemnly.

The Nature of Poetry

My uncle was a man who enjoyed the burden of curious responsibilities. Nothing plain straightforward would suit him. The glebe meadow could grow into a jungle - and frequently did - before he'd take a scythe to it. As for the communal life of the village generally, the little outings, the parish politics, smoking concerts, etc., from these things he withdrew with horror and disdain. His was a private nature which turned naturally to private things.

'Toby!' he shouted to me one fine morning. 'Ain't it after Trinity? Ain't it time for the clock-dusting?'

He disappeared into the brick pantry and returned with two large hop sacks. Shouldering the best leather bellows, he clumped up the lane to the church. I trailed behind him, letting the seeding grasses by the roadside surge against my bare arm. My uncle sang his favourite song, the one which had something to do with the promise a French recruit made to a girl named Lisette. He sang it very noisily and, although it was quite early in the morning, as well as the sound the heady reek of peggle wine drifted down to me. The bellows rode on his broad shoulder with all the gallantry of the rifle he had carried at Ladysmith. It was evident that he was in an excellent mood.

We entered the church, and the gold and purple darkness rushed to meet us. My uncle squinted in the direction of the high altar and gave it much the same kind of nod he would have given old Sammy Flannery in the 'Copper Dog'. Then he foraged beneath the coconut matting near the font for the belfry key. I choked back the slight feeling of nausea the very idea of climbing the church tower always gave me, and then we went up. My uncle went first, bearing the bellows in the position of the charge. Round and round in a dizzy corkscrew of webs, mouse-dirts and darkness we travelled, with my uncle's wide shoulders scratching against the wall and my heel-irons ringing coldly at every step.

'Keep up!' he bawled occasionally, and his voice would spin up the, stair-well like a bullet up a gun barrel.

When we reached the bell-chamber, we put the hop sacks over our heads like cowls, and my uncle fastened mine beneath my chin with an enormous safety-pin. Our feet protruded, still damp and polleny from, the rank churchyard, from beneath the ragged hems of the sacks. My uncle seized the bellows, opened a shaky cupboard door, inserted the nozzle and began to pump away with a sort of controlled fury. The year's dust burst from the cupboard and enveloped us. Although almost blinded, I could just make out the ramshackle machinery of the church clock, a combination of jagged wheels, jerking crowbars, oily rods and snarling springs which miraculously measured off the hours as perfectly as when they had all been fixed together in the reign of King James the Second. Oblivious to our gusty intrusion, time was chopped up into grunting minutes and grating seconds. As the hour approached there was the sound of a terrifying assembling of mechanical purpose, and then a series of *whangs* so deafening, I thought they must be heard all the way to Norwich.

'You do some blowing now, Toby,' bawled my uncle, even his voice having difficulty in making itself heard in the shocking din. He was choking slightly.

I stumbled forward, the hop sack chafing my neck, and directed the bellows at the twitching wheels. And it was at that moment that my uncle began to recite.

It was a thing he had never done before in my presence, and I had certainly never expected it of him. I was very astonished. Even today I can only put it down to his unaccustomed exhilaration at being seventy feet up over the village green on a summer's morning with three tumblers of peggle wine inside him. His reciting was quite unlike anything I had ever heard before. The lines seemed to be wrenched and wrung from him by some violently persuasive method. They sprang smartly from his lips and echoed cavernously in the belfry beams. As he recited he looked exceedingly worried, as though to forget a line would be disastrous. Fascinated - and not a little disconcerted - I lowered the bellows and listened. It was a very, very sad poem.

'*Full oft through memory's burning tears,*' declaimed my uncle mournfully, yet abruptly.

> '*I seek the friends of other years*
> *I turn my sad and weeping eyes*
> *Up to those mansions in the skies;*
> *Where the pure spirits find a home*
> *And hear them whisper, "Henry, come. ."*' '

'But your name is Jake,' I protested.

My uncle swelled up with indignation at my stupidity.

'Toby!' he shouted, and his voice filled the whole church, 'Toby, I ain't a man for boasting, but praise the dear Lord *I* niver reached the age of twelve without acquirin' a knowledge of the nature of poetry.'

He closed the clock door with a mighty gesture, collected the bellows and descended the tower stairs with deliberate dignity, the hop sack floating from step to step behind him. The brilliant freshness of the churchyard restored his good humour. He hung our hop sacks on Mrs Duff's new cross and said, 'Follow me, boy.'

We plunged into the funereal wilds as into a sea. My uncle adopted a tacking motion to avoid the weed-buried graves. Although the ones we stepped over were all without memorials, he kept up a lively commentary on the dead.

'Ol' Argie Brown,' he said disparagingly. 'Ol' Miss Perew - eighty-eight they reckon she was - ol' Pinker Cady, ol' man Heatherby - drank hisself into that hump, they reckon. . . Little ol' Miss Susie...' And where the weeds grew particularly thick and a concealed grave almost sent him flying, 'Ol' Marty Rookwood, blast him!'

We were making for a moss-stained angel in the far corner. The angel was blowing a long marble trumpet in the direction of Saxmundham. When we reached it, my uncle knelt down and tore up the cow-mumble round its base, and I read:

Sacred to the memory of Nigel Aloysius
Crumpetter-Fox, M.A. For twenty-two years
Rector of this Parish.
Blessed are the meek.

'Parson Fox,' said my uncle with feeling. 'I reckon he thrashed me on and off for nigh on four years.'

'*Thrashed* you. . . ?' I stared at him, amazed.

'Of course,' said my uncle. 'How else do you think he could have got the poetry into us? Every Thursday Parson Fox come to the school in his gig to hear what we'd learnt the week before and set us new verses for the week to come.'

'But. . . but. . .' I said, 'supposing you couldn't remember them - all those verses, Uncle?'

'Couldn't?' My uncle was astounded. 'Ain't I been explaining to you this whole live-long day how Parson Fox was a real literary-inclined gentleman? If he couldn't get the poetry into a boy you might as well say that boy had no feelings.'

'And you can still remember the poetry Parson Fox taught you?' I looked from my uncle to the prim angel.

'*Remember* it!' My uncle was almost speechless at my stupidity. 'Toby,' he said, 'you don't seem to understand. When poetry's been put into you it's like tattoo-ink, you got it for life.' He sighed. 'Nobody learns things any more; they just read.' Drawing himself up to his full height and staring the marble angel in the face, he folded his arms across his chest like the advertisements for Sandow's physical culture course and boomed:

> '*Queen Bess will take the air today,*
> *with her princes and her peers,*
> *At the castle gates her coach awaits*
> *with its guards and halberdiers;*
> *Sage Burghley on his mistress tends*
> *And Walsingham is there,*
> *And. . . and. . . and...*'

he repeated miserably.

'Go on, Uncle,' I said.

'It's got seventeen more verses,' he said.

'Try another one, then.'

The proud look ebbed from my uncle's face, to be replaced by one of extreme apprehension. Little crescents of sweat broke out above his eyebrows and his huge hands began to scuffle about inside his jacket pockets. He cleared his throat. 'This one is about the Apostle Paul,' he said, in a very humble voice for him.

> *'The Roman eagle was blazoned in gold*
> *High o'er the canopy's purple fold,*
> *Underneath, on a throne of state,*
> *The Lordly governor, Felix, sate. .'*

' "Sate", Uncle?'

He fixed me witheringly with his fierce, screwed-up eyes, daring me to interrupt him again for as long as the stanzas - endless they seemed - were dragged out of his memory, like a lot of knotted handkerchiefs out of a conjurer's hat. At last it was done. Panting and triumphant, he wiped the sweat from his brow, then swiped the heads of the nearest marguerites with his stick.

'Toby,' he said, as we floundered back to the church, 'have you ever thought what would have happened to y' poor ol' uncle in them hot Africcy places if Parson Fox hadn't strengthened him with the nature of poetry? Why, there wasn't a fear left in the whole wide world after Parson Fox had finished with us lads. We'd used it all up before we were thirteen, gitten the verses right.'

I noticed the jaunty swing of his stick and the elegance of his walk - my uncle was a very fancy walker. I noticed, too, the broad shoulders thrust back, and the thick brown neck rising up from its velvet collar like a column. The brass tip of the bellows winked and blinked in the sun. And then I saw the full glory of it, the strung-out regiment advancing on the Boers, the tat-a-tat-tat-tat of the drums across the veldt.

'Uncle,' I cried, 'which one of Parson Fox's poems did you say when you marched into battle - do you remember? Recite it now, Uncle! Oh *please*, Uncle...'

My uncle stopped dead. Slowly he turned and faced me. His eyes were pressing forward like sky-blue marbles and his mouth was parted, showing his neat yellow teeth.

'Toby,' he roared, 'you're dafter than I thought. Recitin' poetry in battle. . . *in front of me mates!*'

He shuddered, and we reached home, dusty, hot and silent.

The Windfall

The nearer we got to the Bullace House, the more suffocating the day became. 'I never saw nothin' like it!' my uncle panted, meaning the weather. It certainly was hot. The ditches we passed were so filled in with convolvulus and bryony that they weren't ditches any longer. The elms round the edges of the fields quavered up like brownish-green flames when they were near, and like dark blue flames when they were distant. My uncle lunged ahead of me with his feet keeping carefully to the rows between the corn. The corn slipped out from the arch of his long legs in a prickly wash. Because I was ten, and it was August, walking across three miles of ripe corn could be a painful experience. I lagged. 'Keep up, boy!' my uncle shouted.

As I lagged I thought of Aunt, who was dead. Aunt, you understand, wasn't my uncle's wife. She was just 'Aunt' - Aunt to him, to me, to my whole family.

'Why is she just "Aunt", Uncle?'

'Why ain't she Aunt *Minta*? That what you mean?' my uncle hollered back. He never turned his head and his words seemed to bounce against the heat-swollen woods which ended the world we could see.

'Yes - perhaps it was because it's a funny name to say - Minta. . .' I hazarded.

'Maybe you're right,' my uncle roared (he didn't have an ordinary speaking voice like anybody else because of his professions, which had included being a sergeant-major and a town-crier), 'though I reckon Minta ain't all of it and you'd have to make it twice as long to make it come Christian.'

So for the rest of the journey I added letters to 'Minta' to try and make it a recognizable name - which was as good a way as any to make me forget for the moment that Aunt was dead. Poor Aunt, so large, such a bloomy old lady. Indeed, so large and bloomy that one death hardly seemed enough for her! Yet dead she was, or how else would my uncle be clumping across the fields in his best Debenham buskins on a weekday? Aunt lay dead in the Bullace House. I recalled the vast, outlandish spread of comforting skirts across her fat hips and imagined her as a great soft bell lying toppled on its side.

'How old was she, Uncle?'

'Old as her tongue and a bit older than her teeth.'

I gave up, as I was supposed to do. We came to the road. It was only a cart-track really and the Bullace House was about a mile along it. A trap was blinding along towards us. Through the blind - dust and haystalks chiefly - we saw my Cousin Patsy Kettle and his new wife beaming down on us. They were roosting proudly on a high-slung seat covered with a new bit of carpet.

'Jehu!' my uncle shouted, who didn't like either of them. He took off his best hard hat and banged it with his sleeve to remove the dust. Then he did the same service for me, banging my sailor collar until my eyes stung. He was a very neat man. When at last he had recovered his composure he said, with grim satisfaction, 'Well, there's *one* who'll be out of the running. Aunt never took to her from the start!' He meant, of course, my Cousin Patsy Kettle's new wife.

'We won't have to see Aunt?' I then asked in a sudden upsurge of alarm.

'You were pleased enough to see her when she was hale and spruce!' retorted my uncle illogically, lopping scabious heads off with his stick.

I sank into horrified silence. We were passing Aunt's orchard. It stood apart from the Bullace House and was entirely surrounded by an enormous hedge, which was more like a fortification than something growing. A tiny locked gate was the only break in it. Aunt used to take me into this orchard and poke about in the rank grass with her polished cane until, suddenly, there was a *clunk*. 'One there, Toby,' she used to say. The windfall would, as often as not, have a disgusting wet cavity where it had lain on the ground and wasps would scuttle out of it. Aunt would then take it from me, shake it, breathe on its good side and rub it against her skirts. Then she would solemnly pass it to me. All round us were apples. They nodded against the sky and poured down the shiny boughs in pale yellow streams - more apples than Aunt could ever eat, sell or want. But never once did she actually *pick* one for me and when she said, 'Let's go and find an apple, shall we?' she meant exactly that.

Cousin Patsy Kettle's trap was already outside the Bullace House when we arrived. It was a beautiful trap; I dragged my finger along one of its dusty spokes and the paint glittered through - a rich red -gold, like sucked toffee. A big space had been made in the back of the trap as though Patsy and his wife expected to be taking something away with them. When my uncle saw this space his face went campion purple and he banged his cane on his buskins. Then we went into the Bullace House.

It was already terribly full of people, but the strange thing about cottages is that they always hold exactly the family. So everybody had only to squash up a little for there to be plenty of room for my uncle and me. Aunt's parlour - except for its having so many visitors in it at once - looked so normal, so like it always did, that it would not have surprised me very much if Aunt had come in from the kitchen with the cake-tin and her best hand-round plates. Her pot-flowers were on the sills - the very same pot-flowers she used to pour stout dregs into; her cat purred in the fender. Her clock, which was made like a model of St Paul's Cathedral and went tuk-tuk, tuk-tuk rather breathlessly, was in the middle of the mantelpiece. Her linnet, Bunyan ('because of his sweet, good song'), rocked in his cage. I looked about to find more of these comfortable familiar reminders. Yes, there was Aunt's six-tiered what-not and its avalanche of Gosse-china and there were her china dogs with holes in their backs still full of Aunt's hatpins. It was then that I saw that Aunt's musical-box no longer rested on its bamboo table, but on Cousin Patsy Kettle's new wife's lap. She was smiling and stroking it dreamily.

I had hardly recovered my surprise when a glint in the ample lap of my Aunt Bella Jones showed me that *she* nursed a tea-caddy - Aunt's best tea-caddy. Slowly my eyes wandered from knee to lap all round the parlour and, as though it were Christmas morning, I saw that everybody was holding something - mostly things from Aunt's small crowded tables, vases and ornaments and knick-knacks.

'I expect you all heard Aunt say many times how me and Millie were to have the clock,' my Uncle Edward then said in his narrow refined voice.

My Cousin Patsy Kettle, looking worried, said, 'I never heard Aunt say no such thing.'

The relation with the tea-caddy settled this by saying in a severe tone, 'We marnt be squabblin' - it wouldn't be right! Not with poor Aunt settin' forth to meet her Maker. Aunt was always one to keep the peace.'

But she had no sooner said this, than Uncle Edward rose, crossed to the mantelpiece, took hold of Aunt's cathedral clock and lugged it, tuk-tukking, back to his wife. Then, as if she had to give thanks in some way, Aunt Millie got up, gave a sacred glance at the ceiling and said majestically, 'One last look. . .' Two other female relations then got up and joined Aunt Millie and I heard them tiptoeing up the stairs of the Bullace House into Aunt's bedroom. We all sat and waited in a bursting silence.

It was so quiet I was almost afraid to use my eyes for fear they might click like a doll's eyes. In this silence I saw my Cousin Patsy's new wife hold onto the musical-box with one of her strong brown hands, and with the other stretched down at her side, carefully fondle the carved wood of the chair in which she was sitting. She touched the chair like somebody who wants a thing badly, but daren't run to the cost of it. The cost, presumably, had something to do with the way my uncle was glaring at her. Saying that she'd better make tea, a cousin I hadn't seen before traipsed out to the kitchen and sang snatches of a sad hymn, though this didn't drown the sound of the teaspoons being counted.

What I noticed particularly was that nobody touched any of Aunt's belongings without first saying something like, 'Aunt always said I was to have this, or that' and that once this little ceremonious sentence had been uttered no one said, 'Oh no she didn't!' Even my uncle, who at first had maintained a disgusted aloofness, was now beginning to look rather anxiously at Aunt's big dough trough, which could just be seen through the open kitchen door.

My Aunt Millie and the other ladies came down, smoothing their dresses and looking politely upset. 'Your turn,' they said to my uncle, who rose obediently.

I sat like stone.

'Well,' he demanded in a stentorian whisper, 'don't you want to pay your last respects before Aunt's screwed down for ever?'

My answer was to run out of the Bullace House into the garden and then out of the garden and up the lane. And I didn't stop running until I came to the orchard gate which, of course, was locked. I climbed it like a kicked kitten and dropped voluptuously into the cool dense grass. I don't think that even during all the many times I had been to the orchard with Aunt I had seen apples as they appeared on that brazen August afternoon. The trees were roped with them. They hung singly in fabulous globes and myriadly in flushed cascades. I ran from tree to tree, brushing the apples with my hands, feeling them nidder-nodder against my cheeks, pressing my nose against their cool skins and sniffing their crisp freshness. When I reached the precious pearmain tree I stopped - I remembered Aunt standing and just *looking* at the magnificent pearmains. I looked too, but only for a second. Then I stretched out my hand.

I don't know to this day what prevented the heavy apple from snapping off in my hand; I had grasped it quite determinedly. But for a split second it resisted and in that sliver of time I saw in my imagination Aunt's parlour with everybody sitting round picking and prying and aching to be off with her little treasures. And now I was as bad as they were. Or about to be. Deeply ashamed, I turned my back on the glossy pearmains and began to walk slowly towards the orchard gate. To take the edge off any feeling of self-righteousness I deliberately searched the tangled grass and picked up the first apple I saw. It was slug-bitten to be sure, as anything would be which had lain a day or more in such dankness, but I shook it, polished the good part of it, then ate it. It was sour and rather beastly, but I devoured it, every still-tolerable scrap of it for Aunt's sake. Then I climbed out of the orchard and began to walk miserably back to the Bullace House.

Parson Widgeon, I noticed, was coming from the opposite direction. He was hurrying. I hurried too, thinking that I might be able to get to the Bullace House before he passed me and said, 'Hello, my little man,' a greeting I detested. But when I hurried Parson Widgeon appeared from the other side of Cousin Patsy Kettle's horse and trap. He was flushed. 'Hello, my little man,' he said, and to my astonishment followed me into the Bullace House.

But my astonishment was nothing compared with the surprise of all the relations when they saw Parson Widgeon coming through the door. This wasn't the day of the funeral, you will understand, this was last-look day when the Parson generally made himself scarce.

'I'm late, said Parson Widgeon, 'but not too late I see. . . ' He glanced round at Aunt's partly-dismantled parlour and then out of the window, where Cousin Patsy's trap stood with its tail-board already let down. Last of all he glanced at me. 'Ahem,' he began. He unfolded a small, but important-looking piece of paper and after asking, 'May I?' began to read in his beautiful old voice:

'I, Araminta Kettle, being of sound mind and judgment, do will and bequeath my cottage known as the Bullace House, its contents and the orchard in Pig Lane to my great-nephew Toby John Kettle in the hope and trust that one day he may be able to live there and make it his home.'

There was a huge pause, then my Aunt Millie said incredulously, 'Everything - to *him*?' And my Cousin Patsy said, 'Ah, but there's got to be witnesses.'

Parson Widgeon never entered into argument with anyone. He had done what he had promised Aunt he would do and now he folded up the piece of paper, smiled at us with his small yellow teeth and said with gentle finality, 'It is a proper will, properly drawn-up, properly attested.' He bowed to the ladies and left the house, but not before patting me and saying, 'Congratulations, my little man.'

We were nearly home and had struggled through five tall cornfields before my uncle bawled, 'Well, boy; what's on your mind?'

I gazed at the elms, now a dull rose-colour against the evening sky. 'Araminta,' I said slowly. 'Funny, I never thought of that...'

The Church Mouse

The almost matutinal sun flooded the quatre-foils, the lancets and all the stone traceries, awarding rainbow brilliance to her side of the church and to his. The Parmenters in their hereditary pew were purblind with the gaudiness reflected by their own memorial window and dappled shafts which, hectic with motes, transfigured Saul and ignited the jewels of his relations. Unlike the Parmenters, who blinked and fidgeted, the Rephidims floated in the bright refulgence with great contentment. ('Rephidim... ?' said Lorna's friends, reading of her engagement in *TheTimes*, 'what kind of name was that? Where would one find it?' The answer, had they been given it, would have proved to be more anxious-making than the question, for it was, 'in the Book of Exodus'.)

It was Lorna's idea to be married at ten o'clock in the morning. It might easily have been eight had she had her way, though the caterers stalled her there. She had a dewy vision of a dewy bride returning from her nuptials to breakfast proper, and not to some extraordinary bean-feast in the middle of the afternoon with everybody tumbling over the guy-ropes through ennui and alcoholic exhaustion. Saul had complied docilely enough. The whole business was mildly bizarre to him anyway. His complacency on every aspect of his wedding, except that of its legality, was absolute.

Lorna arrived on her brother's arm, a bit early, naturally. She wore the traditional white although she and Saul had been full lovers. Twice. A narrow fender of brilliants pressed a gauzy nylon haze down upon her head and she carried the ritual branch of stephanotis. Edward, her brother, wore his hired tailcoat somewhat indulgently, as though intent on getting his money's worth out of it, and gawpers in the churchyard made aaahhh-ing sounds of proper admiration. Through the yellowing trees (for it was October) Lorna could see the marquee billowing on the Rectory lawn and the brewer's dray from Norwich backing towards it. Enraged rooks flung themselves about above the churchyard elms, AA men prowled through the lanes of

Land Rovers and Ford Consuls, and the pub dog barked and barked. Lorna was faintly enrapt by her contemplation of these things when Edward began to sidle into the church, drawing her with him. As they squeezed along the exceptionally unaccommodating aisle towards their father, tall, sloping and white like a lighthouse in the surplice Lorna had ironed for him the night before, they made an attractive pair. For Lorna, too, was tower-like. Her bones, beneath their overlay of ash-pale flesh, had an aspiring nature, causing her head to look high and proud, though she was neither in the very least. She was a branchy kind of English rose, the long-stemmed sort that would wither handsomely. She was neither clever nor particularly good, but also she was neither stupid nor bad. She might have married anybody - and *was*, her friends were thinking. But they Christianly amended this verdict by adding that Lorna was the one person they knew who could marry an 'anybody' and stay what they were, for Lorna's level-headedness was famous even in a notoriously level county.

Saul stood in front of Canon Parmenter and a trifle to his left. So did his best man, whose name (Hur or Jethro or something) Lorna had forgotten. She would know it when she heard it. Both men were arrestingly still, their plump black backs oddly eloquent, their necks too nourished and their ambience too telling. Even Lorna's dimmer friends felt that they were beginning to know quite a lot about Saul and hoped that it would be all right.

Lorna pressed on, but taking her time. When she remembered to, she kept her eyes down, though this was not often. Usually, she gave little hostess-like glances to every corner of the church. This was quite reasonable behaviour for a motherless woman of twenty-seven who was about to give a reception for two hundred people for herself after being married by her father and whose whole life, in fact, had been crowded with spiritual and social doublings. *Her* side of the church twisted round as she approached, getting a good look and making no bones about it, though they didn't grin or offer recognition when Lorna's roving eye met theirs. They knew better than that. A kind of 'state make-up' covered the healthy East Anglian rawness of the older women. Thickly powdered and vaguely hierarchic, their strong country hands clutching bags, car keys, crumpled gloves and the service sheets printed with Saul's and Lorna's silver monograms, they cloaked their intense nosiness with a gently smiling interest. After all, she was 'their Lorna'. The men, who included at least a dozen who had thought that Lorna might 'do', as they privately considered their own marriages, caught a glimpse of the bride in her frothing nylon and thought, blast! she would have done very well, though too late now. Then, being rather nice people, they allowed Lorna the benefit of the vague doubt in their minds and wished her well with her Saul.

The tolerance poured over Lorna and irritated her very much. They had no right to let her go so easily. If Saul was marrying 'out', then so was she and surely her country friends should resent it a little? But here they were, in their tribal rig, quite obviously resenting it not at all. Only avid and curious, and kind only as an afterthought. Quite needlessly oppressed all at once, Lorna nipped Edward's arm and was answered with a jolly it-will-soon-be-over-darling nudge.

At this point - for these fleeting moods fell upon Lorna in rapid succession and only lasted a fragment of a second before they were overlayed by some fresh worry - she reached Saul's side of the church, where the Rephidims and the Schwanns stood in brunette ranks, and where not even their children, each a lustrous peach-skinned doll, shifted an eyelash as she passed. Seeing them altogether, when she had only met about six of them in the past, gave Lorna quite a shock. She had settled Saul in her mind as a comparatively lonely creature. Now she saw quite plainly that he had his world and had no need to make the slightest claim on hers. The Jewish ladies in their elaborate silk and fur seemed to coalesce into a single aromatic and bejewelled feminine darkness and the Jewish men into a single suave male authority. The bloomy darkness and the masculine worshipfulness were mystically, timelessly, in bond with each other. There was ritual in the way a shiny handbag swung from a fat wrist or in the way the superb eyes of the children glittered. 'And ye shall be my people. . .' thought Lorna, it being second nature to her to find a suitable text. Then, just as she reached Saul's side, and with a force that shut out Edward, her father, the altar and everything but the twigs of the alder tapping away at the east window, 'But how can I? They're *foreign...*'

Lorna's life with Saul in Chester Square was not entirely a surprise to her. She wasn't so naïve as to expect the bare truths of Norfolk in Belgravia. She had expected some kind of submergence, some total eclipse of life as she knew it by life as Saul intended it, and she offered no resistance to his plushy universe. Saul was enchanted. In the first place he was flattered and in the second place he was very excited, for he was thrilled by docility in women. He liked them lush and waiting, like ripe figs in the dusk. Being accustomed to the icy rectory, Lorna spent the first few months of her married life in a state of arrested asphyxia. Central heating of varying intensity sprang out at her whenever she opened a door and was puffed from the wall-to-wall carpets with every step she took. Arrayed in dressing-gowns by Jelenk or Charvet, Saul courted her at all hours of the day and night. The hot bedroom, with its Dunlopillo wastes and the professionally swagged curtains which kept London in its place, became a temple for Saul's rather showy devotion. Lorna had expected some practical lessening of this after their honeymoon in Morocco. After all, there was the safe seat and all those meetings and dinners necessary to keep it warm for Saul. And there was the business in Great Portland Street and there was just life itself. Life, the thing which somehow wasn't there when Lorna wasn't rushing headlong through the day, kitchen, dogs, letters, weeding, talking, shopping, alertly catching tasks and passing on facts and fancies to her country team, each member of which knew his or her duties exactly. Watching Saul brushing away at the thick black curls at his nape one seasonless morning or afternoon - it was hard to tell which, seven months after their marriage - Lorna did begin to wonder when life would have to be lived again.

Pushing her head against the pillow, she began to long for the old challenges, a piercing draught, a dreadful bill or a conviction that she would die an old maid. Saul heard her movement and glanced across his shoulder at her. It was a faultless repetition of the look he had given her when they first met during a performance of Billy Budd at Aldeburgh, and for a second or two her senses reeled. She was back once more in the full glamour of that evening when every non-East-Anglian face had for her a look of hope, salvation and even genius. Saul, with eyes as big as plums and a thick copse of hair shooting up from under his collar-stud, was a poet, she decided. By the time she knew that he wasn't in the very least, that he was young Mr Rephidim of R. and L. Modes which even had a branch in Castle Street, Norwich, she had made up her mind to love him. Submission, she found, was the best and indeed the only way to do this. For weeks she had scarcely been able to believe her good fortune. Everything she had previously desired from life had been simply slaved for, sometimes for years. But to get this little dark bear of a husband with all his undisguisable adoration and his extravagant homage, all she had to do was to behave helplessly. The movement of her head against the pillow betrayed this necessary uselessness. It was the jerk Lorna's head always made when she remembered that she had to lag the kitchen pump or drive her father, who couldn't drive, into Lynn for a meeting. Seeing it, Saul frowned.

'Happy?' he asked.

'Mmm,' said Lorna, who wasn't at that moment. The wordless murmured agreement seemed to satisfy Saul, which was sad and cruel, though inevitable. For, although she was not to realize it for years to come, it was at that moment, seven months, six days and about as many hours after they had knelt before her father in the village church, that Lorna lost faith in Saul. The delicious aura of his magnetism popped suddenly and irretrievably like a bubble. Lorna wasn't to know this. All she felt as she slid from the bed and threw open the window to let in the plane-scented air and the soothing noises of cruising cars was that, although it had been nice being whatever that bewitched and mindless woman had been in Saul's arms, it was nicer to be her old self.

Saul took swift steps to quell this dangerous independence. Dashing past her, he crashed the window shut.

'Sweetheart!' he said. 'What are you trying to do? *Kill me*?'

Whether her Rephidim in-laws, with their ultra-sensory instincts for the clan danger, had tuned in to the sounds of an idyll fracturing in Chester Square, or whether there was some kind of custom about not disturbing young marrieds during the first six months or so, Lorna was never to discover. But it did strike her later that Saul's relations did begin to fill her house immediately his enchantment left it. They came from Hampstead and Golder's Green mostly, though old Aunt Ruth still came from Southwark. Their large eyes swam with interest at everything. There was warmth in their hugging of Lorna but also some cautious ceremony. This is how a Chinese or an African would feel if Saul had married one, she thought. Nevertheless, she liked them all very much and enjoyed the evenings when they came to sip sticky wines, eat sweets and tug at the pearls round their short necks. The men had silky hairs on the backs of their fingers and Lorna never glimpsed this without a start, recollecting how she had trembled in the spare bedroom at the rectory when, in the darkness, her hands had sunk into the warm pelt on Saul's shoulders. She had been surprised but she had not flinched, and so had been laid the foundations of all that followed. Nothing could shock her more or be so intriguing than her first knowledge of Saul's strong yet soft and aromatic body, which repelled as it conquered. He used it with skill and authority. It was as if the Rephidims knew these private things, for Lorna was to see their good-mannered acceptance of her turn to unspoken criticism and this to a kind of muted anger. The male relatives were particularly affronted. The goy wife who was married to the head of the family was barren. They could not forgive her. She should not have looked in his direction. She had her own horizons but she chose his, where all their hopes lay. They could not appreciate the truth: that, son or no son, this tall, fair unmysterious daughter of an English country priest still possessed assets for Saul far greater than his Aston Martin, his election to Pratt's, the securing of a ninety-nine years' lease in Chester Square, his sleeping membership of Lloyd's - even his youthful patriarchy of the family. Which is why Saul did not put her from him (or allow Lorna to escape him).

There followed a delicate form of imprisonment. It lasted for nine years and was tolerable enough even when related to the average circumstances of a most convenient marriage. And all might have continued tolerably enough until Lorna became, in the fullness of time, Lady Rephidim - for that was the direction Saul was travelling - had not another glance, as life-changing as that which Saul had given her as the opera audience gossiped on Aldeburgh beach, made it possible for Lorna never to be faithful to her husband again.

The morning it happened, she had walked to Ebury Street to get a taxi to take her to Harrods. But once outside, the beautifully warm and bright early summer's day had taken control of her and she found herself striding towards Knightsbridge in the same way as she used to stride down to Lower Park Farm in the old days. When she reached the French Embassy she felt so hot and bothered by this sudden and nonsensical exertion, that she crossed to the Park and flopped on a bench just inside Albert Gate. For several minutes she sat there feeling nothing except the tightness of her suit, shoes and gloves, and a stiff little pain in the middle of her back; seeing nothing but the brilliant chiaroscuro of trees and couples. Then the gaudy swirlings of brightness and darkness began to make sense. A fat old woman knitting. A child endlessly rolling. Two lovers almost at her feet, the boy with a gold medallion swinging out of his orange shirt over the face of the girl, whose eyes, legs and hands were all closed to this Danaë approach. Feeling guilty, she looked away and then saw what she hadn't noticed when she sat down - that lovers were everywhere, heaped like flowers on the new grass, each tangled mass generating its own isolation, so that the Park, although littered with bodies, had a dreamy incomprehending wonder, like a garden at night in which all the flowers are blooming in the dark. The trees balanced pyramids of motionless foliage against a sky which was a jazzy blue-gold, as though someone had spread thin cobalt over a brass plate. Lorna blinked. She put out a hand as if to stave off all this glitter and then had the wit to let it straighten her hat, but there must have been some lack of control in the gesture because the next thing she knew was that she was touching something rough and complicated on the seat beside her.

'Reckon I'm takin' up all the space.'

It was the new postman (old now?), the young bell-ringer, the boy who did the garden on Saturday mornings, the tractor-driver; any one of the men who played football on the glebe. Except it was a very young soldier with a babyishly full upper lip and spiky colourless hair.

'My home is in Norfolk, too,' she burst out.

He nodded at her encouragingly, as though she had scored in a guessing game. 'Oh yes,' he said politely.

'Near Lynn.'

'Near Lynn, eh!'

He scrabbled the muddle of webbing closer to his side, then waited for her to continue. His eyes were turned full on her with what she realized was respect. They were big and milkily blue and quite foolishly beautiful. He used them without comprehension and Lorna suddenly understood how little they had seen. The rest of him was all squared-up overheroically, like one of those stocky Kennington drawings of Second World War fighting men, the shape of his body lost in the battle-dress boxes. The leather band of his beret had left a dark pink circlet on his brow and his boots rested on the gravel like monuments.

'Off to Cyprus,' he told Lorna. 'Called back off leave.'

He smiled, suddenly enjoying the drama. Then they talked, Lorna telling him a host of things about Cyprus, about London and indirectly about herself. 'Oh yes,' he said now and then. They seemed to be talking in the Park for hours. Didn't he want to go off and have a look at the sights, she asked him, as he hadn't been to London before? 'Oh no,' he said. Her eyes had now caught his staring trick and scarcely left his face. Although it was a face on the brink of life, it could not have been any different were it near to death. When at last she stood up - it had gone four - she longed to thank him for what he had no idea he had given. At first, Lorna believed it was his utter reality, but later she recognized it as his virtue. Perhaps there were carriers of virtue, just as there were carriers of diseases, and the virtue carriers were as unconscious of their contagious state as were typhoid carriers of theirs. 'Until death do us part,' she promised Saul, and promised it in front of her father! Which was not how most brides had to promise. But death *had* them parted, the death of love - the death of lust, even - years and years ago, and the handsome public thing called their marriage was nothing more than window-dressing for a busy works which clacked away day and night, manufacturing Saul's fame. Would fame fail him if she failed him? Not now, Lorna thought with relief. Not if she walked out of Chester Square gently, slamming no doors. That wouldn't knock him off the Prime Minister's List, not in these days. Anyway, she had no choice. All her common sense told her that while she was talking away to this stranger there had been some total transference of her love and respect, not to the boy - to nobody as yet - but withdrawn from Saul all the same. What a relief thought Lorna. She could kiss the soldier!

Now she was on her feet, the Park seemed to have risen too. The vertiginous moment passed and she held out her gloved hand.

'All this snoggin'!' he laughed, squeezing her finger-tips.

Lorna followed his gaze through the trees to the littered couples.

'All this snogging!' she agreed.

At Albert Gate she turned and gave a little wave. He answered it with a scarcely perceptible nod and a held-back grin. These quite adequately concealed his mixture of relief and disappointment.

How? Why? Lorna was asking herself hours later. She was home again. The house was faintly scented with bath-water and tea. She was with Saul in their bedroom and he was dabbing at his chin with a styptic pencil. Supposing the Schwanns hadn't been bringing the Minister to dinner and the soldier hadn't gone off to Cyprus? Had they been saved - or lost - by their appointments? No, that was ridiculous. Not herself and that boy. He was just the catalyst, or whatever they called it. Just! Feeling almost too free now, like someone thrust from a prison and finding roads leading in every direction, Lorna sighed and began to wriggle into her dress.

'Need my help, darling?' Saul asked in a funny voice, his mouth all twisted so that the shaving nick didn't start bleeding again.

'No thank you, darling.'

Darling. Why not names? Why not Saul and Lorna? Too intimate, she supposed. Too full of identity.

'Now don't forget,' said Saul, still talking like Mr Punch, 'when they get here, your job is to monopolize old Buckley while I get the Knotts and Calvers together. You understand?'

Lorna said she did.

'And put plenty of jewellery on, my sweet. I oughtn't to have to tell you every time...'

Lorna stuck rings haphazardly on her fingers and mounted two big clips, which she detested, on the neckline of her dress. Saul watched her do this in his looking-glass and she saw him watching her in hers. He was naked. New Kolmer-Marcus underwear still lay in its New York wrappings. Talc frosted his furry legs.

'If you're ready you could go down and see if everything is ship-shape,' he said accusingly. 'Stand up. Turn round.' He crossed to her and ran his hand in a feather-light movement across the rich fat bun of pale hair which Lorna had pinned low on her sun-marked neck. 'Isn't it getting just a wee bit heavy, darling? We mustn't let it get too heavy, must we? Right, off you go!' He patted her bottom to show that he was pleased and proud. And then Lorna moved away to take her place with Saul's other possessions in the drawing-room, her heels making sad little wounds in the apple-green carpet. She went straight to the tray and poured herself a huge gin and Cinzano, drank it thirstily and then took the glass into the kitchen to wash it up, very deliberately, in front of Mrs Butcher.

'You've caught the sun,' said Mrs Butcher.

'I sat in the Park - Hyde Park - all the afternoon.'

'I had a lay down,' said Mrs Butcher. ' "Sat in the Park". Well! hope it done you some good.'

The Knotts arrived first, each of them rather squashed-looking. Miriam Knott bounced at Lorna and landed a moist kiss on her cheek and Aaron Knott gave her the wrong hand to show her a special affection. Lorna, who liked them both very much, gave them smiles and hugs. (What were the Knotts going to say when it 'all came out', or whatever it did?) Saul was speaking to her with his eyes over their bobbing heads, something like, 'Never mind the Knotts, your job is to stay with old Buckley. Do as I say *this minute...*' Normally Lorna did what Saul said but tonight she knew it was all quite pointless and futile. The next moment old Mr Buckley trotted straight towards them, crying, 'Well, well, well!' and apparently overjoyed to see them at Saul and Lorna's party.

'*Do something,*' Saul hissed in Lorna's ear. But Lorna did nothing, neither then nor during the remainder of the evening. And when everybody was saying good night, she knew that for once it had been an impotent entertainment and that there would be a row later on. And then, after the row... When Lorna thought of after the row, the first fear of the evening struck at her. She felt suddenly weak and sick. This fear communicated itself without difficulty to Saul, even in the uproar of farewells and car doors slamming, for he knew Lorna very well. The good-byes took a long time. The Knotts, with the extraordinary resilience of the very rich, were trying to drag people on to an impromptu party at the Savoy, and Lorna was cowardly enough now to want to join them. Then all at once the terror left her and she wasn't frightened of Saul anymore. She became the woman she was nine years ago, the personality she had had to set aside in order to make her marriage work. People, she now knew, would debase their true identities out of all recognition in order to do this. It was sometimes called devotion. Her chief thought as she let down her hair and heard Saul throwing his clothes on the floor with rage was that whatever his storming led to now, it could not lead to bed. Not realizing this, of course, Saul worked his way through the routine of his wrath. After the banging about, the pent-up silence. Then the first menacing sentence.

'What's wrong with you?'

'Wrong?' Poor Saul, thought Lorna, can't he see what's right with me? 'Wrong. You bloody well know that we don't have people like the Knolls and old Buckley here just for the fun of it!'

Oh, that kind of wrong, thought Lorna. The Knotts. Mr Buckley. For a second she thought Saul had noticed something far more important.

'Well, Saul,' she said, 'you saw what happened.' The calm in her voice bewildered her more than it did him. It seemed immoral to be as brave as this without making the least effort. 'They met and they talked. Nobody could get a word in edgeways. And that was *that*.'

Saul was incensed by this casualness and a very deliciously real anger raced through him. Lorna realized then that she must try to indicate to him this total return to her old self, for it seemed only fair. Also because if she let him go on shouting and raging he would rage himself into sex, and she didn't want that. She must say something, only what? Idiotic things ran through her mind, then horrible things. She tried to stop the horrible things, holding her hand to her mouth like somebody taken shamefully ill in public. But it was no use. A revolting, long-contained bile sprang from her. It amazed Saul. He sank on the corner of her bed with his beautiful little oriental hands squirming against the quilt.

'I'm sick of being paraded in front of useful people,' she intoned. 'I'm sick of having my house turned into a reception centre. I'm sick of being told what to wear and when to talk and having long hair and being given two pounds a day for taxis and coffee and "being careful" and.....and...' And here Lorna's voice became screeching and foul, so that she didn't recognize it, and her eyes filled with tears because she was sorry for Saul having to see her and hear her like this. When she had said everything and was pure and weak and empty inside, she walked through into the bathroom and leant against the cold white aseptic wall.

Saul continued to sit on her bed. He, too, looked drained and refined. A vein pulsed at his temple and his fingers were pressed together now, partly in supplication, partly in a small judicious arch. What had gone wrong? he asked himself. When had it begun to go wrong? What would happen now? If they had had a child, perhaps. . . ? Could there still not be a child? She was thirty-six - too young to give up. When Lorna returned to the bedroom and sat at her dressing-table, he walked to her and, standing behind her, held her thin shoulders. His mouth burnt on her hair.

'Saully's sorry,' he said.

Lorna was deeply shocked. She picked Saul's hands from her arms, tenderly and one at a time, for although she could never again bear the nearness of him, she must not hurt him more.

'You bitch!' he hissed, his mouth still where it had kissed.

That was better, thought Lorna, for it was more necessary to dislike him than to understand him at the moment. There would be time to do that - years and years of it - when she got back to Norfolk. God might not forgive her but she thought her father might.

At Liverpool Street, the soldier collected his things from the Left Luggage Office - his kit bag, his small pack and the small fibre attaché-case. He had made two mistakes on the underground but was still in good time. The rush hour uproar dazed him. The welter of dull, uncaring flesh, the tumultuous anonymity, and through it all, the way she had looked at him! Her scent was still on him as though, instead of all that going to, she had touched him. And all those blokes and girls on the grass and the way she looked at them. And her clothes and her handbag. They cost a packet. But the way she looked at him. *All the time.....*

The other three were already packing their kit into the reserved carriage. 'Watch out!' they shouted. 'Here he comes! Hide y' missus!' They were regulars in their late thirties and his extreme youth and good looks were a constant source of ribald pleasure to them. Suddenly he needed both to shock them and to confirm his own thudding recollective excitement.

'Where'd you go? What did you do?' they demanded, stowing his luggage, fussing round him.

'I met a bloody tart,' said the boy. 'That's all.' Something had been taken from him. The day was dark and he was trembling.

Take Your Partners

'I suppose you dance?' enquired my grandfather.

'Dance?' I was startled, brought sharply from a reverie of flickering firelight to a sudden comprehension of the old man in his shadowy chair. I saw the flames leaping in the mirrors of his fobs, his ring and his dangling glass, the little luxuries he still pressed about his aged person.

'We all went to balls - that's what they called them. Not dances. Summer and winter alike. Ah, you young people, you haven't a notion about those summer balls! A whole house would be turned upside-down for a ball. All the windows were wide as we danced and the music sounded all night across the fields. I remember one particularly - indeed I'm hardly likely to forget it! Younger than you I was. No more than eighteen. A laddie.'

'A summer ball?' I asked, simulating an interest I scarcely felt.

'No!' he said irritably. 'This was at Campion's. They never gave summer balls.' His faded eyes brightened a little with the aggrievement he felt for those whose ignorance could be so abysmal.

Campion's was a house very familiar to me. It was dead. It stood darkly on a small eminence caught in a loop of the river with desolate chimneys and serried windows blackly glowing through the chestnut trees. Rustic gods, mossy Pans and Dianas rested in nooks of the tumbling garden or gazed with lichen-dulled sockets from ruinous arbours. Their pedestals were banded green where the river found its limits in flood-time. People rented it sometimes. But mostly it was empty, a lovely, half-regretful place, its gutters stuffed with nests, its great rooms cold. It had never occurred to me that my grandfather could have known Campion's in other circumstances. For one so continuously reminiscent it seemed a curious omission.

'It was the first ball I ever went to,' he continued, 'and there couldn't have been a better one to start with. You see, Campion's *was* the ball. You can imagine the excitement there was when Dolly and I got cards for it! The guest-lists from Campion's were always sent to the newspapers. If you had been invited to Campion's you knew you were safe for the whole year, tennis, the Bishop's garden-party and no end of other little beanos! I said so to Dolly - but you remember what your Aunt Dolly was like. She just sniffed and said I was being vulgar! But I knew she was even more excited than I was. Why, you would have thought that it was her wedding she was preparing for instead of a party! You see,' he said almost apologetically, 'they were mostly very quiet times.'

He bent and poked the fire. The coals raged nervously for a second or two, making pictures and ornaments golden and uncertain.

'So we went,' he continued. 'In a carriage hired specially from a livery place, I remember. Your Aunt Dolly had a new dress which she'd started putting on after tea, although we weren't to be there before nine.'

I must have smiled too knowingly, for he suddenly wagged a finger at me.

'Your Aunt Dolly was a fine girl,' he cried admonishingly. 'Make no mistake of it!'

I said I had always thought so and began to hope that tea might come to rescue me from the thraldom of retrospect which binds the old. The day was fading quickly now. Lances of light played on glossy surfaces and the curtains, yet undrawn, hung soft and shapelessly like massed plumes. In the violet comfort I almost envied my grandfather what seemed to me at that moment, the serenity of his years.

'And did you enjoy yourself?' I asked more solicitously to cover the mockery he had wrongly suspected.

'Not a bit,' he said, 'that is, not at first. And certainly not afterwards, but between-whiles was the strangest happiness I have ever known.'

He paused to consider if this long-withheld confidence could even now be proceeded with in the light of my levity. And as I watched I knew that this was no ordinary snippet of recollection growing more and more malformed with the years, but was one of those misty experiences which time alone can clarity. Make crystal at the last. My interest and sympathy must have been apparent, for my grandfather leaned back in his chair, and when he next spoke, it was quite without the tedious banter with which the elderly generally inform the young.

'When we arrived at Campion's I was so nervous that my gloves were miserably damp before I'd had a single dance and my collar rode up and down my neck limply. Dolly began to dance at once with Mickey Tranter (you didn't know him, he's been gone for years) and I was left standing near the old ladies. Old ladies crammed the edges of ballrooms in those days, fluttering and fanning and making trouble. In front of us the ball swept by like a sea. Each time Dolly and Mickey passed she stared crossly at me. She knew that the only dance booked on my card was with her and my fecklessness irritated her. She found it irksome to be responsible for my gaiety as well as her own. Well, I tell you, what with one thing and the other and in the midst of all the music, I began to feel so miserable that I wished I hadn't come. Worse, I knew that I was being discussed by all the old ladies and that it would only be a matter of minutes before I would be sent on endless errands for forgotten shawls and turkey sandwiches. So hardly realizing what I was about, I went off into the garden-room. I vaguely intended to get some cup or something to cheer me up. I ought to have said that they set the sideboards in there. Do you know the garden-room? It is really a kind of conservatory, but more comfortable and they always did call it the "garden room" at Campion's.

'That's where it all began. The room was empty except for a girl with her back to me. I coughed, so as to make her aware that someone else had entered, but she took no notice. She was staring out of the window, standing very still between the mimosa trees. She must have heard the ladle click against the bowl as I took some refreshment, for she turned round. She seemed even shyer than I was, for when I offered her some cup she didn't say a word. Just shook her head and smiled. Thinking that perhaps she was waiting for someone, I finished my drink hurriedly and began to return along the passage to the ballroom. I hadn't gone a step or so when I realized that the girl was following just behind me. We both walked slowly, myself reluctantly, loath to join that assured throng. As we reached the door I held it open and was vain enough to hope that people would notice my beautiful companion and conclude that we were friends.

'You know, Nicholas, there is an eternity between the man and the boy. No woman, except in kindness, would wish to dance with the thin, pale creature which was myself at eighteen. It wasn't until that moment, as I watched the darkly-flushed males whirl their women in the intricate loops of the waltz, that I knew I must go and bide my time until the years should grant me such deserts. But I was sad, nonetheless. I felt a pricking in my eyes and it was only the thought of weeping at a ball that made me smile!

'So full was I of my plan to desert the carnival, that I had forgotten the quiet girl from the garden-room. Rather than wait any longer where I felt so alien, I began to thread my way between the dancers at the far end of the room to get to the door.'

For a moment the old man paused, gazing into the fire as if there dwelt a secret contemplation. Then he continued his story, feeling carefully now for the right words, hesitating often and proving by occasional confusions that this was one memory which had never reached language before.

'You see, she must have asked me to dance when I spoke to her in the garden-room. That is why she had accompanied me back to the ball. At any rate, when I walked into the dancing where the couples were most sparse I found to my horror that instead of escape, I was - how, I shall never know - about to be borne into that confident mêlée! Even now the terror of that moment when I knew there was no escape from the treacherous wastes of chalky floor spreading out before me is only equalled by the wonder that succeeded it. For you see, instead of the stumbling, colliding progress I feared, my feet and brain growing more and more estranged from the music as had always been their fate at the miserable classes I had attended in a vain attempt to make myself a worthy guest for such a night, I discovered myself *dancing*, more even, confident, sweeping down with a lovely girl into the very flood of the waltz!

'For what seemed an aeon I noticed nothing, knew no feeling, had no perception of anything except the dance, the wonder and the intoxication of it. I had always been told that a "good" dancer could take the poorest round, and although I felt that there was something more than this in our absorbed partnership, yet the saying made my wonderment rational, comforting me somehow. It must have been after this realization, as we fled so accurately through the waltz - they were played fast and long in those days - that, my fears quite gone, I was able to look about me. I must confess that my chief reason for doing so was vanity! The old ladies, I thought, what were their sharp tongues shaping now as the huge blue skirts of my unknown partner fluttered their card-tables? What did the young men feel towards me as I passed and repassed, no longer slighted or their equal even, but a chap to be envied! A lucky dog! Most of all, what did Dolly think? Dolly and her pedestrian Mickey when we sped by them on wings!

'People certainly were looking, so much so that I had a little taste of old qualms and for a moment found myself in a funk which quite spoiled the bravado of a turn. I apologized to my partner, and by her encouraging smile I thought she was about to speak. In fact it was only at that moment that I remembered that she had been absolutely silent since our first meeting. Then remembering too my own speechlessness, it seemed no longer strange. We danced on.

'It must have been immediately after this, or perhaps the result of my new awareness, that things began to change. True, the band still played, but less convincingly. The waltz was sustained, but a disenchantment dulled its rhythms. It was like a musical-box which one fancies is tinkling to a stop when a few last bars are worked out by its reluctant revolutions. The fiddlers fiddled, the bassoons throbbed; but they waited for only the smallest nod from the conductor to cease suddenly, inevitably; even never to sound again. It might have been from my glorious exertions that I felt a heaviness, a languor and would have at that moment led my partner to the side, but as though suspecting my thoughts, she became as wonderfully animated as in that first moment when she drew me irresistibly across the ballroom and instead of retiring we danced more gaily than ever.

I say "gaily", yet it wasn't quite that, but rather with an urgency or even a desperation which, as we descended for almost the last time among the thinning couples, seemed to be in a direct and sad conflict with the music. It was as if we challenged it. All this, which takes so long to tell, must have occupied a few minutes. There was nothing I longed for now so much as escape. Obscurity. The floor was almost deserted. I caught a vague glimpse of Dolly and Mickey. They looked perplexed. Above everything I was aware of a new note in the music, a wheedling sweetness adopted for the recalcitrant. A disagreeable charity. "Thank you," I remember saying. "Thank you, let us go back now." But she grew full of wild intentness and stubbornly strong. Determined to end what was now a terrible fear, I stopped dancing and began to walk with long, wooden steps away from the floor. For the briefest moment my partner seemed as if she was about to resist, then dropping her arms to her sides and with the gentlest reluctance, she followed me across the room. As we did so the band stopped abruptly.

'I had only one thought. The garden-room. We reached it without speaking. Now that we were free of audience, I wondered if I had been boorish. The thought that I may have been to one who had been so good to me gave me pain. We stood near the window, she staring out into the night and much as she had been when I had first entered in what seemed to me then, another year.

'We had not moved when Dolly found us. She came in alone but I was aware of others near. I could see that she was in the kind of temper which she stuffed down inside herself until she could no longer contain her indignation and then the most fearful tirades would spurt from her in a positive fountain of anger. Desperately I sought to calm her and by an elaborate mime tried to indicate my late companion who stood partly obscured by the curtains. But even in the midst of such anxieties - and Dolly's temper wasn't a thing to be easily forgotten, I can tell you - I felt some even stronger emotion. A sudden coldness, a chill as though a door had opened and dead hands had entered and drawn all the comfort away. Dolly's wrath seemed less terrible. Without looking round, I knew we were alone. .

'Dolly wouldn't speak to me for about three miles. We sat opposite each other in the carriage with our feet rustling in the straw. Dolly was so tight with rage I thought she would have burst! When she did finally speak; well you'll never believe this, old chap, but do you know what she said? "You're drunk." Drunk! - and I hadn't even had cider-cup! I felt wretched. "Tell me," I beseeched her, "tell me what I've done? Don't just sit there like a volcano!" "I'll tell you," she screamed at me, "and what's more, I'll tell Papa! You danced nearly a whole waltz by yourself in front of the county and if you weren't drunk, then you're - you're *mad*" '

'The lady,' I asked gently, 'did you see her again?'

'No,' he replied, 'but then we weren't asked again.'

Dear Dead Pippa

Miss Pippa, departing at fifty-three, put an end to all their calculations, although had it not been for the excitements of the funeral there was no knowing to what wild limits their grief may not have extended. As it was, Miss Jacynth (their father, Mr Lent, had well-nigh worshipped Browning) soon discovered that there are few things more socially onerous than a funeral. She wrote one hundred and ninety-two letters, all the time gnawing at her pen-holder distractedly in her efforts to work out so many formulae for the acknowledgement of condolence.

'That's what you get for hanging about church doors when the service is over!' grumbled Miss Firenze (then nobody can call her Flo, Mr Lent had decided with satisfaction).

'Why...' declared Miss Jacynth, as she drew yet another sheet of writing-paper from the compendium, 'whatever do you mean?'

'Exactly what I say,' said Miss Firenze. 'How else should you suppose Pippa could have known one hundred and ninety-two people? No one minds replying in the ordinary manner, but to have to correspond with a congregation.. .' She failed to conclude her sentence because Crane burst in, red-eyed and accusing. Even her apron-corners were puckered with snivels.

'You're not still howling!' cried Miss Jacynth unfeelingly.

'He was all I had,' wept Crane.

'He was a good age,' said Miss Firenze.

'Fourteen,' gulped Crane. She clanged the fire-irons together in a fasces of gleaming brass. The noise did her good. 'They should live much longer than that,' she said.

'What was he actually?' enquired Miss Jacynth. She had written, 'Dear Doctor Liverpool, my sister and myself would like you to know how much we appreciate your sympathy at this very sad time....'

'Airedale,' said Crane.

'What, *all* of him?' asked Miss Jacynth, sincerely surprised.

'Three quarters,' conceded Crane.

'Ah!' said Miss Firenze, shaking her small polished head. 'Then it must have been that alien quarter which failed poor Gyp at the last. We are one quarter Winterhouse and it would seem must endure a like predicament.'

'Poor Miss Pippa,' sighed Crane. She squeezed out a token tear.

'She is with God,' said Miss Firenze in a very sensible voice.

'Like Susan, you know,' added Miss Jacynth. 'Dear Lady Trot,' she wrote. Her pen twirled across the paper.

It was on Midsummer Day that Miss Firenze, beating a path through *The Times*, looked up to say, 'It's exactly two months since Pippa passed over.'

'Too soon for a notice, I suppose?' asked Miss Jacynth. 'Crane has broken both the yolks again - you look.'

'Ugh!' said Miss Firenze with genuine repulsion. 'You know I couldn't! Of course it's much too soon for a notice - you are obliged to wait a whole year for that - but there is something else that we have to do. I wonder if you can tell me what it is. . . ?' She spoke as though there may have been a prize.

Miss Jacynth removed her rimless glasses the better to see, and smiled. 'I have not forgotten,' she said. 'The stone'.

'What had you in mind then?'

'An obelisk mostly.'

'Oh,' said Miss Firenze, 'I confess I have not been thinking in quite such terms . .'

'Then we must see what is usually the case,' said Miss Jacynth. So they did. They took a number seventeen to Highgate Cemetery in a fine shopping mood and discovered at once, as one does in Harrods or the Army and Navy, that too great a choice is no choice at all.

'There's enough marble here for Heaven,' said Miss Firenze.

'We should have tried Stoke Poges first,' lamented Miss Jacynth,. 'where they have just a few of everything.'

But they remained cheerful. The day was so warm and beautiful and the inscriptions so diverting that they almost forgot the duty they had to perform.

'Oh, my dear, just look at that one! Only its situation could persuade one that it isn't what it could so suitably be. But it's obelisks we're after. . .' Miss Firenze fumbled in her bag and produced a list which said, 'Bridge-scores, small Dundee, Gee's linctus, 1. Obelisk, 2. Curb, 3. Tablet, 4. Angel. "Evergreen" on at Gaumont, Putney.'

'We must do our best to let it be Pippa's choice,' said Miss Jacynth.

They trudged on and on until the angel won. Obelisks proved to be altogether too lively and curbs, on the whole, seemed to limit that greater freedom they now assumed to be Pippa's. So it remained just to choose what kind of angel. Miss Jacynth favoured the dimpling Cupid kind and Miss Firenze a strapping Gabriel and they settled finally on a shape between these two, prodigiously winged, obscurely breasted and clasping a pink marble book which, in this instance, read 'Pippa Winterhouse Lent. Aet 53. Requiescat in pace.'

When they reached home they told Crane all about it. But she would not be comforted. She cast her left, most lachrymose, eye in the direction of the shrubbery where Gyp lay buried; the other pupil, her right, glared sullenly in front of her. 'He was my all,' she said, and banged the teapot down.

That evening they discussed Crane's extraordinary behaviour. It wasn't hard to understand. She was jealous of the attentions lavished on Miss Pippa whilst Gyp, poor beast, had been merely hurriedly interred among the arbutus roots in the shrubbery. 'After all,' said Miss Firenze, when they had made their decision, 'there can be no harm in it.' So Crane, bearing marigolds one morning to the depths of the shrubbery, discovered a neatly engraved tile, 'Gyp - a dear friend' and a quotation from Sir Thomas Browne, which foxed her. This memorial, of course, was the worst possible thing the two ladies could have thought of. Gyp at once became no longer a pet, a dog, but something very much more. He was 'a dear friend' and beguiled by such terms Crane made no attempt to keep her mind off the wretched animal; it obsessed her. She was barely polite in the mornings and positively rude in the afternoons and when she ran the Ewbank over the carpets, she grunted bitter little tunes. This went on for a very long time, so that when, one evening as Miss Firenze hung out of the wisteria porch for a mouthful of air and she heard Crane singing fairly gaily 'I cover the waterfront', she was pretty astonished. She told Miss Jacynth.

'Then you didn't see the kennel?' said Miss Jacynth. 'It's all been fresh painted.'

'Pippa gave her that,' said Miss Firenze. 'Did you notice my hair? I've got it up all round.'

'And yesterday she went out and bought two pounds of Spiller's Shapes. If you have it up all round, you'll show your wart.'

'Well, it's better than howling at any rate,' said Miss Firenze. 'Somehow I feel that dear Papa wouldn't have had Crane in the house at any price. Do you remember how we made Pippa interview her when she applied?'

'That is something we shall have to do for ourselves in future.'

'Do you suspect as much?' enquired Miss Firenze. She fixed on another silver-wire bangle, which made eleven.

Curiously enough on the day that it actually happened they both overslept. Miss Jacynth woke first, indignantly aware of the deprivation of tea. Thrusting her teeth in, she flounced off to the kitchen. She saw nothing unusual at first, only the door wide to the garden and in the garden, singularly, Crane with a spade. She was cleaning dirt off it. Miss Jacynth heard her singing in a free and balmy way. She turned furiously to put the kettle on herself. It was then that she saw it, a wheel-barrow in the middle of the kitchen, made stately as a catafalque by the addition of the best Ulster linen dinner-cloth thrown splendidly across it. There was something in the tense quadruple humps pushing up the tablecloth which decided Miss Jacynth against removing it. There was, too, a strange odour, dissolute; musk-like. On the dresser she observed a brand new dog collar, lovingly engraved; fourteen dog licences, a sorbo ball, a Vim case crammed with shavings and saw-dust; a neat pile of bandages, a copy of the *Amateur Taxidermist* and a book that was once Mr Lent's called *The Mummy* by Dr E. Wallis Budge. There were other things, but Miss Jacynth did not see them. 'Firenze! she shrieked.

Breakfast was delayed that morning for it took some minutes for the ladies to recover. When they had, there was much to be done in the clearing-up line.

'If there's one thing I object to,' pronounced Miss Firenze, who had been obliged to wheel Gyp back to his grave, 'it's putting things away after servants. What's she doing now - you look.'

Miss Jacynth removed her glasses and peered into the garden.

'Smelling the lilac,' she said.

'Smelling the lilac - but that lilac's been dead for weeks! Jacynth, I'm never going to forgive Pippa for landing us with that creature, full knowing that she hadn't got a reference!' Another thought struck her.

'We haven't actually ordered the angel, have we?' she asked.

Miss Jacynth shook her head.

'Good,' said Miss Firenze. 'In that case we'll keep her waiting until next year, and plant antirrhinums instead... Do you remember how they always brought her out in a rash?'

The Schism

It was being in a strange land, so to speak, which made the brief announcement in *The Times* possess an added poignancy. I was travelling among the islands of the Inner Hebrides, which are a far dream from Suffolk, and I was led by longer days than I have ever known elsewhere to reading the newspapers with an analyst's thoroughness. Hence the complete sorrow I now felt when, bigger and blacker, more meaningful, more dazzling than all the rest, I saw the name Foxfellowe in the Deaths column. What need was there to read further? Yet it was interesting to see that besides Adelaide, which I knew, she had also borne the names of Miriam and May. Neither was her age, or at least its approximation, quite unknown to me. Yet there was majesty in seeing 'ninety-three' in black and white.

Of the two bright images which filled my mind at seeing her obituary notice, one would have surprised Miss Foxfellowe. It might be better in this present case to mention the one with which she was so familiar.

Miss Foxfellowe in an age of charitable plainness was uniquely, surprisingly ugly, and, although my recollection of her commences when she was already a very old woman, I knew that what I witnessed was not just the conglomeration of time set in the body, but was virtually the sculptural remnants of an uncompromising, lifelong hideousness. The effect of such a disadvantage upon the mind and character may be found reiterated many times in those now unread works of physiognomy, but the conclusions generally drawn in those gross volumes did not apply to Miss Foxfellowe. Beauty and ugliness are accepted by their bearers with pride or fortitude. Only plainness is combated. As soon as Miss Foxfellowe realized the uncompromising nature of her mortal shape, and had grown impervious to the involuntary flicker in the attitude of those newly making her acquaintance, she abandoned the race whose only prize might have been that of compassion and threw herself into the study of archaeology.

This happy decision was made more than half a century before. Canon Retort introduced me to her. During the lifetime before I was born and grown to manhood the unique person of Miss Foxfellowe had wandered at will over the English counties in search of triple piscinae, corbels, priest-holes, and rare genealogies. Her peculiarly bowed figure had penetrated the doorways of numberless learned societies, and her brisk handwritten corrections would blot the purple of many a fine phrasist who, to her way of thinking, had shown a pretty imagination where she would have preferred good, sound, unalterable history.

My first attendances at the meeting of the High Suffolk Archaeological Society were somewhat marred by my uncomfortable awareness that I was at least thirty-five years the junior of anyone else present. Canon Retort was treasurer, secretary, and editor of the Society's publications. Mr Wynn was chairman, and we shared with a great many other institutions a fragment of the public life of Lady Bugle. She was our president and our undoubted *entrée* to the Adam drawing-rooms and state bedrooms of our more county neighbours. Each of these officers was re-elected over the years with the certainty of springtime and harvest. The rest of us were country folk and clergy. Dominating every gathering of the Society was the figure of Miss Foxfellowe. Her place was always in the centre of the front row. Her hair, like colourless unravelled string, was scrabbled beneath a large wicker hat, her tweed coat, oddly protuberant, was liberally flecked with hairs from her two fat cats, and about her whole person there hung the stale redolence of dinner-wine.

At the time when I joined the Society, resentment against her was becoming very marked indeed. Grand and arrogant as she had been there many years, old age had brought a special arrogance. Vague and unfashionable as her clothes were always, they were best epitomized in Mr Wynn's malicious word 'clobber'. And it did not require malice to know that 'dinner-wine' was a purely euphemistic interpretation of the odour with enveloped her. But, as though in recompense for these many failings, her splendid voice became more sternly resonant with the years, and, being possessed of a lucid mind and a first-class classical education, she could continue where most had to leave off, and never failed to spin verbal rings round such members of the Society as she had selected for her particular approbation.

'I have very great pleasure in letting the Society know that Lord Breen has most kindly given his permission for the visit to Breen Hall,' announced Canon Retort at the opening meeting of my second year's membership.

This was most exciting news. Breen Hall, with its great gallery of Italian pictures and Renaissance panelling, had withstood the Canon's blandishments in the many letters he had written to its owner for a quarter of a century. Lord Breen had a proper, if out-dated, conception of the seats of the gentry. It decidedly contained no clause for meddling historians. The very idea of a score of trippers paying half-a-crown a head to tramp his drawing-rooms would have killed him. The Canon had obtained his permission somewhat ambiguously. On a rare invitation to dinner he had managed to persuade his lordship to allow him to bring 'a small party of friends to see the Hall'.

'I have discussed the matter with Mr Wynn,' continued the Canon, 'and he has concurred with me that the most that one could politely contain on such an invitation would be twenty people. As you are aware, we have eighty-four members, and in further concurrence with our chairman, and with Lady Bugle, I think the fairest thing would be to have a ballot.'

Anxiety rather than pleasure marked this proposal. It had long been the custom of the Society to fill three omnibuses and all to go sight-seeing together. Anxiety, too, marked the faces of Canon Retort and Mr Wynn. A good impression on this auspicious occasion was essential, and ballots often carried fairness to the point of inconvenience, 'the fringe of inconvenience' was the nicer phrase in the Canon's most private thoughts. For the first time in almost fifty years an august presence might be missing. At this latter possibility

Mr Wynn smiled perceptibly, and the Canon, not daring to utter his thoughts, caught his breath.

The slips were placed in an old candle-box and we all filed by and gingerly extracted our fate. Miss Foxfellowe showed no sign when the twenty names were read out and her own was not included.

As it was such an unprecedented occasion and our numbers were so reduced, it was decided that after the morning visit to Breen, instead of the customary sandwiches, luncheon would be taken at the 'Copper Dog' in the village, and that after luncheon the jambs of Nortley Church might be inspected. It was to be a full, happy day.

I still remember a thousand details of those now far-away outings. Such societies are articulate above all things. As the comfortable omnibuses filled with the chattering company, the bland, elderly ladies at the windows, curates on the outside, Canon Retort would walk up and down, his pencil and list poised in enjoyable stage-managership. We would set off early, at nine, the sun already showing signs of great warmth, and we knew that by eleven our progress would be halted in a fronded lane whilst the drivers pulled back the long sliding panels in the roof. Lane dust, petals, and summery air would blow in our faces as we proceeded. We travelled slowly, never more than twenty or so miles an hour, and we never stopped except for those monuments listed on our agenda.

These outings have acquired an idyllic patina. In remembering them now I understand more fully an incident in my father's own experiences which he related to me. How that during the 'eighties, as he was riding in a narrow lane, he was obliged to rein his horse into a field to let a broad flower-garlanded brake pass. It was a village outing, but the villagers were unknown to him. They had presumably been travelling for some hours, and my father had met them at a time when their happy voices had flagged and grown silent. Four decorated punches drew the long flat vehicle upon which women and children in pale voluminous dresses were heaped like blossom under the high June sky. The only sound came from the creaking axle-trees. From their unknown hamlet to their unnamed destination they passed between the heavy trees. It was like a dream. My father never forgot it.

It was five minutes to the hour when I arrived at the bus. Canon Retort was distinctly self-congratulatory. The delicate selection had been achieved without a hitch. Three or four minutes to go - and then to Breen Hall. In his happiness he hung from the door as conductors do, and so doing was afforded the appalling sight of a most familiar figure with an only-too-well-known back-slipping walk making her way towards the bus. In her arms she bore a thermos flask and a volume of the Historical Monuments Commission. In her face abstraction vied with determination.

'Time to leave! Time to leave!' called the Canon.

'Lady comin' up yet, sir,' replied the driver solicitously.

'I say start up at once,' cried the Canon angrily. 'Our number is made up. We must start immediately.'

The driver's reaction to this was to smile. Didn't he know their funny ways? Why, if he 'adn't rounded them up out of them old churches, sometimes they wouldn't never a got 'ome. So, remembering the whip-round which always came at the end of the day as a gesture of their corporate gratitude for the way in which he put up with their queer goings-on, his knightly character came to the fore. As we all gazed in stupefaction from the windows and Canon Retort, agitated, swung from the handrail, the driver gently led Miss Foxfellowe up the steps of the vehicle and patted her into the front seat. I remember thinking that it was proof of the vanity of our supposing that we should give her the slip in this way that this seat, so long her own indisputable position on many scores of such journeys, had not been taken.

There was nothing to do but proceed. Some members, not wishing to appear as uncharitable as they felt, began animated conversations, as though all was well. Lady Bugle found the reference to Breen Hall in her 'Little Guide', dropped the book, found it again, and commenced to write vigorously in the margin. The driver, satisfied that no more of them were about, touched his forehead to the speechless Canon, and we started.

Sunshine and familiar joys repeated destroyed our antipathy. Soon we were all laughing and talking, pointing at a cottage here, an outside bread-oven, the Donkey and Buskin - *hopelessly restored* (a letter to the county newspaper regarding this); and soon, as the air grew sweet and golden with the morning heat, we drew up with grotesque aplomb before the pinnacled gates of Breen Hall. Distantly gleaming between the widely-spaced hornbeams was the splendid house. And inside were the pictures. Miss Foxfellowe passed under the crested arch with that superb sense of 'belonging' which I so admired, and which made the delta of fragile veins in the Canon's nose darken with irritation, causing it momentarily to have the appearance of an anatomical drawing. So confidently did she press ahead, with such determination, that I would not have been surprised to see the great doors of Breen Hall flung wide by lackeys to let her enter. Instead, she startled us by announcing, with that extra enunciation which made her slightest utterance seem instructional, that as she had seen the pictures, and the panelling, she would take the opportunity this visit afforded her to view the gardens. 'My uncle, Bishop Foxfellowe, was particularly fond of the gardens,' she added as a parting shot at the Canon. 'He often came here - once with Paxton, I remember, whom he had "borrowed" for the day to instruct the eleventh Lord Breen on tulip-trees.'

We watched her go with her slow, lurching walk, dragging her trodden-down old shoes over the crisp lawn. Our own reception at the famous doors was most cordial. Inside there was an almost purple gloom, such as one finds in a chantry, and there was a smell of luxurious decay, such as one observes when a church chest containing rich frontals and ancient embroideries is opened. It was before the period of elimination and conscious 'good taste'. Twenty generations had encrusted the house with twenty most individual ideas. There was, for instance, the idea about armour, which, not content with the usual human accoutrements, had insisted upon huge pieces of horse-armour to swing from the walls. There had been a Chinese embassy during the eighteenth century, and this had brought vast vases and ferocious temple-dogs to snarl from every mantelpiece. Greek gadgets from the Great Exhibition rubbed against whole assemblies of Hepplewhite 'made for the house'. A dark little Murillo, glazed and varnished to an almost mirror-like effectiveness, was corded under a tall Millais. Near to this odd pair was a full set of sporting prints in shiny maple frames hung closely together to make sufficient room for a French looking-glass bracketed with gilded candle sconces. The rooms were set in the grand manner, but the great vista they were intended to afford was reduced by the immense quantity of furniture to the appearance of a good day at Sotheby's.

Lord Breen himself showed us round. After our inspection we were drawn, with the kindest insistence, to the library, where we were offered coffee and sherry and some dull, yet memorable, stories. Without a doubt the visit had been a great success, in spite of all our forebodings. The Canon was already wording the sentences with which he would describe the outing in the next 'Transactions'. It was, indeed, with reciprocal graciousness that Lord Breen and his guests shuffled to their leave-taking, and it was with equal horror that host and guests, appearing on the terrace, were confronted with the sight of Miss Foxfellowe struggling towards the drive, her hat awry, her arms filled with floral spoils from his lordship's immaculate garden.

We motored glumly to the Copper Dog. Between stifled remorse and scarcely stifled anger Canon Retort thought of the grovelling sentences which would have to be fitted into a very prompt letter. The rest of us gazed at the summery landscape with lack-lustre eyes. Miss Foxfellowe had stuffed the rifled blooms into the mesh-carrier above her head, and the jolting bus, loosening their profusion, had caused them to hang like a canopy above her battered hat. Seemingly oblivious of the muted outing, she bowed her ruminative countenance to within an inch or two of the Historical Manuscripts Commission and made careful corrections in its margin.

The Copper Dog was an inn in a transitional stage. No longer a coaching-house, it was only possible to obtain food in its meandering depths by the most elaborate prearrangements. The arrival of our party was resentfully catered for after the passage of several letters and a final reassuring telegram. The public rooms were ill-defined. The smoke-room led into the proprietor's sitting-room, and this in turn into a long, echoing, cheerless annexe, where the Buffaloes and similar organisations flourished. This room had been pressed upon the Canon, but he had been firm in his requirements, and so we found ourselves in a large Tudor room, lined with vast sideboards - a room shiny and emphatic with sliding surfaces and stale air.

The place seemed to fascinate Miss Foxfellowe. By the time luncheon was served many boot-cupboards and little doors had rendered to a degree their musty secrets to her investigating eyes. As we sipped our sherry we heard the unconcealed satisfaction of her penetrating voice as the chenille drapes of mantelpieces were pulled aside to disclose smoky acanthus carving or Caroline bevelling. On being sent to bring her to table, I found her with well-planted feet before an ancient settle, upon which huddled a crumpled wretch of a man. They were drinking beer out of quartern mugs as she added to her remarkable erudition the mysteries of pargeting.

Our advancements and our downfalls hinge upon such slender potentialities. Innocence can be accorded a vengeance such as duplicity can never know. So philosophising, I watched Miss Foxfellowe tackling her food with that enviable appetite to be found in adolescence or in extreme old age. The dull dining-room possessed an ancient genius which permitted us on this hot summer's day to settle in its almost chilly depths and savour with delight the warm smells from the nearby kitchen, smells of rich golden crackling, green vegetables and heavy, comforting soup. No lettuce leaves or fruit salad. Food was an oven arrangement at the Copper Dog. Summer and winter its matted wattles sturdily sandwiched between parget and panel kept out the weathers, and its small, flower-crowded windows most of the light. It was as if an antique peasantry, obliged to be so long each day in the wind-riven fields, had snugged the wood and plaster about them to make a sanctuary from the ubiquitous elements, a private place where no climate might touch them.

Beer for the meal was drawn from the first of a row of barrels in a brick passage. From where Miss Foxfellowe and I sat we could see the pleasing operation. I watched as, oblivious of the general conversation, she turned her curiously-hooded glance to the various features of the room, as if in search for some secret essential. When she came to the little passage with its neat barrels, its scrubbed boards made as bright as a golden detail in a Dutch interior, she leaned forward a trifle as though in sudden recollection. Then turning to me she said: 'Tell Sempkin I will have mine in the nice old pot I left in the bar.'

The heroic measure was set before her and, to the alarm of little Miss Wynn sitting on her left, Miss Foxfellowe pulled it forward and drank long and appreciatively. Towards the end of the meal it was refilled at her request. As the rest of us rose for coffee, she, too, sought a more comfortable seat, bearing the pot libation-like before her, like a deplorable Ganymede.

If things had not continued to happen from this point, if, for instance, the bus had been on time, or the landlady had not begun to possess a hardly-concealed desire for our swift departure - thereby settling us the more determinedly in our seats - all might have been well. The county would not have the embarrassing wealth of *two* archaeological societies. The Historical Commissioners, instead of being led into controversy over practically every issue, might have received a single authoritative report, thereby preventing the appalling sensationalism - which even leaked into the popular press - when the vaults of Aktonbury were opened in a search for the Lydgate pyx. This apart from the row over the hearth-tax and the scandalous nature of the disclosures in the Tanfield Correspondence, which was not supposed to have been published until the last member of the Reevey family had died. All this, and more, might have been avoided.

And all this caused by, or to be traced to, an accident of physiognomy! As one upon a rare and delectable occasion sees in the passing crowd a young man with a proud and reminiscent head so like the faces on Torrigiano's tombs that it seems a secret blend of patrician blood has lingered in time, bridging half a millennium by a countenance, so one perceived in Miss Foxfellowe more than a hint of the eighteenth century. It was as though she had arrived straight from the clumsy rooms of William Kent to meet our modern niceties with a robust, yet aristocratic, vulgarity.

As the last drains were tilted from her beer-mug, she became suddenly aware of the ostentatious charade of the coffee-takers, who, seeking refuge in numbers, crowded upon each other's shoulders holding their cups high. Faintly from the taproom came the sounds of muffled song. Whether the rustic merrymaking offered a prompt escape from our self-righteous company, or whether Miss Foxfellowe imagined that in that ancient mirth she might, like Cecil Sharp, find a bucolic pearl of greatest price, we never knew. We only saw her rise with care and, clutching her mug, leave us.

It is difficult to know what exactly happened after this. A considerable interval must have passed, for I remember that, the crisis momentarily banished, we had settled down and were busily covering with a soothing film of conversation our old irritants. So engrossed had we become, indeed, that none of us noticed when the singing from the taproom stopped. When a distant shout of some majesty was heard, we continued to talk, each of us hoping that we might be guilty of an individual hallucination, yet all privately convinced that something was amiss.

The distant noise by this time had grown very strange. To me it was for all the world as if I were in the vicinity of some ancient rite. Now there could be no mistaking the measured voice. But what was it engaged in? A little lecture to the labourers? A terrible public remorse for her social failings - with fragments of the Litany thrown in?

We rose and hurried towards the taproom. With one door less between us and the voice, I was reminded of those drama critics who compare unfavourably the emotional stature of a modern actress with some legendary figure of the past whom they imagine no one is old enough to remember except themselves - Rachel, Réjane . . . It was such voices as that which we heard now that filled their ears and made all our present utterances seem thin.

This brief soliloquy of mine was rudely interrupted by sounds of utmost confusion. A sort of howl interspersed itself with the splendid lines. 'Disgusting!' we heard a woman screech, and then, in the very height of complaint: 'And you a *lady*, too.' Further protestations were drowned in the familiar and blissfully oblivious sonority.

A fantastic sight met our gaze. The narrow ledges serving for seats around the bar were crowded with uncomfortable looking yokels, their buttoned-up faces registering every emotion from leering pleasure to pent hostility. Before them stood Miss Foxfellowe, her hat quavering, but her hands rigid and steady as she swung aloft her great quartern pot.

'Why - why, she's *drunk*!' murmured little Miss Wynn as we crowded in the door.

But Miss Foxfellowe was beyond criticism, and, in the eyes of Canon Retort, plainly beyond redemption. The hop had worked as nobly as the grape and had transported her back to some Attic glade of swains and woodland deities. ' "For the nymphs of the springs, the glorious goddesses mountain-born, I beg a dole! 0, Hermes, hearken!" ' And with this fragment from Euripides she tipped her beer-mug in high libation before we could approach her. The mug wasn't full, but it might well have been. The amber flood was astonishing in its richness. The almost stupefied yokels leaped from its splashing pool. The general hostility began to penetrate the warm classical miasma in which Miss Foxfellowe floundered. Summoning her dignity, she addressed herself to the furious landlady. 'Kindly inform Canon Retort that Miss Foxfellowe will await him in the omnibus, my good woman.'

'Tell him! I'll tell him,' shouted the woman. 'You disgusting old creature - a *lady*, too. I'll tell him if it's the last thing I do!' She turned towards us, beside herself with anger. 'Out! Out!' she cried. Her face was purpled and puckered like pickle-cabbage. 'Out - every one of you! *Disgusting*!'

In vain did Lady Bugle place two fingers in great kindness on the landlady's flushed arm. In vain, too, the Canon's firmness and dignity. It was 'Out' and 'Out' growing louder and louder. In a daze of humiliation we groped for our hats and papers and stirred towards the door. The bus met us with slightly mitigating coincidence as the inn-door banged behind us. The Canon's mouth worked nervously as he considered the many difficulties which had beset him in the past and added to them this latest effrontery. To be thrown out of an inn!

The driver was told to drive straight home. On the back seat the committee huddled round the Canon as he told them that they must believe him when he said that the limit had been reached. Unknown to Miss Foxfellowe an obscure ruling was remembered and she was expelled from the Society.

Miss Foxfellowe's answer to the Canon's chilly letter bearing this news to her came towards the end of that same summer. It arrived in the form of an elegant card of spiralling copperplate. This announced that the *New* Suffolk Archaeological Society, under the leadership of Miss Adelaide Foxfellowe, FRSA, invited me - my name was crabbed in her unsteady hand - to a visit to Pavely Castle. The invitation proved to me that my interest in her was of the most charitable kind, and in compassion for what I imagined to be her lonely state I accepted.

There was considerable difficulty in getting a seat on the bus. It appeared that my charity was shared by forty-three other members of the Canon's group. I noticed that they were the people whose opinion had never been requested at any time and who had tolerated the whims of Mr Wynn's committee for decades. Before us, as we travelled along, the great wicker hat dipped and rose. Occasionally its undulations became more precipitant as Miss Foxfellowe scotched some nonsense in a small book on pudding-stones which the British Museum had thought fit to send her.

Immediate Possession

It stood just a fraction back from the main road, a 'dwelling house' the tipsy board said. Shrubberies pressed up to its walls jealously and the flaking white gate was manacled by spear-grass. Miss Trebble, motoring into market with her brother, the Major, had seen it many times. In time she grew to covet the house, though secretly, since at her age the most stifling desires are referred to as fads when others get to hear of them. The front door intrigued her most. It was what the house-breakers - and pray God that they never appear! - would have termed an important door. It had broad panels and its tarnished fittings of wrought brass made in the time of King William IV, and its scallop porch of saffron plaster, not much chipped, made her pleasure quite tumultuous. The felicity of the door blinded her to the threatening, sightless windows and the sagging wormy loggia which should have tempered her enthusiasm for Handel House. As for the suppurating nests under the guttering, into which swallows sped like darts, Miss Trebble did observe these once and thought them quite charming. When at last circumstances allowed her to purchase the house, she astonished the agent, familiar as he was with the temporary insanity in which a property deal is concluded, by her avid haste to move into it. It was only fair, he thought, to repeat what he had said about the condition of the rooms in their plum-dark damp flock wallpapers.

'You will need to spend quite a bit on it,' he advised her.

Miss Trebble scarcely listened. She merely said what she had already said a dozen times, 'I shall love pulling it round slowly. . .' Her brother was sailing with his regiment. That left the child and the governess and herself. Between them they should be able to resuscitate poor Handel House. She did not, however, explain all this to the agent because he was very young and smelled of shaving-soap and, she could see, was soundly prejudiced in favour of a hygienic view of human existence. So she nodded and smiled as he advised her to get the whole place stripped and clean, murmuring to herself, 'Mortification! Poor house, it doesn't deserve that!'

It was April when she moved in with her nephew and the governess. Tight pyramids of lilac, the double kind and extraordinarily forward that year, nodded stiffly in the garden. Horse-chestnut sconces quaked in the wind. Ghost-like under the impenetrable gooseberries and stagnating perennials, there was another garden, a Victorian dream of Tuscany, in which box hedging made formal patterns on the snail-sour earth and bits of balustrade came and went in the miserable ivy. Not knowing what to do first, Miss Trebble and the governess gardened. It seemed a sensible decision. The weather was quite lyrically fine. The birds sang. Now and then they stopped gardening to call out, 'Edmund. . . Edmuuuund!' to the small fair boy, and watched for him to creep from the shrubbery, as nervous as an okapi. Or they would watch him at a very private game which involved the reeling sundial on which was inscribed, *Time remembered is grief forgotten.*

'He's sure to fret a little at first,' said the governess, whose name was Miss Joan Brown. 'But we mustn't worry, he'll soon settle down.'

'Come over here with Auntie, darling,' cried Miss Trebble, who was acquainted with the terrors of solitude. But Edmund rarely came. 'Come to Nanny, Edmund!' shouted the governess, generously demoting herself for his sake. But he usually managed to keep his distance. May arrived and then summer spun in.

It was then, when the real warmth came, that the governess began to wonder if she really enjoyed so much gardening. She was the kind of person who rushed at it, tearing and chopping and raking; exhausting herself and almost perversely ignoring the restraint necessary for the performance of such a task, the care which makes it priestly and a kind of cleansing. Miss Trebble, with her hedged and limited happiness, grew painfully oblivious of the governess's weariness and the boy's real loneliness, although in neither respect was she callous. It was only that for her own peace of mind she had taught herself to find great joys in small things for so long, that any condition of the spirit outside these things rather bewildered her. 'A simple woman' is how she had once heard herself described. Could it have been a compliment? She often wondered.

Meanwhile the days passed fresh and bright. Edmund was fed and clothed and taught and smiled at. Miss Trebble, for simplicity's sake, took all her meals with the governess. At night they retired to cold lofty rooms looking out on the tarry main road. Whenever she remembered it, Miss Trebble walked round to the front of Handel House to contemplate its beautiful door and its perfection sent all her fears to sleep. Once a week a letter from Major Trebble would glide through the, now glittering, letter-box. So all went well. The two women arranged, tidied and reinstated. Their being so busy made Edmund's silences seem less unnatural. He would watch them hoeing and mowing. And if he obeyed them and brought them something they needed - bass or the scissors - there would be a strange 'considered' quality in his action. Neither of them could be indifferent to his detachment. It was so deliberate, so obvious. Not caring for what she saw, Miss Trebble grappled with the weeds and did her best to dismiss it. As for the governess, her understanding of the young was dominated by a frigid common sense. Besides, she happened to be engrossed in a far more subtle situation and one which, to give her her due, was entirely new to her. *'Dear Elfrida ...'* She found herself sighing, as Miss Trebble, in her magnificent innocence, smiled across at her.

It was on the third of June, to be exact, that Miss Trebble interrupted the snakes-and-ladders game. They had been gardening as usual, but an indication of their delicately changing status in the eyes of each other was evident in the more independent freedom of their bowed forms on the iris bed. Until now they had been inclined to tackle separate corners of the garden, the governess hacking away at the earth with wasteful unprecision and Miss Trebble lavishing upon the weeds the same rich absorption she brought to her embroidery-frame. Now they worked side by side. Occasionally their hooked maiden figures would unravel to full height like august ferns as they addressed one another. Their conversation was trivial in the extreme, as conversation frequently is when much is at stake.

'I really do think that it's going to be the best summer ever,' the governess said for the hundredth time. The repetition indicated her cat-like content.

Miss Trebble nodded and agreed. 'It would be a sin to be stuck indoors on a day like this.'

'Edmund doesn't think so!'

'Oh dear,' Miss Trebble said, 'I honestly did think he would have settled down by this time. I never thought I should be looking forward to the day he went to school when the Major asked me to look after him. Fancy sulking in the house in this weather! Aren't children extraordinary!'

'It's not just today - it's every day,' insisted the governess. 'He just hates being outside, that's all.' She looked up as she spoke, thinking to see Edmund staring down from the nursery window. Miss Trebble looked too, and said:

'Heavens! I've forgotten to leave my bedroom window open. It will be like an oven.'

'Let me - Elfrida,' the governess said, greatly daring.

'No... no,' Miss Trebble replied, as though she could not have heard. Dropping her trowel, she darted away. Handel House stretched up before her, its height vying with the monkey-puzzles and making a grim oblong against the speckless sky. Sparrows clung to its chimneys and drifting Himalayas of cloud turned each window into a gloomy negative of the sky. The eaves were more corroded with nests than they had ever been and the sills and cornices were streaked with white. Miss Trebble observed all this with satisfaction. Others could say what they liked, but she preferred such plain-jane strength in the building in which she had chosen to end her days.

Edmund was in the nursery. He was sitting on the scrubbed floor shaking a dice in a scarlet box. There was a snakes-and-ladders board in front of him. He looked up quickly when Miss Trebble entered.

'I'm busy,' he said defensively.

'So I see, darling. But why not be busy outside?' Her voice quaked with a forced intimacy. 'Do you know, I found a robin's nest in the lilac? Yesterday, it was. It has three eggs and it's quite low down. Come and see!'

'I'm busy.'

'We're all busy,' Miss Trebble said, though with more asperity than she intended. Children bewildered her.

Edmund regarded her sullenly.

'We - I want to finish the game.'

'What's wrong with finishing it outside - in the lovely sunshine?' Another thought occurred to her. 'Tell you what,' she said, enormously jolly, 'let's *both* play snakes-and-ladders! We'll play it on the lawn, shall we? You're sure to beat me, though.' She laughed brightly.

He offered his rare, beautiful smile.

'I'm busy,' he said.

Miss Trebble understood defeat when she met with it. For a full minute she stood perfectly still in the cold bedroom, which had so resolutely refused to be a nursery in anything but name. Not that she had not done her best in the latter respect. She had pasted cut-out elephants and teddy-bears across the welter of purple grapes and dun chrysanthemums of the original wallpaper, although now, as she stared around her, she realized this had been a mistake. The result was vaguely terrifying. Murky natives peered through the fruit and flowers, their faces plaintive with a morose ardour. It had all become a kind of travesty; a cheapened Rousseau. She regained her composure and said in a grown-up voice she found quite despicable:

'Very well, Edmund. We'll expect you at tea then. I don't suppose you'll be too busy for Fuller's walnut cake.'

'He was playing snakes-and-ladders,' she told the governess.

'What - by himself?' the governess dragged herself upright, committing her long lisle legs and her bare freckled arms to a forlorn repose. Groundsel heads and leaf mould trickled from between her fingers. She was flushed and tired.

Seeing her so, Miss Trebble said, 'Don't you think we should call it a day?' 'Joan', she nearly added, but then was glad she didn't.

'Shall we...all right.' The governess concealed her heartfelt thankfulness.

'We'll have our tea on the terrace steps. That's sure to bring Edmund out. I told him about the cake.'

'Why is he playing snakes-and-ladders by himself? I mean, how is he playing it?'

'My dear,' said Miss Trebble, '*you* should know what children are!'

There was a hurtful silence. The governess knew she had been snubbed, chased back into that dismal realm of other people's brats. To 'Miss Brown knows best'.

'I'll get the tea,' said Miss Trebble, as though innocent of a cloud in the sky.

The governess rubbed her earthy fingers together, resenting that there should be gritty crescents in her nails and mud all round her neat black strap shoes. Very well then! she thought. If she was to be the governess, she'd *be* the governess and blast the gardening! She shuffled her rage into the warm dark soil.

Edmund sat on the top step for tea and the two women, in softly draped attitudes, took their places a little lower down, one on either side. The tablecloth was like a white carpet going in and out over three steps. It made the bread and butter and the silver tea things look wonderfully lavish - sacerdotal almost. The walnut cake mopped up the governess's indignation like blotting-paper.

'And who's been playing snakes-and-ladders?' she demanded archly, winking at the small sedate figure on the top step.

Edmund stood up. He gripped his plate and cup. 'I think I'll take my tea indoors,' he said.

'But-' Miss Trebble protested.

'It's the sun; it hurts my eyes.'

The governess waited to be asked to intervene - in vain, it transpired. Miss Trebble said nothing and Edmund simply walked away. They watched him do it. For a second the yellow of his hair burnt like a lamp in the black interior, then he vanished altogether.

Why do you give in to him like that? the governess longed to demand. Such cossetings! It made her sick. But her confidence had already received a buffeting, so she munched her cake instead, and it was only by the deliberate manner in which she splashed tea in their cups that she gave vent to her disapproval. June passed. Curious unsuspected perennials sprang up in the garden and there was an abandonment of ancient roses everywhere. A whole tournament of spiky aquilegia forced its way through the box hedging. The grass was rich and sparrows crouched in the moss cushions and on the tall red walls. Miss Trebble decided that she was happier than at any other period of her life. Happier, she told herself, than she had any right to be, experience having taught her the value of humility. She took her place among the flowers and sat in a wicker chair, and the lace-work trickled from her lap. Now and then she looked up. The governess might be waving to her from an upstairs window - she was so friendly these days. If there was a movement in the ivy, Miss Trebble waved back just in case. Miss Joan Brown was proving an inestimable creature after all. Handel House would have still been in a sorry state without her.

One morning, as though awaiting her cue in Miss Trebble's soliloquy, the governess appeared at a particularly early hour. She was unexpectedly clad in a soft floral frock and a hat of pale rough straw. She manifested a Tissot brightness of white arms and long gleaming neck. She was altogether changed, and knew she was. She proved that she was one of those creatures who for too long had abjured the one state for which nature had intended them. She had dipped into and sampled experiences that were not rightly hers, and which she had to admit had brought her occasional grief. But now, disdainful as she had been to begin with, she knew she was entering the real and predetermined sphere of her happiness. At fifty-six Miss Joan Brown was about to wrench off the hateful harness of her profession, the stiff linen which left its stigmata at her throat and wrists each night; the prissy barriers which kept her back from the adult world. She knew now that she *hated* children and cared for nothing so much as sitting in the garden with Elfrida Trebble. 'If only

I had realized it before!' she lamented, too green in her new ways to suspect the fierce warmth of so late an affection. She was a born companion.

Their rôles became interchanged. Now it was Miss Trebble who hurried into the house from time to time to keep an eye on Edmund. The governess nipped brown roses off, tugged the wicker chairs further and further beneath the myrobalan's shade and, when they were both quite settled, read to Miss Trebble the works of Florence Barclay, beginning with *The Upas Tree.* If she spoke, it was more into the future than out of the past, since there was little in her recollections, she decided, worth the dredging for. She even went so far as saying that she adored Handel House, which she privately thought quite horrible. In her heart, she knew it was a terrible house; cold and malignant and for ever manufacturing its own darkness. But what worried her most was what would happen to her in October when Edmund went to school. Would it be yet another household and more new ways to learn? God forbid! She shivered in the sun. If not. . . and here were possibilities she scarcely dared to contemplate. Miss Trebble . . . Elfrida.. . No, no! Yet there *was* the possibility. She knew it; felt it. She was engrossed in such dreams one morning when Miss Trebble's excited cries took her running to the stables.

At first she could see nothing, not even Miss Trebble, who was pulling and tugging for all she was worth somewhere beneath the canopying webs. Desiccated hay flew up and choked them both.

'Give me a hand!' Miss Trebble was shouting. 'It's so heavy it's killing me.'

'What is, dear?' asked the governess, edging her way past the crippled shafts of a carriage. Miss Trebble was struggling with a large plank in the corner. 'Oh -*firewood!'*

'Not firewood,' Miss Trebble panted, 'it's a see-saw.'

'A see - *Really?'*

'I expect it has been here for donkey's years. It's most frightfully well made.'

'We must get it out.'

'I'm doing that.' Miss Trebble appeared exasperated.

Between them they dragged it as far as the paved courtyard. It was immensely strong. Its stout bar was hooped with iron handles and it had been made long enough to carry an entire nursery of flouncing Victorian children. For a minute or two they stood looking at it thoughtfully, sending it up and down gently with their hands. It grated.

'A duster and some oil,' Miss Trebble said. 'Yes, yes,' agreed the governess, and flew to get them. Here was the answer to stuffy little boys!

They cleaned it up and in no time it had settled so naturally that they felt sure it had soared beneath the very same tree in summers long ago. 'Edmund! Edmuuuund!' they sang. And the pigeons moaned softly.

They took their places, gingerly at first, rocking only as far as their legs would allow. The governess had chosen a timorous side-saddle, then, preferring safety to propriety, she slipped one long leg over the plank and trailed it down until her toe rested on the ground. 'Edmund!' they shouted again. With daring, Miss Trebble drew up her feet and sank a little towards the ground. She gripped the iron hoop so hard her knuckles bloomed like white flowers on her sunburnt hand. 'Oh, oh, oh!' the governess laughed, feeling herself rising, but in embarrassment not mirth. She hated to seem ridiculous anywhere. For Miss Trebble it was different. Absurdly elated, first with her find and now with the motion, she pushed recklessly against the flagstones with her feet. The garden wheeled and diminished. A joy seized her. Now she was high above the lowest of the myrobalan's branches, now low as a kitten. Her dress frothed out in the tilting ascent. She laughed again, tipped back into girlhood by this heady geometry. Floundering before her was the governess, quivering with the emphatic laughter of the victim. She was beating a protest with a clenched hand on the plank. Her legs dangled wildly when in the air and scrabbled distractedly when on the ground. 'Stop, stop, stop,' she begged and her frock billowed up and blinded her. She had never felt such a fool in her life. Edmund then appeared and they were at once decorous.

'Look, darling,' Miss Trebble cooed. 'Don't you love it?' With their legs cricked safely, they showed the see-saw off. The governess's face was red and distracted. A coil of hair stood out grotesquely from the smooth cusp of her head. She trembled. Miss Trebble's eyes were unnaturally bright. With the utmost solicitude they made it easy for each other to dismount.

'Now me,' said Edmund.

'Of course, dear,' they both replied. But when Miss Trebble tried to partner him, in whatever place she sat, her weight sent the boy up to a dizzy height where he stuck helplessly. So she had to stand and work the plank up and down with her hands. It was hard work. This, like everything else, won't last long, she consoled herself. He'll soon tire of it, she thought. But he didn't. He clutched at the safety hoop, not from fear, but from a determination to stay on. His eyes were brilliant. The heavy yellow hair slipped up and down on his brow like a cap. 'Go on! Go on!' he shrilled rudely.

So Miss Trebble went on. She brought the weighty plank down until she thought her back would break and then let it up until it strained her aching fingers. And all the time Edmund aired his extravagant pleasure by yelling, 'Go on! Faster. . .*faster!*' Then the governess took over with a good grace which perceptibly soured as Edmund shouted at her. At last she lost her temper and let him down with a thud. His screaming anger made her think at first that she had really hurt him.

'Nothing wrong. No bones broken!' soothed Miss Trebble. Edmund's knees were harboured in her long thin hands.

'Nothing wrong with him,' the governess remarked bitterly.

'Why, dear, have you hurt yourself then?'

The governess could not reply. She was outraged.

Without turning and still crouching low at the boy's side, Miss Trebble said, 'We're all a bit tired, aren't we? It must be the heat and one thing and another. Let's go in and make some tea.'

Still the governess did not speak. Her silence was multiplied over and over again until it seemed that it would be too momentous for it ever to be broken again.

'She did it,' Edmund said.

'*She*' Miss Trebble prompted.

'Miss Brown - she did it,' Edmund muttered abjectly. 'She let go to kill me.'

'Edmund! What a wicked, wicked thing to say!'

'She wants me to die, I know. . .' He turned his face away. It was grave with self-pity.

Miss Trebble was on her feet at once. She used up all her height. 'Edmund!' she cried, so loudly that the birds flew out of the currants, 'say you are sorry to Miss Brown at once. *At once*, do you hear!'

It was his turn for silence.

'This is ridiculous,' Miss Trebble said, half-way to tears herself and with her hands snatching helplessly. They each stood there miming their passion. It was the governess who broke the charade. Turning abruptly she slouched off towards the house. Her grief was indulgent, her trudge apocalyptic. Seeing her thus caused Miss Trebble to recover immediately.

'You just behave yourself,' she said darkly to Edmund. Then she too walked away, but with a wide, swinging step.

It was much later, but the same day. It was proper tea-time and they were having it in the drawing-room. Outside there was the rhythmic grating of the see-saw. Grate... grate.... it went with metronomic regularity. He was pushing it up and down with his small nervous hands, they thought. He'd been sulky all day. The noise was a nuisance because it reminded them of the scene in the garden earlier on.

'Do you think that I should go and see?' Miss Trebble asked, feeling that something ought to be done.

'Look? Why?' the governess said abstractedly.

Miss Trebble didn't know quite 'why' so she busied herself with the table.

Feeling faintly victorious, the governess selected a subject and began to air it. She discussed furnishings. A new wallpaper for this room, for instance. Wouldn't that be a good idea? What did Miss

Trebble think? The present one gave her, the governess, the creeps. Her words were chopped up into small pieces by the grate, grate, grate of the see-saw.

'It does get on one's nerves,' she admitted.

'I expect he's all right,' Miss Trebble said in her turn.

'I'm fifty-six,' the governess said quite suddenly.

I know that, thought Miss Trebble; it's in her references. But she nodded and smiled and said, 'And I just sixty.'

They regarded each other haltingly across the lacy cloth. The room stretched around them in amorphous wastes. Like twin signatories to a pact not yet fully agreed upon, they hedged and hawed with their words. Grate, grate, grate, went the see-saw as the governess uttered those things not to be discovered in her credentials and grate again, as Miss Trebble fought for answers to questions she could never have imagined existed, had they not clanged like great bells in her ears. The afternoon drifted by as they talked and the tea grew cold and rinked with tepid cream in the Rockingham cups. A vista of a thousand such afternoons was spread enticingly before them. Days and days when they might sit so, and talk so, and be so. Yet. . . yet. . . Miss Trebble glanced about her uncertainly. Was that what she wanted? She must be sure. Wisps of darkness swept in and settled upon the normally serene horizons of her mind.

But the governess was thinking, 'She's a beech-nut - that's what she is! A nice brittle, polished creature!' She dropped her gaze to Miss Trebble's hand where it lolled on the red mahogany sofa ridge. Small criss-cross pads of toil tipped each finger. 'Elfrida -' the governess said carefully. It was still a new word to her.

Miss Trebble watched her own hand where it rested against the mahogany roses. In fact she discovered herself thinking of the hand in terms of extreme detachment. Its stillness and its whiteness filled her with a dull compassion. Would her hand welcome this new intimacy? she wondered. It had always known great independence in such matters. Would it need friendship - such a fancy business it seems! What was she being offered that her hand had to burn and freeze at the same time? Contentment? Not that surely. Contentment was something she'd known on and off always. Love. . . But who ever heard of such a thing! She brought the hand back to the tall silver hot-water jug, but deathly conscious of the fixed eyes of the governess. *Could* she be happier -? Miss Trebble was beginning to ask herself and then the see-saw made such a horrible noise that she leapt to her feet and exclaimed:

'Edmund! We've forgotten Edmund and it's past seven!'

The governess smiled but did not move. 'Never mind Edmund,' she said.

Miss Trebble wavered. The governess sat in a tense arc, as though she might be able to preserve the dangerous present by her sheer physical immobility. The grating of the see-saw was like some dreadful clock geared for eternity. It pierced Miss Trebble's ear-drums to the exclusion of every other sound. Half a century away she heard her father saying, 'Always be polite, Elfrida. Politeness always tells.' She turned to the governess and said:

'I'll see to the child, Miss Brown. You had better clear away.'

Outside the garden glimmered as stiff and bright and motionless as a waxen garden under a huge bell-shade. The sun shone from the west, a silver sun which was like the moon. Miss Trebble saw all the trees as flat and lifeless as stage-props and looking as though any minute they would be tugged away. In the cardboard shade of the myrobalan tree was Edmund. His feet never touched the ground as he dipped and rose in the airless evening. Grate, grate, went the see-saw, up and down with merciless precision. Up and down went Edmund, but alone. The opposite seat was empty.

One thing was certain, Miss Trebble insisted to herself. On no account must she call for help - such help as might be had from the static presence in her drawing-room, for instance. She must neither faint, nor fail, nor fly. But above all she mustn't scream, *'Joan. . . Joan....'* She leant against the half-door of the stable and began to pray. After she had got to 'But deliver us from evil', she couldn't go on and the tears ran across her rings as she buried her head in her hands.

Edmund regarded her goldenly, sometimes from the heights, sometimes from the depths. He sat the plank limply, a pathetic, manipulated creature. He was exhausted; she could see his weariness from where she stood. She watched him, full of pity and with her hair dragged down across her cheek by a cold wind which seemed to affect her alone. He was looking in her direction and as he looked he seemed to urge, to supplicate. He was demanding something of her with his ebbing strength. And all the time the see-saw rose and fell to persuade her that she wasn't mad. 'Edmund!' she cried and panic rattled against the stage-prop trees. That would never do, Miss Trebble told herself. She made an immense effort to summon together every snippet of reason and sensibility that still remained and when she heard her voice it sounded ordinary and level enough.

'Why, goodness gracious, child,' she said, 'what are we all thinking about! Still having tea and it's hours past your bedtime.'

The governess left by the front door. For a second she hesitated beneath its shell-like porch as if the evening light was too much for her. She carried a coat and a case. The rest must follow. With these clasped to her she clambered into the hired car, not hearing, not seeing and, at the last, not seen. Her hand was a smudge against the window as she sought to lower it. Her fingers fluttered. Valediction they implied. Farewell to the noble door and the sweet recovered garden. Farewell, my dear, farewell! The hired car trembled - was moving. The governess pressed her face to the window and saw Handel House like a doll's house, its façade gone, its secrets given up. There was the drawing-room and the tea things still scattered about round the fireplace - she had refused to clear them. There the hall, the dining-room, the one, two, three, four bedrooms. Oh, and there the nursery - so brightly lit by the westering sun. An elderly lady sat in it reading to a small boy, who was nuzzling against her breast. The governess turned wretchedly against the hired car's stern upholstery. '*Fool. . . fool!*' she wept.